The Rite
of
James Biddle

The Rite
of
James Biddle

A *Novel by*

Andrew Bailey

BAYEUX ARTS
DIGITAL-TRADITIONAL PUBLISHING

The Rite of James Biddle
© Copyright 2014 Bayeux Arts

Published by Bayeux Arts, Inc.
119 Stratton Crescent SW,
Calgary, Canada T3H 1T7

First printing: June, 2014.

www.bayeux.com

Cover and Book design: Judd Palmer and PreMediaGlobal

All comments in the text are the author's own, and do not reflect the views of the
Publishers.

Library and Archives Canada Cataloguing in Publication

Bailey, Andrew, 1979-, author
    The Rite of James Biddle / Andrew Bailey.

ISBN 978-1-897411-78-0 (pbk.)

    I. Title.

PS8603.A4426R57 2014   C813'.6   C2014-901509-7

Printed in Canada

Books published by Bayeux Arts are available at special quantity discounts
to use in premiums and sales promotions, or for use in corporate training
programs. For more information, please write to Special Sales, Bayeux Arts, Inc.,
119 Stratton Crescent SW, Calgary, Canada T3H 1T7.

The ongoing publishing activities of Bayeux Arts, under its "Bayeux" and "Gondolier"
imprints, are supported by the Canada Council for the Arts, the Government of Alberta,
Alberta Multimedia Development Fund, and the Government of Canada through the Book
Publishing Industry Development Program.

Contents

PART I

Gathering of the Community

"God hath created nothing simply for itself, but each thing in all things, and of every thing each part in other have such interest, that in the whole world nothing is found whereunto any thing created can say, 'I need thee not.'"

—Richard Hooker

1

Chapter

1

He was happy for her. He was. He'd helped get her through theological college. Recommended her to the Old Man as having a knack for pastoral care. Sung her praises to everyone he met, even though she was at times lax in her liturgy and he still wasn't sure if women should be priests. She had distinguished herself as both deacon and curate. For six years she had served with him at St. Matthew's. Together they had created a number of initiatives, including a bake sale in February, the Flea Market in April to go along with New-To-You (which had been a Thanksgiving tradition since as long as anyone could remember). Her slightly evangelical, populist, liberal yet inoffensive style had brought young people into the congregation. Not as many as could be hoped but enough to make the Nine-Fifteen a true family service again. No small feat in these times. She was sincere in her faith and sincerely a good person. Soon to be the first woman rector of St. Stephen's, Langford, a small working class parish in the suburbs. She would be wonderful at the job.

He really was happy for her. It was he who organized this congratulatory get together. Invited the whole staff, as well as the youth who had come of age. Invited the Sewing Circle. Invited the Old Man and his wife. Gathered money for her gifts: a gold leafed concordance and a bottle of scotch. He had himself contributed more to the cause than anyone. No one could accuse him of being bitter.

And he wasn't bitter. Sure he'd put in the time. The years. The late nights. The early mornings. He had given his every waking hour to devotion. To proper liturgy. To probing, literary sermons. Sure, he'd brought in the new choir director who was a hit with everyone who still cared about church music. Sure he knew nearly every Christian philosopher or saint. Could name the Seven Deadly Sins and Seven Cardinal Virtues in the time it takes to speak them. Knew Dante from the Italian and Thomas More from the Latin. For two years taught a zero credit course on Erasmus for UVic before it was cancelled due to lack of support. Sure he'd had top marks throughout junior high, high school and university and would've had top marks throughout elementary school too except that half-way through his district began experimenting with a wishy washy liberal-fascist "grade free" system much to both his and his father's dismay. He could have been nearly anything he wanted. His guidance counselor said that in high school. His thesis adviser repeated the sentiment.

But he had a vocation, a calling, to which he had devoted himself with every atom of his being. He prayed several times every day. (Never for himself.) He never said a curse word worse than "bloody", "hell", or "damn". Never watched *American Idol* or *Canadian Idol* or any show with "Idol", "Survivor", "Shore", "Real", "Race", "Dance", or "Life" in the title. He might as well only have had PBS, BBC Canada and CBC News. (CBC proper had for several years been cluttered with mediocre and obnoxious scripted programming that would've been dead on arrival if it weren't for Cancon regulations.) In another era he might have replaced the Old Man as bishop by now or at very least been rector of his own parish. Respected and respectable.

But he wasn't bitter.

"Thank-you for doing this, sweetie." She kissed him on the cheek.

"Not calling me sweetie would be thanks enough." He smiled at her, black haired beauty. She was a youthful thirty-five. One year younger than he was. Was ordained three years after him. The Reverend Ashley Tan. Kept her surname. Half Chinese. Slightly Aboriginal. A woman.

She deserved her success.

Her husband shook his hand. A chartered accountant. An American. Sensible fellow. But she could have done better.

"You're a good man, father." Americans always call you father.

"If I'm not I'm in the wrong profession." Quite witty. Good job.

"You know I got her a concordance for her Kindle too."

"You haven't… you wouldn't." The eyes James directed at Ashley were more hurt than angry.

"It's convenient for when I travel. It would never replace hard covers."

"I don't get what the big deal is", said Ashley's husband.

"It was the one refuge technology hadn't touched. The one mode of education and entertainment that hadn't 'progressed'. The one…"

"Bed time for us." Ashley pulled her husband towards the door, the two of them smiling at him one more time as they left. He checked his watch. Eight-thirty. *I go to all this trouble and they leave at eight-thirty.*

He sighed, watching the door swing closed. The whole Sewing Circle had gone already too, as had anyone with two X chromosomes. The youth had all moved on to better parties. This left the Old Man, whom he certainly didn't feel like talking to right now; the Rector, whom he never felt like talking to; the Choir Master whom, though he'd helped bring in, he had yet to have a real conversation with; and the new Deacon, who referred to the Lord God as "Creator".

"James!" the Old Man called. He gestured for James to come sit down at the corner booth with himself and the Rector. It was going to be an awkward conversation. James knew it. He'd hoped organizing this get together might throw them off the scent. He could deal with disappointment. That was a part of life. But talking about disappointment. Talking about his "feelings". That was downright humiliating.

"It's a suburban parish", the Old Man started. He was bishop now. James' father had given him his first parish. Molded him. In another era the Old Man might have returned the favour for James. "They're families. Working class mostly. The sort of people Ashley is best at communicating with. She was a better fit for this particular position. That's all. But I want you to know everyone is very happy with your ministry."

"Absolutely", the Rector agreed, his mouth half full with nacho. A small bit of guacamole on his chin. "Your gift… excuse me…" he swallowed "…and it truly is a gift, is with the elderly.

It is such a comfort for them to have you, James. We couldn't do without you. Who else could give the Eleven O'clock Service its proper liturgical grace?" The Rector hated the Eleven O'clock Service. Hated that it existed. Wouldn't be able to distinguish liturgical grace from a condiment for his beloved nachos. His words were completely hollow.

Still, James appreciated the flattery.

"You're still young, James. Your father wasn't made rector until he was well into his forties. Your time will come."

James thanked them both for their kind words. Assured them he was pleased with the ministry he was doing and that he could not have been happier for Ashley.

All that crap.

James excused himself and then got in line for the bar. (He'd never had much patience for waitresses.) One more black and tan and then he would go. But he needed alcohol and he avoided drinking alone when he could help it. The Choir Master cut in line beside James. He was a handsome young man with carefully tussled hair, thick stylish glasses, stylish jeans. He looked as though he tried hard to look as though he didn't try hard to look as though he was stylish. Just the sort of fellow James normally detested.

But his musicality was exceptional.

"The Reverend James Erasmus Biddle. Rumour has it you're the one I need to thank for my new job."

"Harriet recommended you. I just passed it along." She had impeccable taste.

"That's at least good enough to owe you a beer. What are you having?"

"You really don't have to. I really didn't do anything. It's us who owe you." James had been working on this form of social interaction: "Black and tan. Thank-you."

"The least I could do. Two black and tans please." The bartender began pouring. "You know, I listened to you during the service. You have perfect pitch."

"Certainly not perfect."

"No. Not perfect, but decent. What are you doing in the backwaters? I mean I'm young. I have to pay my dues. But you're…"

"I'm thirty-six. Victoria is not a backwater." The bartender gave them their beers. They headed to an empty table.

"You don't feel isolated? Living on an island, I mean."

"Victoria has a greater population than London in the time of Shakespeare. Than Athens in the time of Socrates." If anything there were too many people.

"Is that true?" They sat down.

"Yes."

"But you have to admit there's a lot of old people."

"I like old people."

"I didn't mean anything by it." They both took sips of their beers. Both looked out to the street. "It's pretty. It's much warmer than Toronto."

"I'm sorry. I didn't mean to sound so defensive." Yes you did.

"So what do people do here? Outdoors stuff I take it."

"People do. I go for walks. Or read a good book."

"No wonder you like old people." James looked at the Choir Master, who was smiling roguishly. *He* did have perfect pitch. Why would God give such a gift to such a git?

"It was a joke", said the Choir Master. "Say, have you bought a Kindle yet? It's great when you have to travel."

The new Deacon came to their table, filled with youthful energy. He was muscular. Blond. An Aryan poster boy. He looks like every bully I had to endure in high school, thought James. Yet I'm actually glad to see him.

"Thank-you so much for inviting me James. It really made me feel welcome. I'm meeting so many new people. I had a great conversation with the youth. I love it here already. It's wonderful."

I take it back.

"Who's this?" asked the Choir Master.

"This is the Reverend William Johnson. He's our new deacon. He'll also be doubling as Family Minister until the new one arrives in August."

"William? Too formal. I'm Bill. Though most just call me Big B. That was my nickname in hockey. Or you could just call me Reverend B, or Plan B or Busy as a B. You're new here too I take it?"

"This is Rodger Richards." The Choir Master and the Deacon shook hands. Something occurred to James: "Are your parents Rodgers and Hammerstein fans?"

"You're the only person that's ever got that."

"Really?"

"God no. But now we're even for my insults to your fair city."

"It's a great city. I love it here", said the Deacon. "So Kim and Alex invited me to this music group they're going to. You guys should come too."

"Is this praise music?" asked the Choir Master.

"Yes it is."

"Don't you think I get enough of that with my job?"

"Ha! I like you. What about you, James?"

"It's getting close to my bedtime I'm afraid."

"One day we're going to get you to let loose and have some fun." The Deacon patted James on the back. "You know what guys? I think we're going to have a great time together serving the Creator." And just like that he was off.

The Choir Master whispered, "Is he for real?"

"As far as I can tell", said James.

"I think he needs a nickname."

"A nickname? Okay. How about…" James pretended that he was searching his brain. He'd thought about this for quite some time. "…The Venerable B."

"I don't get it."

"Well he calls himself 'B' and the Venerable Bede was a medieval scholar who, for the time, wrote in a very transparent writing style so…"

"I like it James. I do. But it's not quite there, though I think you're on the right track with the 'B'. Maybe B.O. or… his last name's Johnson. Maybe we should call him Reverend B.J."

James thought this over for a moment. "Butter and jelly?"

"Blow job. As in I bet he gives a good one."

James was shocked. He knew choirmasters sometimes participated in locker room talk, but he had never heard it for himself. "That's a bit mean and though I'm not personally offended, we do have several openly gay parishioners so I don't know if we should…"

"James, I'm in church music. It's not bullshit for me to say I have a lot, a *lot*, of gay friends but both me and them enjoy mocking people who are so obviously in denial."

Many thought that James was one of those people. "I don't know."

"C'mon, he calls God 'The Creator'." James laughed. Maybe the Choir Master wasn't such a bad guy after all.

Chapter

2

Prince Edward Island. The late Victorian era. The schoolhouse. He is one of the pupils, twelve or thirteen years old. The bell rings. All the students line up to wish their teacher good-bye for the summer.

"Good-bye, Miss Shirley."

"Good-bye, Jacob. Good luck with your job at Mr. Henderson's orchard. I hope the bees don't bite you like they did last year."

"They won't, Miss Shirley."

Child after child runs out, exchanging good-byes with their red haired teacher. Then it is his turn. He's been dreading this.

"James, a word if you will."

"Yes, Miss Shirley?"

"I couldn't help but notice how you don't spend much time with the other children in school."

"I prefer books, Miss Shirley."

"You know, James, I'm something of the bookish sort myself. My favourite part is when I first open the book." She begins to unbutton her blouse. "I don't know what wonders I am going to discover." Her blouse is open now. She pulls him towards her. His eyes level with her perfect bosom. She pulls him in. Closer. Closer.

James awoke. This was definitely his least favourite recurring dream but, for one part of him, also his most favourite. He showered thoroughly and put on a clean pair of pajamas.

He always kept a spare.

* * *

James lay in bed awake stewing straight through till morning. That dream had always given him a grave sense of loss. The mini-

9

series came out on the CBC just as he was reaching puberty. Just as his mom was getting sick again. People had called her death "tragic" but that was technically not the case. Tragedy is a specific genre of drama with characters of high societal status (usually royalty) who usually, though not always, fall from grace due to a flaw, traditionally a sense of overweening pride (ὕβρις). It shows men and women of such high status that they mistake themselves to be as gods, until Fate cuts them down to size, reminding them of their mortality and the wide gap between the human and the divine. His mom was a wonderful woman, but certainly not a queen, and she did not have overweening pride. She was caring and humble.

Even colloquially speaking, it did not qualify. She was supposed to have died years before. The time James did get to spend with her was a precious gift. He never lost sight of that fact. She was twenty years younger than his father, warm and generous of spirit. But she was also sick—fragile—for most of his childhood. She did not have healthy marrow. He was terrified of ever upsetting her. Terrified he would say or do the wrong thing. Terrified that thing would bring the cancer back. So he did his best always to do the right thing. He studied hard and kept out of trouble. Other children seemed hell bent on causing trouble so he steered clear of them, which suited him just fine.

He would, at times, feel lonely. Those times were known as recess and lunch hour. He'd sit alone reading to himself. The children would come and tease him. Take his book from him. He would rise above the fray. Eventually they would have to give his book back lest he report them to the principal's office. He could wait. They could take his book but they could never take his dignity. They would flick his ears and laugh. Push him down and laugh. He was a pacifist, he informed them. They could harm his body all they liked, but it would not do one jot of damage to his immortal soul. That's when they started punching him too.

He was delighted to discover that the library was open during lunch hour. They couldn't touch him there: a librarian was always on duty. It was filled with books, which he liked, but most of them were much too young for him. So he brought books from home.

Shakespeare. The Book of Common Prayer. Greek and Latin lexicons.

With the exception of P.E., James was a straight A student. Then they stopped handing out letter grades. Even so, his "Effort Marks" were top notch. Nonetheless, his mom worried about him.

"How's school going?" she'd asked.

"They have a wishy washy liberal grading system but Mrs. Morton assures me I would be getting straight A's."

"I meant friends. You never seem to bring anyone around. Are you making friends?"

"At school?!" He hadn't meant to react so melodramatically. James assured her that his church friends were enough. (Kids had to be nice to him at church. God was watching.)

"Sweetie, I want you to know that it's okay to make mistakes sometimes. It's okay to fool around." That was when she held his shoulder, so he would know the next words were of exceptional weight and merit. "Life is short: live it! Okay? Have some fun!"

He'd tried to obey her on this front but was not sure how best to go about it. As far as he knew what he did was fun. It was fun to teach himself Greek. Fun to have the top grades in class (when they'd had grades). He was sure this was not what she'd meant, however. He had to find something that he might enjoy and, most importantly, that would stop her from worrying. Church provided the answer. A counselor from summer camp made an announcement before the whole congregation. Sign up forms were at the back. A number of his church friends would be going too.

Perfect! Camping. Swimming. Fishing. Canoeing. Archery. These were the sort of things kids were supposed to do for fun and it would be in a church environment, so no one could be mean to him for the whole four weeks. Plus it would give his parents some much needed alone time. He had read somewhere that good marriages needed that.

When he arrived, all the counselors seemed to be far too excited, even for evangelicals. They all saw God as "Fun!" And the music, if you could call it that, was nothing but 60s pop ditties with rehashed lyrics, set to out-of-tune guitar: *House of the Rising Son*. That's not even clever. And he had never heard the word "awesome" so many times in his life. God was awesome. Jesus was awesome. The Holy Spirit was awesome. God's people? Awesome. (James hoped they might be doing a translation of δεῖνος but he doubted it.)

Camping. Swimming. Fishing. Canoeing. Archery. These were the sorts of things that James had no aptitude for. He could swim in the sense that he didn't sink, but he tended to be the slowest, girls or boys. Plus, over the winter, his bathing suit had lost much of its elasticity, meaning he had to constantly pull it back up, which he was quite careful to do. Nonetheless, on one occasion, the suit did, for a short moment, fall to his ankles. The lifeguard (a nineteen-year-old who wore sunglasses over the brim of his hat rather than over his eyes where they might have done some good) gave James a stern talking to. Word of James' embarrassment soon spread throughout the camp. "Biddle's got a little diddle", became a popular phrase that rolled off people's tongues whenever he walked by. That, or "Fag".

They canoed to a secluded island the local Aboriginals had given them permission to use. They camped there, the whole lot of them. Sleeping bag jutted against sleeping bag. James was stuck in the dead centre. He kept thinking, "What if I have to pee?" And the more he thought, "What if I have to pee?" the more he had to pee. The more he thought, stop thinking, "What if I have to pee?" the more he kept thinking, "What if I have to pee?" and the more he had to pee. Five times he got up in the night, each time waking up a dozen or so other campers. The popular phrase was lengthened to "Biddle's gotta piddle with his tiny little diddle" and set to a twangy jingle. At least they don't hit me, thought James. Then someone (he didn't see whom) tripped him from behind and ran off into the bushes with a group of other kids, laughing.

Then they had the sharing circle. Three or four cabins joined together to discuss their personal feelings about Jesus. Most of the kids had positive but rather superficial things to say: "He's nice." "He's loving." "He's kind." "I couldn't get through life without Him." James said that his favourite thing about Jesus was from the Gospel of John: "'God so loved the world, that he gave his only begotten

Son, to the end that all that believe in him should not perish, but have eternal life.' He let His own child suffer and die, which is the hardest thing anyone could do and yet He did it for us, despite our sinful nature. Jesus isn't simply man or God but is, truly, the deepest expression of love the world has ever known."

There was a moment of stunned silence. Everyone stared at James as he sat back down. "You're my hero James", said George, a boy from church whom James had mistakenly considered to be his friend. Everyone laughed. Yes, James thought, I'm different! I've already been informed of this fact! But James was not sorry for what he'd said. It was a Christian camp. Were they there to share their love of Jesus or not? James was who he was. He had nothing to be ashamed of. The counselor settled everyone down. Said that James' words were true and beautiful. (Of course, he only did this after laughing himself.)

As the crowd was dispersing back to their respective cabins, a number of the campers told James, "You changed my life, fag." "Real deep, fag." "So Jesus gave you a big brain to go with your small dick and bladder... pussy." (At least there was some variety.) James, by this point, had realized his error in reasoning. The kids at church seemed nice only because there weren't enough other kids to make cruelty worthwhile: they didn't gang up on him because there weren't enough of them to make a gang. But at camp there were more than enough.

James was about to give up on humanity altogether when a black haired girl of about ten ran up to him. "I just wanted you to know that I liked what you said and I didn't laugh." Then one of her friends called and she ran away. James watched her go, fighting not to tear up due to this unexpected kindness. Bloody hell, what they'd call me if I cried. (He didn't realize it until theological college, but this kind girl was Ashley. James did not consider this to be a coincidence, however. "Anglicans of our age make such a small community, really. We've all already met each other.")

As much as he hated camp, he wished his time there hadn't been cut short. His mom's cancer had gone bad. Very bad. It had relapsed before he'd left, but she hadn't told him. It had taken a serious turn not long after he'd arrived but she had refused to let anyone contact him. She didn't want to spoil his good time.

She looked like a different woman when he came to her hospital bed. She asked him how camp had gone. He told her it was the best time of his life. He had seen enough movies, and read 1 Kings 2 enough times, to believe his mom would then give him a piece of wisdom that would sustain him for the coming years. She did not. She simply smiled. Said, "Good." And then fell asleep.

She never woke up. His father was kept busy that week and though James offered to help, he soon discovered it would be best if he just stayed out of the way. He tried reading Plato's *Kratylos*, but his thoughts raced too much to concentrate on the words. Having taped both *Anne of Green Gables* and its sequel, he watched for hours on end, wishing he knew a bookish girl like that. He liked how they developed her character when she became an English teacher. Not because of his dreams, which didn't start till years later, but because she was filled with doubt and worry, and yet acted the part of authority. Acted like things didn't bother her. That's all any of us can do, he thought.

He cried at the funeral, but not out of sadness for his mom. She was a good woman. She had died in the faith. Her soul was bound for heaven. He cried because he didn't like change. He cried because he was worried. Would he be able to get through his adolescence without her? It seemed melodramatic to say now but, before he'd lived them, those five years seemed like they would be impossible to survive without a mother. So he prayed to God. Prayed that He would watch over him. Prayed for Him to guide his actions.

Never before or since had James' prayers been answered so quickly. Before he could cross himself he felt overwhelmed by the best kind of love. By 'αγάπη—the word from Paul that sometimes was also translated as "charity". The love that rejoiceth in the truth, beareth all things, believeth all things, hopeth all things, endureth all things. The love that was patient and kind. The love that was steadfast. He felt time melt away. He felt his soul reaching upwards and all around him dissolving into the great Oneness. There was no future and no past. Only now. Only love. And then, in an instant, he was himself again. But James knew that everything would be all right because God was with him and his mom was with God.

Tragedy? He hated when people misused that word. His mom was in heaven and he felt overwhelming love: both of them had been raised to grace, not fallen from it. Tragedy? Tell that to the Lost Boys of the Sudan. Tell that to anyone born within a hundred miles of the Congo River. Tell that to Jo-Marie…

He sat up. He turned to his phone. No. That had turned out as it had. She didn't want anything to do with him. She had made that more than clear. (Besides, it was barely dawn.) He hoped she was okay.

"Love hopeth all things." Yup, that was one of them.

Chapter
3

James got out of bed resolved to feel happy. His life was a good one. He lived in a first world nation in the early part of the twenty-first century. Even the homeless were well off, relatively speaking. He'd bought his house before the jump in property values and was wise enough not to sell his parents' home until after. He'd paid off his mortgage and had savings to boot. The house was a modest but respectable place in the 1300 block of Vining Street between Stanley Avenue and Fernwood Road. Built in 1913, it had stained glass windows and steam radiators, which were good for his asthma. It was far enough from town to be part of its own neighbourhood but close enough to walk most places. It had a small garden in which he grew tomatoes, cucumbers, squash, green beans, cabbage and potatoes. He was not the green thumb his parents had been but he enjoyed it as a pastime and believed, with patience, his skills would improve.

He looked in the mirror. He had always been a bit gaunt, but was in generally good health. He liked his name, which he shared with his father and grandfather. The only drawback was that he also shared it with Captain James Biddle who, by formally claiming Oregon Territory for the United States in 1818, aided in the betrayal of David Thompson's diligent and meticulous adventurism.

He pushed down the toaster handle. Both classical and church music were still respected and loved in this city. Not a week would go by without a concert to attend. (If he felt like going out that was.) While church was poorly attended, he still had the beautiful liturgy of the Eleven O'clock Service, worshipped in the beautiful language of the Book of Common Prayer.

He took out some marmalade. Red Fish Blue Fish made a fantastic seared tuna tacone. Spinnakers Pub served excellent wild salmon. The Belfry Theatre, while rarely showing great plays, certainly showed competent ones. And the new gelato place had just opened up across from it. Paulo's Gelato, despite the obnoxious name and being slightly overpriced, made the most fantastic nocciola you could imagine, served straight, in a freshly made waffle cone or, on more adventurous days, with espresso—and it was less than a five minute walk from his house!

he was blessed he was blessed he was blessed

* * *

James arrived at the Jubilee hospital and got out of his 1997 Toyota Corolla Sedan. He hadn't wanted a car, but with all the pastoral work he did there wasn't much choice. He simply bought the most reliable model he could find on the cheap.

He walked up to palliative care, nodded a hello at the nurses' station. He entered Mrs. Henderson's room. "Is that you, James?" she asked. Her eyes were still kind even if they were no longer so good as eyes.

"Yes it is, my darling", he said, opening his fat black leather case. It contained a vial of holy water, another with wine, a chalice, a wafer box, and a purificator, each set in its own special compartment. Everything he needed for Communion. "You look as lovely as ever." James took out his Book of Common Prayer. Turned to page 576. Mrs. Henderson had her own copy. She was already at the correct page.

"'Peace be to this house,'" said James, "'and to all that dwell in it.'" The service brought comfort to her. He could feel that. It brought comfort to him too. The Gospel was one of his favourites: "'I am the good shepherd; and I know mine own, and mine own know me, even as the Father knoweth me, and I know the Father; and I lay down my life for the sheep.'" ' αγάπη, thought James.

* * *

He placed the host upon her tongue. "'The body of our Lord Jesus Christ, which was given for you, preserve your body and soul to everlasting life. Take and eat this in remembrance that Christ died for you and feed on him in your heart by faith with thanksgiving.'"

She chewed and swallowed. He waited patiently. It was not easy for her anymore. He should've dipped it first.

James put the chalice below her lips. Helped her drink. "'The blood of our Lord Jesus Christ, which was shed for you, preserve your body and soul to everlasting life. Drink this in remembrance that Christ's blood was shed for you, and be thankful.'" James wiped the chalice with the purificator.

"'Unto God's gracious mercy and protection we commit thee. The Lord bless thee, and keep thee. The Lord make his face to shine upon thee, and be gracious unto thee. The Lord lift up his countenance upon thee, and give thee peace, both now and evermore.'"

Mrs. Henderson concluded the service by saying, "Amen."

James began to put away the sacraments.

"Are you here for a visit?"

"If you'd like. It's always wonderful to be in the presence of such a force of nature as yourself." Her spirit was fading; he could sense it. Victoria was the retirement capital of Canada. The funeral capital also.

* * *

The Sewing Circle met at Swans Pub once a month, usually on a Saturday afternoon. The Old Man hadn't come, but the other old clergymen had. Apart from James, not one of them was under sixty and most were on the far side of eighty.

These were James' favourite people, former colleagues of his father. As a teenager he would talk to them during coffee hour, impressing with his knowledge of Greek and Latin. His father took him to theological lectures where James impressed everyone with his knowledge of Scripture. Then his father started taking him to theological conferences where everyone was both surprised and glad to see him, young as he was. Before James knew it he had become one of the gang. Finally, real friends! He kept in touch with them when he went to theological college in Vancouver and was happy there were still people around who knew how to write proper letters.

"You should have been Rector", said Canon Conroy, at sixty-eight the spring chicken of the group (next to James and The Old Man when he bothered to show up). "I don't know what David Skinner was thinking."

"Let's not be too hard on him", said James. "It's not easy being Bishop."

"James is young yet", said the Venerable McCall. "It's rare you find a rector under forty."

"James is exceptional though", said Canon Conroy. "He's been preparing his whole life for this. He's earned a better lot than being assistant to Canon Welker." A murmur of displeasure went through the group at the sound of Welker's name.

"Your father would have been proud of you", said the Reverend Doctor Leonard White. "Do not be hard on yourself for your lack of advancement. Times have changed. Your father never had to face what you're facing."

"Ah yes, the Very Reverend Biddle. Good man. Good man", said the Reverend Doctor Zi-Wei Lim, born and raised in Fujian province, China. "I could not find the right location for my sabbatical year. He said, 'Go to Strasbourg.'" Zi-Wei used to be an associate priest at St. Matthew's. The old ladies called him, "Our very own Chinese monk." But he'd left because of Canon Welker. Somewhat hot tempered, he'd also left the Anglican Communion itself. Joined the Orthodox Church, which met off the highway. Converted by Father Hansen. That slick used car salesmen of a priest. (He actually was a used car salesman—Orthodox Clergy had day jobs. You had to admire the work ethic.)

"So, young Biddle, what is your opinion on gay clergy?" Zi-Wei always asked this question. The other men looked to James with compassion and anxiety. I'm a tidy bachelor who loves cooking and Broadway musicals, thought James. I suppose I'd think I was gay too.

Zi-Wei still looked at James, expectant. You had to be careful with your answer. *Via media*. Always remember *via media*.

"I agree with Desmond Tutu: 'What is all the fuss about?'"

"Spoken like a prophet", said Zi-Wei.

"The issue of homosexuality is not central to the Christian faith one way or the other. There are much bigger issues such as war and AIDS..."

The Venerable McCall jumped in: "If they think Robinson is the first gay Bishop they're fooling themselves." I've known a few, thought James. The High Church has always been good at looking the other way. Was tolerant a hundred years before any of these liberals that's for sure.

"Whatever happened to *via media?*" said James. "Just don't ask the question and you don't have to argue about it. We'll think what we think, others will think what they think, but we don't have to split the church apart." Why do people have to be openly anything? Why do people's personal lives matter to anyone else? Harold and Jonathan are wonderful people. They are a fine couple and good parents. Can't we just leave it at that?

The conversation turned to the Book of Common Prayer.

"Canon Welker won't get rid of the BCP. He wouldn't", said the Venerable McCall.

"I wouldn't put it past him", said Zi-Wei, smiling knowingly at James.

"I hear he's planning to get rid of the Eleven O'clock Service altogether", said Canon Conroy.

"I'm sure he wants to," said James, "but he isn't doing it. He specifically told me he needed me for the Eleven. He can just do the Nine-Fifteen and leave the Eleven to me. Go home early. One of you old coots can assist me. It would suit me fine."

"There is the modern service and then the traditional", said the Reverend Doctor White. "That way everyone is happy."

If I got married all the groomsmen would be over seventy-five, thought James. It would probably be some sort of record.

"*Via media*", said Canon Conroy, smiling at James. Everyone nodded in agreement. James looked around the room. He had known them all so long he sometimes didn't notice how creased and sunken their faces had become. Their hands tired and withered.

When you all are gone what then will I do? Who then will I talk to?

* * *

James left Swans at 5:17 pm. He had been careful to consume no more than one drink per hour, and had given forty minutes since the last drop of alcohol touched his tongue. As he put his key into the driver's side door, he froze. Turning up Pandora Avenue was a beautiful woman with auburn hair and freckles. He was too far away to see the colour of her eyes, and yet he was sure they were a striking blue. Her right index finger was set in a metal splint. He couldn't recall them ever having met and yet he felt that he'd always known her. He found women attractive from time to time but to be struck like this was, without question, exceptional. For a moment, a brief moment, he considered running up and talking to her. Telling her how he had been struck. Of course he thought better of it—it was neither dignified nor sensible—but, before he could turn away, her eyes caught his. She smiled at him. He smiled at her, then fumbled his way into the car, frightened and breathless.

Chapter

4

James, freshly scrubbed, put on a clean pair of pajamas and returned to his sullied bed. Another of those damned dreams. It was the mysterious woman who caused it. Was she even really mysterious? It was probably just that her red hair reminded him of Anne. His Anne. (No. Never his.) He'd long mixed her up with the Montgomery/CBC/Disney one. He shuddered at what psychiatric professionals might say about it.

Perverts!

They'd met in Classical Studies 420, "Intermediate Classical Philosophy". Back during his year of doubt. His whole life he'd expected the call to be a priest but it still hadn't come. He had survived high school, for which he was thankful. He'd found the Sewing Circle, for which he was thankful. But he was well into his twenties and hadn't felt God's presence since his mom's funeral. Had that even been God's presence or had James, desperate for reassurance, projected the experience with his own mind? He was starting to feel lost and without direction.

Then Anne walked through the lecture hall door, backlit and radiant.

He'd mentally tried to will her to sit down beside him.

"Is this seat taken?"

"Not that I know of."

Soon enough he was tutoring her before class. Aristotle. Plato. Xenophon. (He knew them well, having used their texts when first teaching himself Greek.)

But after two months James realized he didn't know her name. He couldn't ask. They'd known each other too long. One moment, when her head was turned, he leaned over to see if she'd written it on the top of her essay…

"It's Anne."

"Hmm?"

"I know what you were doing. My name is Anne."

"Anne?" And she had red hair too!

"I'm aware."

"Aware of what?"

"I have red hair. My name's Anne."

"I'd say your hair is more auburn…"

"No. It's red."

James studied her hair, carefully. "Is it?"

"You're lucky you've been so helpful." She seemed legitimately agitated: the fiery personality!

James could not stop his brain from being excited. Anne! He knew an Anne. He sat beside an Anne. "An Anne", he said to himself. It was fun to say or think. He would be sure to play it cool next time he saw her of course. But he couldn't think about playing it cool or he definitely wouldn't be cool. He'd tried that before. Already the fact that he was thinking about playing it cool would almost definitely mean he would be unable to play it cool…

Aaargh! Why did he have to be him?

But next class he was actually not uncool, though that was probably because her blackened eye had distracted him.

"Are you all right?"

"I don't want to talk about it."

Not talking about things was something James respected. It wasn't his business. It's not like he knew her very well and…

Tears. Whimpering. Streams of mucus. People were staring at them. He offered her a packet of Kleenex he happened always to carry in his old leather briefcase. She looked up at him, almost dazed, before the tears completely overtook her. She rushed from the lecture hall. He considered following, but thought it improper to intrude on her grief.

Next class she apologized for her outburst and, before he could say, "That's quite all right", she was going on about her relationship with "Joss". How he'd made her pregnant. How he'd accused her of having a baby to trap him. How he drank too much. How she wished she could bring herself to leave him.

"I just bought a new house. I have extra room."

"Oh no, James. Thank-you. That's too much."

Of course it was too much! Idiot. What made him say that? How could he abort?

"It wouldn't be any trouble." That's making it worse! "I'd say that to anyone in similar circumstances." Aaargh!

She looked at James strangely. "Thanks all the same but I'll be all right, really."

Well, thought James, that's ruined. He sat in a completely different seat next class, assuming she'd want nothing to do with him. But no, she sat beside him. Said she'd moved in with her mother. Asked him if he'd tutor her for finals.

For three weeks they met on Sunday and Thursday nights. He'd bake chocolate caramel cookies with a pinch of chili powder so the place would smell wonderful when she arrived.

"According to Aristotle the opposite of a vice is not a virtue, it's another vice. It is a vice to be a spendthrift and a vice to be miserly. Recklessness is a vice. So is cowardice. If the two vices could be represented numerically, the virtue would be the mathematical average between them. The Golden Mean." *Via media*, thought James.

"So a person could be too nice?"

"This is where I disagree with Aristotle. You see, I believe Jesus sacrificing himself on the Cross was the nicest thing anyone's ever done and I believe it was virtuous. I also disagree with Aristotle on women and slavery."

"I thought you didn't believe in Jesus anymore."

"I believe in him", said James. "He was a real person. Maybe even God. But even if he wasn't, even if he only thought he was, I still think it was a virtuous thing. Anyway, I'm sorry. I led us into a digression."

"You're adorable."

"How do you mean?"

"You're always so serious."

"I'm sorry. Is it off putting?" Anne smiled at this. Bit her upper lip, trying to stifle a laugh. She then took his hand into hers.

"You're a nice guy aren't you?"

James shrugged.

"I think it's good that you're nice but I also think you're too nice."

"Why's that?"

"Haven't you wanted to make a move on me?"

James blushed.

"I didn't invite myself over just to learn about *The Nicomachean Ethics*."

"No?"

She briefly kissed him on the lips. "No."

The next kiss was not brief. Nor was the next touch. He almost wanted to stop it before it led too far, but pre-marital contact wasn't against Scripture. Well it was debatable. And though he preferred strictness on such things, when Anne caressed him it felt right. When she kissed him it felt like something that was always meant to happen. When they lay down in bed together he felt like he had arrived home at long last. When they had relations, it was lovely. (Okay, a bit slimy and sweaty and their bodies rubbing against each other made farting sounds, but lovely.)

Jo-Marie had feared him at first. She was Joanne then, named after both her parents (Joseph and Anne-Marie; her grandma's name was Jeanne, so that almost worked too). She rushed away when she saw James. Hid behind Anne's leg. "Joanne, be nice. James is a nice man. Give him a hug." Don't force the poor girl, thought James. She's afraid. She doesn't know me. She's being honest. Why do people think there's something wrong about not showing affection when maybe that's not your thing?

James found himself opening up to Anne. Not something he was normally fond of doing, but with her it felt natural. He told her how he feared failing the spirit of his father. Feared his watchful eyes looking down from heaven. Feared what he'd think if James never became a priest. Feared the judgment of those eyes more than the judgment of God.

He introduced her to the Sewing Circle. She charmed them all. "When will you two be married?" asked Zi-Wei.

"It's lovely that you've finally found a *woman*", offered the Venerable McCall.

As the summer went by it became unbearable not to reveal his love. The way she looked at him so deeply, through the eyes and into the soul. Like she needed him to tell her or she would break.

But perhaps he was just projecting.

"I think I might be in love with you." He'd carefully considered this exact wording.

"I am in love with you. You think you might be?"

"I know I might be in love with you." She laughed. He'd even meant for it to be funny! "I know that I absolutely am in love with you."

Anne's mother kicked her out. She had been spending "too much time on this Protestant who has no respect for the sanctity of a real family."

"Technically Anglicans are neither Catholics nor Protestants and at the same time are both", pleaded James, but to no avail. He did not want to admit it, but there was a part of him that thought Anne's mother might be right. That he was an intruder on a family, albeit not a happy family.

"Do you still have room for us?" Anne had asked.

"Yes", said James, in that moment deciding to delay his application to Keble College, Oxford. His father's school. Instead, he took some 500 level courses that would be applicable if he did choose theology. For the next eight months (was it only eight months?) he'd had a family. People to cook for. People to clean for. It gave purpose to these things that for too long had felt like empty rituals.

Joanne was talking up a storm. (She no longer feared him.) She would give him a toy that he, honoured, would treat with the utmost care and consequence. Her stuffed puppy *was* a puppy. Tig *was* a tiger. Her baby Jasmine *was* a baby (and so we must be gentle). A three-year-old takes play seriously. James took everything seriously.

He should have been studying for exams but there's something about a child who adores you that is just impossible to ignore. Nor should you ignore it. You miss the little things like that you miss life. If he hadn't learned that from all his books, he hadn't learned anything. Siduri told Gilgamesh to "cherish the little child that holds your hand." That was from the Old Babylonian Version, circa 1700 BC. Had truer words been written since?

His grades had suffered, but not that much. It may have been the difference for Oxford, but that didn't matter anymore. They were a family. And he'd shown her the proper way to pour tea: warm the pot first! Jasmine, Tig and Mr. Snugglesworth were very appreciative of the care put into this.

He looked at Joanne and felt overwhelmed. I will do for you what I'd forgotten God has done for me, he thought. I will protect you from every harm. I will make a home for you to grow happy and strong. This was the love he'd felt after his mom's funeral, but more powerful. The love God had for him James felt for this little girl. This, he thought, is why we say "God the Father". He loves all His children as I love this child. This boundless love I feel for one child He feels for all creation. It was then that James started calling her Jo-Marie: Mary and Joseph. She was a sacred child to him.

And it was then, at that precise moment, that James knew he had to become a priest.

There you go! James turned onto his side. The Lord worked in mysterious ways. God had given him direction. Just what he'd been praying for. Things worked out as they were supposed to. Why couldn't he just believe that? He was a priest. Believing was a big part of what he was supposed to do.

It just takes a mustard seed of faith.

It's the easiest thing in the world.

Chapter

5

There had been an unexpected snowfall—snow in Victoria was always unexpected. It wouldn't last long, it rarely did, but for the moment the city was at a standstill. There were few ploughs and while most people had shovels you certainly couldn't expect them to clear in front of their homes or businesses early on a Sunday morning. Most cars didn't have snow tires. The elderly could not get from their homes. The radio specifically told them not to try.

It was hardly a surprise, therefore, that the Eleven O'clock Service was poorly attended. Alice and Ruth both lived at the seniors' apartment complex next door. Carol lived just up the street, as did her husband Frank. Even with the short walk any one of them could have fallen and broken something. At their ages that could get complicated. That they had come at all on such a day was a testament of their devotion both to God and to proper liturgy.

So the Rector blindsided James in the vestry when he said, "I've had a talk with the wardens. We're going to see about phasing out the Eleven."

James was pretty sure he'd heard wrong. "You're what?"

"You see how sparsely it's attended these days. I've never been to a service with the numbers so low."

"It snowed."

"We still had decent numbers for the Nine-Fifteen. I'm sorry, James, I know how much this service means to you."

"Not just to me." James noticed that some servers were watching the conversation intently. "Perhaps we should talk about this privately."

"Perhaps we should", agreed the Rector.

"Should I come too?" asked the Deacon.

"I was hoping you would", said the Rector.

* * *

James sat in an old wicker chair in the Rector's office. He looked at the Deacon who smiled warmly but was at least bright enough not to try to engage him. James was still livid. Correction: more livid. He'd had time to stew about things. To come up with excellent counterpoints to anything the Rector might throw at him. This had been a long time coming. The Rubicon had finally been crossed but, unlike Rome, James was ready.

Returning to his office, the Rector gave James a cup of tea. James nearly spat it out it was so poorly made. Had the man never heard of steeping? Never heard of warming the pot first?

"This is delicious", said the Deacon.

"Are you planning to get rid of the BCP too?"

The Rector sat down in his chair, sipping his tea. "Listen, James, the fact is we need to build up a new generation of parishioners. We've only stayed afloat these last few years by dipping into our savings that, as you well know, are fast dwindling. We're desperate for a new roof. We desperately need to hire a security company with all the crime in the neighbourhood."

The Rector was not exaggerating. The roof leaked. It should have been replaced a decade ago. Parish Council kept putting it off and putting it off until financial times were better, but financial times only got worse. Drug use on the church grounds was rampant. Not a day went by without James stepping over a needle or a street addict or a streetkid. His car window had been smashed twice, netting the hoodlums a CD of the choir from St. George's Chapel, Windsor Castle and approximately sixty-seven cents in loose change. The office had been robbed on three occasions. Someone even stole the lighting board during Friday morning meditation. "Stealing light from a church", the Rector had said. "That'll bring you bad karma." The mixed religious metaphor had nearly made James scream but he'd held it back. He'd held everything back for far too long.

"More people will leave if we lose the Eleven", said James. "It's not like it costs us anything more than a few wafers and a little wine. If it's too boring for you, then don't come. Have your Nine-Fifteen with your guitar music and modern language Book of Alternative Services service." Take that! "Why do you have to take away the service with proper music and liturgical grace in the process?" And that!

"I admire your passion, James, but imagine a prospective new parishioner coming in to see ten people in the congregation, all well past retirement. Do you think they'd want to come back? Do you think they'd tell their friends?"

"If they can't appreciate beautiful liturgy they are privileged to share with people who fought in the war, then that's their problem." Speak it!

"We can't afford to scare off new parishioners."

"What about scaring off the old parishioners?" Zing! Keep it up. "What about the Sternes, the Dormans, and the Hudsons? These families have been coming here for generations. Ethel Cleaver has been coming to the Eleven O'clock service every Sunday since 1934. That's before the rectory burned down. That's twenty years before you were even born. Timothy Edwards fought in the war. He still has Nazi shrapnel in his left shoulder. You know how Simon Douglas has always had trouble with his eyes? He fried his retinas when he saw an explosion through a scope while serving on the HMCS St. Laurent. He was part of Convoy ON-154! They have served their country, served their God and served this church. The Eleven is the service they know and love and are familiar with and there's not much in this world left for them to be familiar with. Where do you get off taking it away from them?"

"It is wonderful that you care so deeply for them, James. It does you credit. But, you know, when I went on sabbatical last year my research showed that the best way to attract new parishioners is offer them an exciting atmosphere."

What sort of person goes to church for excitement?

"We are a church, not a business. Not a television show. Not a blog." Pow! Pow! Pow! "We weren't put on this earth to be popular.

We were put here to offer salvation." James couldn't believe how fast he was coming up with this stuff. But he noticed his hands, shaking. Don't forget *via media*. Otherwise you're no better than they are. James calmed himself. "We must maintain a sense of dignity."

"These things aren't mutually exclusive, James. But we need new parishioners. We have to do some outside the box thinking."

"I like the box. I miss the box."

"It's hard when things like this have to change. I think it's a beautiful book. It has beautiful liturgy. It's a gift. It's most unfortunate this decision had to be made."

He's patronizing me like I'm one of the elderly. To his unconscious mind I'm ninety.

"Innovation, James. Evolution. We need them for our survival. It is the way God made the world. The Church has had to evolve before. The Book of Common Prayer was part of an evolving church. The King James Bible too. They were innovative in their times. And that's why I wanted Reverend B to be here. Ha ha." The Rector and Deacon shared a short laugh. "He's got an idea that I think demonstrates the sort of thing we're looking for. It's sure to deliver some youthful vibrancy to worship. You're just the man to help him with it."

Am I now? Ten years of ministry and I get to assist a deacon. Fifty years ago I might have been something. Joined the Rotary Club and the Masons by now. (To be fair the Masons, in the guise of Canon Jones, had invited him, but he decided against it. Anyone under fifty who still wanted to be a Mason was a little bit pathetic. Even James could see that.)

"I'd love your help, James", said the Deacon. "I need your help."

"Help with what?"

"Well", said the Deacon, "it's called a U2charist. Basically it's a Eucharist but, instead of boring old hymns that nobody cares about anymore…" James gave him the death eyes. "I'm sorry, that intimidate some people…" The Rector looked at the Deacon proudly. "… instead of those hymns we use songs by U2. Their music is surprisingly spiritual if you really listen to the lyrics."

"Is this a joke? A set-up?" James turned to the Rector. "Are you trying to get me to leave?"

"Joke? No. Of course not." The Deacon handed James some papers he'd printed off the interweb.

"These have been popular for years", said the Rector. "They've helped bring people back into churches by generating excitement. It's reminded people that church can be fun."

James looked at the Rector with utter disgust. "Have you listened to yourself? 'Popular'. 'Innovative'. 'Fun'. Church should never mix with business."

"Actually," the Deacon said helpfully, "the U2charist is an entirely charitable event."

Via media! Via media! James took a deep breath. "I really appreciate that you've worked hard on this," said James, "but I must respectfully decline."

"I'll do all the grunt work, but I don't know the parish very well yet. I was hoping you could assist me on that front."

"I'm sorry. I can't do it."

"Why not?" asked the Rector.

"Because I'm not Bonotheistic." You should write that one down.

"You see," said the Rector, "even you know *U2*. They're the most popular band on the planet. I hate to be trite, but it will help us get bums in pews."

Bono. Yes James knew *Bono*. That accursed name! First he had somehow made charity unsavory with his slick sunglass wearing appeals for Africa. Then he had made a mockery of the Broadway musical and now he was getting his guitar plucking fingers into liturgy as well? Charity, Broadway musicals and liturgy: three of James' most favourite things ruined by this male Irish banshee!

"We already have a Facebook group", continued the Deacon. "You should join."

James glared.

"We're trying to reach out to you, James", said the Rector. "We're trying to keep you involved."

"You're trying to push me out", said James. "Just like you did Zi-Wei." James stood up. "You can be sure that I will be speaking to Parish Council about the Eleven." And then James walked out. He thought it might be too dramatic a gesture, but for once in his life he wanted drama. He even considered slamming the door but, remembering the handle was an antique, merely shut it firmly.

Chapter
6

James walked rapidly up Gladstone Avenue. Some nocciola. Or perhaps hazelnut. Or coconut. He hadn't tried it yet but had heard good things. He looked down to his shoes. Black dress shoes. In his anger he had forgotten to change into his walking boots. His feet were freezing in the melting slushy snow.

He didn't care. He wanted it that way. He was not completely satisfied with the points he'd made to the Rector. When he said I was needed for the Eleven he already must have been planning to shut it down. May already have had the meeting with the Wardens.

Treachery! Lies!

James was definitely going to treat himself to a waffle cone.

Facebook! Him join Facebook? Ha! There was nothing in this world he wanted to do less. To display your own life for all to see, as if your life were somehow news. They even called it news. (And meanwhile the printed press was all but dead.) He saw it once: the Facebook news feed. Shallow news for a shallow generation. A generation of narcissists and navel gazers. Three generations really if you include the Xers and Boomers. They were into it too. How did the Great Generation create such progeny?

James came to the front steps of Paulo's Gelato. It was most definitely closed. Why he'd expected otherwise was beyond him. The whole city was shut down.

And who would want to eat gelato in the snow?

* * *

James flipped through his record albums. He had over one thousand. When old parishioners died their (rather neglectful) children would sometimes ask if they could repay him in any way. He would say no, he was just performing his duty, but would then glance ever so subtly at the record collection. "Take any you'd like. We would just be giving them away anyway." Both Market Place and New-To-You offered ample opportunity for collecting. He had two or three copies of all his favourite albums. One to listen to, the others for safekeeping.

James finally found it: the original cast recording of Rodgers and Hammerstein's *Carousel*. He precisely lowered the needle onto the opening bars of *You'll Never Walk Alone*. James looked at his watch. The tea had steeped for exactly five minutes. He poured the milk. He took off the cozy. Poured himself a cup through the strainer. Put the strainer onto a small saucer. Took a sip. Perfect. James spread out on his couch. At last he could relax.

RING! RING! RING!

James despised his phone. "Hello?"

"Hi James, it's Rodger. Lovely job during the Offertory."

"Thanks", said James, trying to sound as annoyed as he was.

"I called earlier too. I didn't see you at coffee hour."

"Oh. I hadn't checked my answering machine."

"So that *was* an answering machine. I didn't know they still existed."

"Well they do. Why did you call?"

"I'm meeting some friends at The Penny Farthing."

"Are you sure it's open? I mean, the snow…"

"You Victorians! Yes. We checked. The snow's half melted anyway. I thought you should come."

"I don't know…"

"James, you need to hang out with people close to your own age. It would be good for you." Who was he to say that? How did he know what would be good for James? "Though I should warn you we'll be encroaching on a book club."

"A book club?"

"Yeah. They'll be discussing *Les Miserables*. I haven't read it personally. It's ridiculously long."

James paused. Spoke with a less defensive tone: "I'll think about it."

"That's the best I'll get from you isn't it?"

"It is. Good-bye."

"We're meeting at four. Bye."

James considered the invitation. Sitting by himself drinking tea and listening to Rodgers and Hammerstein, perhaps making fresh scones, was definitely an appealing way to spend the afternoon. However, the Choir Master had taken time to reach out. After his outburst, James could use at least one ally at the office.

He went to the bookshelf for his copy of *Les Miserables*. His mom had given it to him. It was long, but that was what made it rewarding. You truly got to know all the characters. James conceded that it was at times sentimental, but at least there was feeling. At least the author treated his characters with compassion. Bishop Myriel was a childhood hero of James. Monseigneur Bienvenu. James had secretly wished to one day earn that nickname, or something like it. But he never would. He knew that now. He just didn't have the right personality.

Maybe this was a path God wanted him to follow. They just happened to be reading his favourite book? Hardly anyone read *Les Miserables* anymore. Maybe these would be James' sort of people. Surely there must be some of them in this generation, statistically speaking.

Chapter
7

Nobody actually had read *Les Miserables*. Not the whole thing any-way. Not even the first volume. It was so long! Mostly they had just talked about Books 1 and 2, which James had hoped would mean a focused discussion.

Yup. It was focused all right. Everyone grilled him on why priests weren't more like Bishop Myriel. Why was he himself drinking beer with them when there was famine in Africa and children living on the streets? What did he do all day anyway? What's the point to a priest if not to help those in need? Bono was doing his work for him.

James stood at the bar. Ordered himself a stout. "They were just ribbing you", said the Choir Master. "They didn't mean anything by it."

"They did", said James. "They were right. I don't live up to the example of Bishop Myriel. But if they're so concerned, why are they drinking in a pub? Nothing's stopping them from helping."

"They meant it to be funny", said the Choir Master. "Trust me. I know these guys."

James handed over his money and took a sip of beer. "I thought you hardly knew anyone in the city."

"I did a shout out on Facebook." Facebook! Of course. They were as shallow as the rest. Not one of them had even bothered to pur-chase the actual book. They all read it on their iPads and Kindles. Why was he here when he could be making scones? Hadn't he been through enough humiliation for one day? James considered leaving, but he'd already walked out on the Rector. He didn't want to make a habit of it. He would at least have to finish his beer.

The Choir Master and James headed to the table where the Book Club was waiting. There were seven of them. Some similarly dressed to the Choir Master. Some with pullovers. Some with tight fitting jeans. "Don't judge them too quickly", the Choir Master had said when they first met on the street outside. "I know they might seem like hipsters."

"Hipsters? What do you mean? Like beatniks?" James didn't much care for their literature or style or sense of liberal entitlement. In many ways they were a pox on the Great Generation. Their self-righteousness echoed down to modern youth. But he liked some of their ideals. "Beat" from "beatitude" or "beatific". Kerouac himself had said so. Not enough people saw them that way though. Least of all themselves.

The Choir Master had laughed at James, before leading him inside.

James took another sip of his beer before sitting down at the table. The seven hipsters were playing a game. The Choir Master explained: "It's called, 'Who created more lesbians?' You compare two things about heterosexual men that probably turned women gay."

More about gay people! Can't people just be gay without us having to talk about it? Or not gay? Or have sex or not have sex? Why aren't people allowed to be in the closet? Why does every-one have to be on Facebook? Can't people have private lives any-more?

"We're not making fun of lesbians", the Choir Master rational-ized. "It's not really about lesbians at all. We're pointing out what's wrong with the current generation of straight men." Oh, thought James. I should be good at this.

The Choir Master had a go. "Which created more lesbians? Men wearing socks with sandals or the 'Whazzup?' campaign from B*dweiser?" People laughed at this, hysterically. It made James very nervous. He agreed with the socks and sandals part, though he knew women who did the same thing. He'd never heard of this "Whazzup" campaign. B*dweiser tasted like carbonated urine.

James would have to go next. What could he mention? Would they laugh for him too? What did he care? They were just stupid beatniks and not even from the good generation and… he had it: "Which created more lesbians? Men playing video games into adulthood or soul patch facial hair?"

People actually laughed. It made him feel good. Exceptionally good. He was trying to remember the last time he'd felt this good when he caught sight of auburn hair, freckles and a right index finger in a metal splint: the girl again! Her eyes were a striking blue just as he had suspected. And she was laughing at his joke. Where did she come from? What was she doing here?

"It's you", she said, taking a seat with the group. James was dumbstruck. He nodded.

"You two…" (those accursed syllables!) "…know each other?" asked the Choir Master.

"Not at all", she said, smiling at James warmly. Under her right arm she held a paperback copy of *Les Miserables*, dog-eared and slightly battered.

* * *

Their conversation was going far better than he could possibly have expected. At first they'd talked about how it was a coincidence them running into each other again but not really a coincidence since they hadn't really run into each other a first time. James tried his best to be dismissive of her. She wore a similar outfit to the rest of them. The female ones anyway. Far too stylish. And she wore nail scissors—nail scissors!—as a necklace. What was that about?

But she wasn't like them. She was kind hearted. Lovely. She didn't make fun of him for not living up to Bishop Myriel's high standards. "It's not like he's a real person", she'd said. (He was based on a real person, thought James. But Hugo probably exaggerated.) "I've known people who gave up their lives for charity. There can be something selfish about it in real life." She asked him all about being a priest. Were they really consuming Jesus' body and blood at Communion? How many weddings had he officiated? How many funerals? What was his daily schedule? Did you really have to have a calling? She seemed fascinated by everything he said. Genuinely fascinated. She asked him many intelligent and probing questions about Consubstantiation.

Her name was Melissa. One of James' favourites. He'd even built up the courage to tell her why: "It comes from μέλιττα."

"Mehleetah?"

"Yes. It was the ancient Greek word for honey bee."

"I like that. Sweet but with a sting."

"But it's not actually Greek. It's likely not even Indo-European. It's one of the oldest names that exists, from a language family lost to time."

"That's so cool! It makes me feel mysterious and connected to the ages." Exactly how James hoped it would make her feel. "So you took Greek when you were studying to be a priest?"

"Koinic Greek for that. I already knew ancient Greek. I took my undergrad in Classics."

"That's Greek and Latin languages right?"

"Exactly."

"Teach me something else in Greek."

James tried to keep calm. "Okay. Here's one, from Heraklitos, as quoted by Plato: 'πάντα χωρεῖ καὶ οὐδὲν μένει.'"

"Pant aack! Rakee ordern many?"

"Close. Panta…"

"Panta…"

"Khōrei…"

"Kōrei…"

"The Greek letter 'chi' we usually transliterate as 'c' 'h' but really it's a hard breathed 'k'. So it's k-h-ōrei. Kh-ōrei."

"Kh-ōrei."

"Perfect. Panta khōrei…"

"Panta khōrei…"

"Kai ouden…"

"Kai ouden…"

"Menei."

"Menei. Kai ouden menei."

"Exactly. So: panta khōrei kai ouden menei."

"Panta khōrei kai ouden menei."

"You're good at this."

"Thank-you. What does it mean?"

"Panta khōrei… So 'panta' with root of 'pan' means 'everything' or 'all'."

"Like Pan-American Games."

"Precisely. Then there's khōrei, which is our verb. It means 'give way' or 'flow' or 'change'."

"All changes."

"Yes. We'll come back to that. So the rest: 'kai' means 'and', 'ouden' means nothing, and 'menei' means 'stationary', 'static' or 'constant'.

"All changes and nothing is static."

"Yes. Though, idiomatically, I prefer: 'Everything changes and nothing is constant.'"

"Panta khōrei kai ouden menei. I love it. It's sort of like what Abraham Lincoln said in that speech: 'This too shall pass away.'" Was this truly a woman, or an angel?

"You're very good at this. You should've been in Classics."

"What's stopping me? I've studied nearly everything else."

"Really?"

"I started out in music composition before switching to a double major in history and astronomy, then to economics because I thought that would be more practical, but I hated it so I just got my degree in botany. Can you show me how to write panta khōrei kai ouden menei with Greek letters?"

Breathe James. Just breathe. "Sure." James searched for his pen. Where was it? He always kept a pen. He was known for that.

Melissa's cell phone rang. "Hello?" Cell phones were the only things James despised more than regular phones. He still hadn't bought one. Everyone at the office liked to tease him about it but he'd be the one laughing when they all had brain tumours in twenty years. Well he wouldn't be laughing. He wasn't planning on becoming a sociopath who would laugh at other people for having cancer. But he would feel vindicated. And, let's face it, he would feel quite guilty about feeling vindicated. Whatever. Better not to have a cell phone. That was the point.

"I'll be right there." Melissa put her phone away. Started putting on her jacket. "Sorry, I've got to get going. It was really nice meeting you."

"You t... you also." She was already standing. Waving her good-byes. Already heading for the exit. Get up! Chase her! Don't let this one get away!

He remained fixed to his seat. But, before leaving completely, she turned back and looked directly at James.

"Facebook me", she said and then left as suddenly as she'd come.

* * *

That night, James parked his car at the church. As he got out he saw a couple of streetkids seated in the lych gate of the Memorial Garden. One had a needle in the neck of the other. James at first recoiled in disgust. They were dirty. Covered in germs. The needle probably contained hepatitis C. What if they attacked him? What then? He steeled himself. Looked directly at them. Smiled. Said, "Hello."

"Hello", said the one holding the needle. "We'll be gone soon. We promise."

How do I help them, thought James. What if I said the wrong thing? What if, by trying to help, I only make their problems worse? They don't want to talk to me. They just want me to leave them in peace. Let them live their lives. Or die their deaths. Whatever you want to call it. The Street Priest is better suited for this than me.

"Is that okay?" asked the one with the needle in her neck.

James grimaced a response. Turned. Rushed towards the back door.

* * *

James picked up his walking boots. Looked up at his computer. He'd forgotten to shut it down. He moved the mouse, awakening the screen. He sat in his desk chair. Hesitated for a moment. Typed the word "Facebook." Hit return. He clicked on the website. It asked him if he was new to Facebook and would he like to join?

It would be a nice gesture to the Deacon, James thought. James had overreacted to his request. The Deacon was new. Young. Earnest. Doing his best. Anglicans should be accepting of a wide variety of worship provided that the adherents were pious and used the Nicene Creed (and the Apostle's Creed and, to a lesser extent, the Creed of St. Athanasius) as their declaration of faith. Anglicans should be inclusive: *via media*. It wasn't the Deacon's fault they were getting rid of the Eleven O'clock. He had been very friendly from the start and James had been nothing but rude.

Get over it, reverend.

James shut down his computer for the night and then went home to bed.

Chapter

8

He didn't even see the Rector until staff meeting on the following Wednesday. He'd been dreading a confrontation, but the Rector simply asked James if he was feeling better. James simply nodded.

He brought his issue about the Eleven up with Parish Council. They agreed that any changes to the services should be done openly and with the consultation of the entire parish. In fact they had already set it on the agenda for the Vestry meeting, scheduled for the following Sunday. James would have time to speak then.

The rest of the week he devoted to his defense of the Book of Common Prayer and his beloved service. He had just gone to the printer room (actually a closet) when the Choir Master called him into his office.

"Did you enjoy your time on Sunday?"

"Yes, thank-you."

"You and Melissa seemed to hit it off." James had avoided asking him about her, feeling foolish about the whole thing.

"Yes, she was quite lovely."

The Choir Master looked down at his desk. There was a sheet in front of him. "Did they make you sign this Safer Churches crap when you got here?"

They had indeed. Anglican priests could marry and were generally not viewed with suspicion by their parishioners. Still, scandals happened. The Reverend Howard, former rector at St. Richard's, had an extra-marital affair with one of his chalice bearers. He'd been fired and quickly. Eventually he left the communion altogether. People still talked about him in hushed tones. "Judge not lest ye be judged" abandoned people's minds during scandals. James sometimes even felt sorry for the man. But when he was forced to sit through Safer Churches talks he cursed the Reverend Howard's name. Why should his indiscretions make everyone else have to suffer?

"You're not even supposed to hug", said the Choir Master. "What kind of person is so uncomfortable with themselves that they can't even hug without getting all tetchy about it?" James glanced at the ground. Sighed internally. He was thankful to Safer Churches about that and one other thing. On the rare occasion that a lonely woman of the parish approached him, James had a simple ready-made answer to make her back off.

Suzanne Cumberbatch was the only parishioner ever to pursue him after this. "We're destined to be together. We both like historical documentaries." Lots of people like historical documentaries: that's why they make them. She thought that breaking the rules would be romantic. That he would find her flouting of convention to be exciting and sexy. She was wrong. After repeated attempts to clearly but kindly dissuade her affections he had been forced to report the situation to the Rector. She denied everything, of course, saying he was putting words in her mouth. That the problem was his. That was fine with him. At least she left the congregation. Of course they could scarcely afford to lose parishioners, which the Rector could not help but remind him.

"We would have lost more with a scandal."

"You're right of course. You did the right thing."

Rumours were started. He'd felt humiliated. But everything died down after only a couple of weeks. An advantage to people assuming he was a closet homosexual.

Luckily Melissa isn't a parishioner.

What the…? Why had he thought that? Get that woman out of your head.

James nervously laughed at a couple of the Choir Master's Safer Churches jokes before he informed him that he had more important matters to attend to.

* * *

Nearly the whole congregation was at Vestry. The prospect of losing the Eleven had managed to create a little excitement. The Rector had made his case for dissolving it, essentially the same one he had made in his office. Now it was James' turn.

He stood at the podium. He hated public speaking. The fact that he did it every week made him capable of faking his way through. But his nerves never seemed to fade. He glanced down at his notes. While he could not help but appeal to some emotions, his arguments would be, he hoped, literary and thought out. Like the best of his sermons. The BCP was a work of ideas. So too, James hoped, was his speech:

"We must not eliminate the Book of Common Prayer nor its liturgy at St. Matthew's. This is the book that set us apart as Anglicans. That helped define who we are. That made us different from the Catholics and from the Protestants. Anglicans have always taken the middle way between the two. The *via media*. Some may find the Book of Common Prayer outdated. May find the Eleven O'clock Service boring. They may prefer modern language. Modern music. A modern sensibility. By all means. That is their right. As Richard Hooker himself said, our method of worship is one of the 'things indifferent' to God. Provided you believe the words of the three Creeds, provided you are pious, loving, and accept Jesus as your Saviour, God is not concerned about how you worship Him."

"Or Her", someone yelled from the congregation.

"Yes…" this was going to hurt… "or Her."

"And what about Hindus? What about Muslims? Buddhists? Why should they have to accept Jesus as their saviour?"

"This is a Christian church. I thought I might limit my argument to Christianity. To save time, if nothing else." *Via media*. James took a breath. He had lost his place. He looked back down to his notes, nervously, robotically spewing out the following sentence and a half: "Butsomepreferthetraditionalway.Forsomethe liturgyofShakespeareofWilberforceandNewtonofDickens ofChurchilloftheirparentsandgrandparents…" Slow down. You mean these words. Speak like you do. James took another calming breath. "For some this is the only way they can worship God. The old language helps bring them outside of themselves. Helps them leave the mundane modern world to experience the world of the divine. But just because this way is right, doesn't mean the other way is wrong. No liturgy is wrong provided it is performed with sincerity, humility and, above all, piety.

"St. Matthew's has always been known as a church which accepts both the modern and traditional. Both high and low churches. To cancel the Eleven in order to 'put more bums in pews' would be short sighted. It would be an act of desperation. Maybe it would bring a net gain of a parishioner or two, but it would be at the cost of our own identity and at the cost of an entire generation of parishioners. The Eleven might not be important to you, but it is important to some of us, including those who built the church at which you worship and the country in which you live."

James had found himself getting emotional as he approached the end but it appeared to go over well. His passion was obvious. He hoped his logic was too. Some people had even clapped before the Rector's Warden had, rightfully, asked them to stop. Simon Douglas patted James on the back. Whispered, "Thank-you good man", into his ear. James felt their chances were good.

* * *

The votes to eliminate the Eleven were 278 for to 83 against. In seven weeks time they would contract to one Sunday morning Eucharist, starting at ten-thirty, which would use the modern language of the BAS. At that time the BCPs would be removed from the pews and placed in storage.

"Good speech", the Rector gloated. "The vote was much closer than anyone could have expected."

"It was really great", said the Deacon. "I feel like I can learn so much from you."

James thanked them, just managing to maintain both politeness and dignity.

* * *

He sat in his living room, gently holding a 1717 copy of the Book of Common Prayer, full calf gilt, sold by John Sturt (engraver) with permission of John Baskett (printer). Though chipped and rubbed in places it was in excellent condition. He softly caressed the cover. His father had loved old books. Had once possessed the third oldest book in Western Canada which he, of course, donated to a museum. The museum would've liked this book too but no, this invaluable copy of the BCP he had given to James. His high school graduation present. James' father was never one to hug or speak loving words. He never told James he was proud of him or any of that nonsense. But he did express affection. This book was proof.

James returned the book to its safe and shut it tight. Only he knew the combination: 15-4-9. The date of Archbishop Thomas Cranmer's original BCP.

James considered his options. The Old Man would sympathize with him, but side with the Rector. The congregation had voted, after all. St. Barnabas' and the Cathedral still had beautiful liturgies, but they also had more than enough clergy. Become a Continuing Anglican? The cure was worse than the disease. Could he join an order? The quiet would be nice. Living outside of modern society. But all the monks he knew were just plain weird. Besides, he couldn't move away. He just couldn't. James, momentarily, wished there was an Anglican Use church in Canada. They had lovely liturgy, but he could never follow a pope. Besides, you couldn't get married.

Married? What did that matter? Are you still thinking about that girl? It's a silly infatuation based on what? A freak emotional response? The fact that she was interested in Ancient Greek? Her superficial resemblances to Anne?

James went to his antique desk. Turned the key. Opened the top drawer and took out a beige photo album. He sat down on his couch, looking through numerous photos of his younger self. He came to the pictures he was looking for: a series of him with his Anne (never his) and the three-year-old Jo-Marie. They were flying a kite off Dallas Road. Feeding the goats at Beacon Hill Park. Drinking milkshakes together at the Drive-In. In every one of these pictures James was happy. Truly happy.

It broke his heart to look at now. Made him hurt as if no time had passed. As if it all had happened only yesterday. Made the wounds fresh again.

The desired effect.

Chapter
9

No dream this time. No sleep at all. It was his own fault. Looking at those pictures. Had it been to scare off new emotions or indulge the old ones? Idiot. What good was it to keep reliving the past? An empty ritual. But one for which he was the wary officiant.

James still didn't understand why the relationship turned sour. He'd done his best. He would take care of Jo-Marie while Anne was at work, making dinners for them to eat together as a family. Anne would come home, take her plate, go to another room and cry. He would come to comfort her. Ask her what was wrong. "Don't", she would say, before sitting by herself again.

They'd lay awake in bed. "You probably don't love me anymore now that you know what I'm really like."

"I do still love you." It was true. But the love was no longer a source of joy. That was for sure.

"You've really changed." This was entirely untrue. James was the same. His love for her was the same. He wasn't sure if he was even capable of changing on that front. It was like he'd undammed a river and now the rush of water was too strong to plug it again no matter what happened. The more she pushed him away, the more he tried to make things better. He would treat her to surprise poetry. To surprise presents. To surprise nights on the town (as much as he hated both surprises and towns at night). "Just leave it", she would say. "We got by fine before without you."

Every once in a while she'd be herself again. Let him hold her in his arms. She would say that life hadn't been easy for her. Her father, a lieutenant in the navy, used to hit her and her mom before they left him. Joss hit her too. James was the nicest man she'd ever known and she was sorry if she sometimes got moody. She knew she was hard to live with.

It gave James hope. It gave him moments of happiness even. Hours could go by and days and be amazing. That Sunday they spent at Dallas Road and Beacon Hill Park was a pure, glorious, happy day.

But days like that were days too few.

* * *

Lent was fast approaching. It was time to decide what to give up. This was not technically required. It was not doctrine. Not a rule of the church. But it was a rule of his father. James had always loved Lent. He loved Shrove Tuesday (not technically Lent, but Lent inspired). He fondly remembered his father and mom flipping pancakes at the Cathedral hall. James took stacks and stacks of them to the tables. Big stacks on beautiful ornate plates decorated with peacocks. He remembered sitting with all the lovely old people who said kind things to him about his manners. Remembered smothering syrup on his pancakes and "accidentally" getting it on his sausages too.

James loved Ash Wednesday. The priest would smear the cross on his forehead. He loved the way the whole church would change. The veils. The shrouding of the altar. He had always liked giving something up for the season. It just seemed right. Properly religious.

He much preferred it to Christmas. Christmas! He didn't like that it was commercial, but he hated much more that people would get up in arms about the commercialism, mistaking Christmas for an important religious holiday. Important next to St. Swithin's day? Absolutely. Compared to Easter? Don't kid yourself. He especially hated the more recent developments. This war on Christmas nonsense. This fear of the words "Happy holidays". Why should non-Christians have to say "Merry Christmas"? Why should anyone? Oh Christmas was a major feast day to be sure but so was Ascension Day. Christmas was decidedly unimportant in religious terms. Two of the Gospels didn't even mention the birth and when Matthew did it was to help compare Jesus to Moses. Why else go to Egypt of all places? Why else have another slaughtering of the innocent? Evangelicals were ones to talk. What about the war on Lent? The war Zwingli quite deliberately waged by distributing all that meat in the town square. Lent was an important part of all the Synoptic Gospels. An important part of Christianity. War on Christmas? More like rich white people wanting to feel oppressed.

James took a breath. He had to focus. What to give up? It had to be something he truly enjoyed. Historical fiction? He'd given that up too many times before. Besides, he'd already read every book in the genre worth a damn. Until Gillian Bradshaw wrote something new it really couldn't count. The museum? There weren't any good exhibits there this month anyway. The library? Walks along the beach? Didn't seem to be in the right spirit. The pub? Closer, but not the honest choice. No, if he was going to give up something he truly enjoyed it would have to be gelato. James sighed, a sure sign that he had made the right choice.

He looked at his watch. It wasn't Lent yet.

* * *

James headed west down Vining Street. He had decided to stay on at St. Matthew's. He couldn't abandon the older generation. He offered them at least some stability. That gave at least some purpose to his life. He couldn't leave. He couldn't give the Rector the satisfaction.

James turned right onto Fernwood Avenue. Across the street he saw a number of young hoodlums rough housing. Even though he was an adult now, James could not forget the beatings he had received from such fellows when he was an adolescent. Fear gripped him. It was stupid, he knew, but he could not shake it. What if they were to attack him? What could he do? He feared the humiliation.

"Quit looking at us sicko!"

"Help! Police! It's a pedophile priest."

This stereotype irked James. He almost forgot his fear. "I'm Anglican, not Catholic. Also, properly speaking, I think you mean pederast." That seemed, at least, to confuse them. And it was a fair thing to say, mostly. No one had come out of the Residential School fiasco unscathed. Not the Catholic Church, nor the United, nor the

Anglicans nor the Government. Least of all the native children. But at least the Anglican Church had admitted fault, formally apologized and offered recompense. It had been far more forthright than the Catholic one.

James had been raised an ecumenist and he loved Catholic liturgy, but he could never condone some of that church's more political actions. Its corporate attitudes. Its inability to learn from its moral mistakes. Its refusal to budge on anything until five hundred years after it would have meant something (you're welcome Galileo). They wouldn't receive Anglicans for Communion. Wouldn't accept Anglicanism as one of the branches of the true church.

But to be fair, Bishop Myriel was a Catholic (but wasn't particularly real). And Mother Theresa (but wasn't the saint people sometimes thought).

To be fair, Catholics created gelato.

(And to be fair, James thought, he had no problem with Catholic people; he had problems with their church's Ecclesiastical Polity.)

(And Joe Clark was a Catholic. How could he forget? The second greatest political leader in this nation's history.)

As James approached Paulo's he was terrified he'd been followed but, looking back, he saw that the boys had moved on to other things, namely throwing rocks at a wasp's nest. He let out a sigh of relief. The bell dinged as he entered the shop.

The line was long but long lines gave James time to make more careful decisions. Part of him definitely wanted nocciola. It was his favourite and he would get precious few chances to have it before Lent. However, he couldn't wait over a month before he finally got to try coconut.

A young man and woman, university students probably, kissed in front of him. PDA: three of his least favourite letters. He turned back to the gelato. Ding! A young woman entered the shop, cutting in front of James. Hey! (James didn't mind lines, but he hated being cheated his fair place.)

The young woman hugged her friends. James saw her touch the young man's back. Him squeeze her hand. Were they having an affair and the other girl didn't know? No. They were just friends and yet here they were, touching. Being affectionate. Like people were supposed to do.

Ding! James looked back. It made him feel as if his chest was hurtling in free fall at a thousand miles an hour while the rest of him faintly floated into the air like a dirigible: Melissa had just rushed in. She took her place behind him. James noticed his right hand shaking rather rapidly. He steadied it against his leg. Pretended he didn't even notice Melissa had entered. He looked towards the cashier. Didn't dare glance back. Just stood stiffly. Let her make the first move.

Except she didn't make any move. He knew she was there. She hadn't turned around and left. There would've been another ding. He could sense her presence. Almost feel her breath. What was she doing? Breathing, obviously. Hadn't she noticed him? Was she consciously not making the first move too? Was she as awkward as he was?

Fine. We'll just both stand in this line not talking. Not getting to know each other a little bit better. That's probably for the best anyway. Good James. Good. Stay disciplined. Deny yourself what you want. Do not give into temptation. Use the skills you've learned from Lent.

Would he regret not looking back? Would it haunt him forever? Would she regret never talking to him? Would they be two people who were attracted to each other but who never talked because neither could speak first?

He glanced at her. Her splint was gone. She was staring intently at the flavours, unable to decide. She looked at her watch impatiently. She looked towards James who hastily looked away: he hadn't been looking at her. Hadn't been studying her. No ma'am. He was merely fascinated by the tiles that made up the ceiling. By the whole décor of the place. He was just getting a sense of his surroundings. He was a man who paid attention to the details of life. If she happened to enter his line of vision, well he couldn't be held responsible.

It genuinely irked him that she might think otherwise.

Had he been too successful looking away? Had she not seen him? Had she seen him but still decided to say nothing? Had she seen him looking at her, deduced that he was pretending not to see her, and been so offended that there was no way she was going to talk to him now? What if they were meant to fall in love? What if, by not engaging her in conversation he was disobeying God's will? That would be some thing for a priest to do now wouldn't it?

"The nocciola is fantastic", said James.

"Oh God. Sorry I meant 'Oh goodness'. Sorry! I didn't even see you there. I'm stuck in my own little world. How are you doing?"

Whatever you do, don't go into the BCP stuff. "Fantastic. I'm about to eat delicious gelato."

"I know! Yum." She looked at her watch. Why did she keep doing that? "So you recommend the nocciola?"

"Yes."

"I've yet to try it."

"It's like hazelnut", said James. "It means hazelnut in Italian, but there's a subtlety to the flavour that must be tasted to be believed." (You're overdoing it.)

"Well now I have to try it. I love this place. It reminds me of one that was near my house back in Toronto. In the Annex. I went there almost every day. It's a sinful habit. Ha! Sinful. Here I am talking to a priest. It's probably what made me say it." She was quite neurotic. "I tried to find you on Facebook." She tried to find me. "I looked through all of Rodger's friends named James and none of them looked like you." She really tried. "Are you under some weird alias or something? Hiding out from the man?"

"No", he said.

"Oh I get it. You're not on Facebook." James nodded. "I should've guessed that about you. I'm not a huge fan either but it's great for getting out and doing stuff in a new city and hey, it helped overthrow a dictator in Egypt."

"It did do that."

"I wish I had found you. I needed help with my Greek." An opening. James had heard about these.

"It's not too late."

"That's where you're wrong. I found it online and have now taught myself to read and write the whole phrase thank-you very much." She took a pen and scrap paper from her purse. Carefully wrote something out before handing it to James: "πάντα χωρεῖ καὶ οὐδὲν μένει".

"I guess the internet knows everything." Was he actually jealous of the internet?

"But it ain't exactly cute."

That was flirting! Even James could recognize it. She'd looked him up. She'd taught herself some Greek. It would be unreasonable to expect her to hate the internet too. There had to be some differences. That's what gave life flavour. What if hazelnut and nocciola were exactly the same? James began to imagine what their children would be like. Wondered if she'd let him name their son after his father.

She looked at her watch yet again.

"What's the matter?"

"I'm late for a very important date." An actual date or was she just quoting Lewis Carroll? "I should've given it more time. I should've known there'd be a line. There's always a line here."

"There aren't many good dessert places in this city."

Now what? James didn't want to let her cut ahead of him. It meant he'd have less time with her and her date would have more time. Maybe James had somewhere important to be too. Maybe he was in just as much of a hurry. She hadn't asked. He got here first. He wasn't obligated. For once in his life he was not going to do the polite thing.

"Would you like to cut ahead of me?"

"Really?" James nodded, stepping aside to let her past. "You're one of the last gentlemen left", she said. He could feel the blood rushing to his face. He wished he had better control of his involuntary responses.

"Nocciola please", Melissa said to the cashier.

"Would you like a taste?" The cashier held a tiny plastic spoon.

"No need", said Melissa, glancing at James. "I have faith." She elbowed him in the ribs affectionately. It was almost like touching. "I'd like a tub of it please."

A tub? Was she taking it to her date? Was he going to enjoy delicious nocciola because of James? A scowl came to his forehead.

Melissa paid the cashier and headed for the exit, passing James. "I bet it's delicious." She touched his back, making everything feel all right. Maybe she had simply been quoting Lewis Carroll.

And then she was at the exit. And everything felt wrong again. He hadn't even got her number. He could ask Rodger. So could she. She was only being friendly. Only ever being friendly. So what if she liked learning Ancient Greek? Doesn't mean she's right for you, thought James. Get over yourself.

"Hopefully I'll run into you again", Melissa called from the door. "I come here all the time."

* * *

James took a bite of coconut gelato. It was as delicious as he had been led to believe. Even better than nocciola. James took a bigger bite. It wasn't Lent yet and he was still allowed to overindulge.

It gave him brain freeze.

So what? That's part of the experience. He was glad he took the risk. Things could turn out different this time. Everything changes. Nothing is constant. He looked at the scrap of paper. She'd forgotten to take it back.

He didn't have to give up gelato altogether. You weren't supposed to give up everything you liked. James had definitely come close to despair a few times recently. That was a worse sin than not giving up enough for Lent. "You're too much Good Friday, not enough Easter Sunday", the Old Man had told James once. He was right. James would simply give up coconut, delicious as it was, and nocciola. And hazelnut to boot. Those were the flavours he most enjoyed. That was more than enough.

Chapter
10

Nearly two weeks into Lent. Nearly two weeks trying flavours such as Menta, Fragola and Zuppa Inglese and he hadn't run into her once. He'd even joined Facebook but apart from a "Thanks for the add, welcome to the modern era", message it hadn't exactly opened up a communication link. He had occasionally checked her profile to see if he might be able to accidentally run into her at Paulo's but the effort proved fruitless. He'd seen her a few times in the "news". A number of men had written her flirtatious messages. Each one reminded him that his attraction to her was not special. Occasionally she'd even responded. She'd been flirtatious back. James decided it was most unhealthy to obsess over this sort of thing. It was one of the reasons he had avoided joining Facebook to begin with. He'd misread her. Lesson learned.

Fifty-two parishioners had added him as a friend. Some of the pictures they posted: debauchery. Debauchery for all the world to share in, and then you and your friends write messages encouraging more debauchery. Facebook was one big debauchery positive feedback loop. He was already planning the sermon.

But for now he was doing the final touches on his homily for Mrs. Henderson. She had passed away peacefully in her sleep. Her will had requested a simple service using the good ol' BCP. They can't stop us, James thought. Not for this service at least.

* * *

It was not well attended. James made an executive decision to hold it in the Chapel rather than the nave. She'd always loved that chapel.

Mr. and Mrs. Henderson had once been pillars of the community. She'd run New-To-You for over a decade. Had chaired the Anglican Women's Guild for six years. He'd done St. Matthew's books, at no charge, for a generation. He'd died twenty-five years before her. They'd had two children: an older son who'd already passed on, himself nearly seventy, and a younger son, now sixty-five but still filled with the same force that drove his mother. Most of her friends had left this world ages ago.

The longer you remain, the less loved ones you have remaining.

The Sewing Circle all showed up. They remembered all that she had done. They'd given James many of the stories for the homily. They smiled when he spoke, laughing at their own tales. Tales of a woman of great spirit. Who did things her way, but my goodness who did things. There was not a committee she hadn't at some point managed. Not a tea went by without her infamous lemon square. She'd been a nurse on the Channel Islands. Had been a spy in the war. She'd lived, my God, she'd lived.

The server poured water over James' hands during the preparation of Communion. James dried them on the lavabo towel. Bowed his head to the server who bowed back to him. James fondly remembered his father's funeral. How that blessed man had left five pages of instructions outlining every detail. The service was simple, but it was done right. This isn't empty ritual, he'd taught James. Every aspect has deep spiritual meaning. Every gesture matters.

* * *

"'Who shall separate us from the love of Christ? Shall tribulation, or distress, or persecution, or famine, or nakedness, or peril, or sword? Nay, in all these things we are more than conquerors through him that loved us. For I am persuaded, that neither death, nor life, nor angels, nor principalities, nor powers, nor things present, nor things to come, nor height, nor depth, nor any other creature, shall be able to separate us from the love of God, which is in Christ Jesus our Lord.'"

It was pouring rain as James gently spread the first layer of dirt— almost mud—over Mrs. Henderson's ashes. Long ago she and her husband had reserved plots beside each other in the Memorial Garden, next to the sundial, beneath the cherry tree (currently in bloom). Prime real estate.

James recalled the first time he understood death. He was five or six. The cancer was bad for his mom, but to James it simply meant she wasn't devoting enough time to him. He'd been so selfish then.

One day he was walking a forest path with his father. A woman stopped them. Told his father there was an injured bird. Asked him, in hushed tones, if he could put it out of its misery. The Very Reverend Biddle told James to turn around. James did so, but not before catching sight of the bird, shaking. He caught a glimpse of his father picking up the rock. He caught a glimpse of his own hand, shaking. Then he heard a thump. James knew, instinctively, that the bird's shaking must have stopped. He must have seen shaking stop like that at some point, but he couldn't remember when. He knew, instinctively, that one day that might happen to his mom.

That one day it might happen to him.

Some point after, maybe a day or maybe a year, a thought appeared in his mind, unasked for: one moment I will think and the next moment I will not. What happens then? The incomprehensibility of non-existence.

James cast his thoughts to a year or so after his mom had died, when he read about Epicurus, who espoused the theory that death was not something to be feared because it was never experienced: "When you are, death is not. When death is, you are not." This explanation had never really caught on with the masses. Not like Mithraism, the Cult of Isis, the Eleusinian Mysteries and, last but least least, Christianity: death is not the end. A much nicer thought to think. But did he believe it?

James let himself be distracted by the world around him. "Excellent service", said Zi-Wei. "It brought tears to my eye. A lovely woman. Such a spirit."

Jerrod Henderson, the surviving son, grabbed James by the arm. Led him up the steps towards the Parish House. "You were such a blessing to my mother." James glanced back at the Memorial Garden and saw a streetkid sleeping in the lych gate. He wasn't certain, he had only caught a glimpse, but it sure looked like Jo-Marie. How had she ended up on the street? A thousand horrible but plausible answers flooded his thoughts. James wanted to go back and see if it really was her, but Jerrod sought answers about his recently deceased mother. It was James' job, his sacred duty, to comfort the grieving. He couldn't just abandon that based on something he thought he saw out of the corner of his eye.

* * *

He was not at his best during the wake. He was polite, to be sure. His small talk was fine. He was pleasant with Jerrod and all the mourners. Reassured everyone that needed to hear that there was a special place in heaven for people like Mrs. Henderson.

He didn't spill his tea. He didn't drop his pecan square.

But he was merely going through the motions. His thoughts were at the lych gate. His thoughts were in the past. His thoughts were with sweet Jo-Marie.

"Lovely service", said Canon Conroy. "Simple yet moving. A wonderful send off for a wonderful woman."

"It really showed what they'll be losing when the BCP goes", said the Venerable McCall. "Thank goodness for St. Barnabas'."

"I warned you he would do it", said Zi-Wei.

"At least James is still here for services such as this", said Canon Conroy.

James excused himself from his friends. He went to the lace covered refreshments table. Picked up the healthiest cookies he could find and wrapped them in a napkin. He poured a cup of tea into a coffee mug. Put in three scoops of sugar (a ridiculous amount!) and a splash of milk. He headed for the back door.

* * *

Jo-Marie wasn't at the lych gate. No one was. No one was at the cottage nor at the steps to the Hall. James checked the alley: four or five junkies shooting up but none of them Jo-Marie. He checked the courtyard. Nobody.

That left the Well.

The Well was a sunken area between the sidewalk and the crypt, about fifteen feet below street level. Almost the length of a city block, hidden from view of the casual pedestrian, it was the perfect place to shoot up, to deal. It stunk of hot stale urine, human excrement and body odour. He avoided it at all costs.

He descended the steps. Cautious. People were often strung out down here. They could be violent. They could have hungry vicious dogs who'd never had their shots. The stories the vergers would tell him made James shudder. Nonetheless, he continued to the bottom.

There were six junkies in front of him. "We were trying to keep this private", a rippled mean looking junky shouted. He obviously hadn't shaved in months and his skin appeared to be made of dirt. "Where do you expect us to go?" A wraith-like woman held him back. James pretended not to hear. He didn't see Jo-Marie. He probably hadn't even seen her at the lych gate.

James turned to leave and saw, in the alcove between the crypt and the stairs, Jo-Marie, sitting on the ground with a couple of unruly urchins. This was a frightening development. The lych gate was one thing, but you had to be pretty hard up to be hanging out in the Well.

Chapter

11

James offered her the cookies and tea.

"I was taught never to take candy from strangers."

"I know", said James. "I taught you that."

"Can we take the candy?" one of her companions piped up.

James hesitated. "It's not really candy." Deciding this wasn't a very good point he handed over the cookies.

"What's that?" said the other companion. "Tea?" James was very reluctant to hand over the mug. It was decorated with the Spartan helmet, from the Department of Classical Studies at UVic. He himself had donated it.

He watched her two companions sharing the drink. Two sets of germs. We'll never get it clean, thought James. No. That's ridiculous. I'll merely need to put it through on hot. Twice.

"Your father probably misses you." Jo-Marie turned away from James. Stared at the wall. "Well if you're having problems with him then you can stay in the spare room at my place."

"Hear that everybody? A priest wants a thirteen-year-old to spend the night at his place."

Jo-Marie's companions could not stop themselves from laughing.

"I won't let you spend it on the street. Look, you knew I was a priest here. You knew I might see you."

"It wasn't even my idea to come." Jo-Marie glared at her friends.

"I'm sure you could have convinced them otherwise. You can be very persuasive when you choose to be."

"Don't act like you know me."

"I will not stand here arguing. You're coming with me and that's final."

"Only if all my friends can come."

"We have a night shelter in the crypt at which they are welcome to stay."

"I'll go there too."

"No, you're coming with me. I want you to be safe."

"The night shelter's not safe?"

"Of course it is. It's the streets that aren't safe." James looked over his shoulder at the junkies, staring at him. "This well isn't safe."

"Shouldn't you want Ink and Tru to be safe too? Aren't we all God's children?"

James looked at her two companions. The girl had multiple eyebrow, nose, ear, cheek, lip, other cheek, and tongue earrings. The boy was covered in tattoos from head to foot, several of which championed the values of anarchy. James hesitated. "I don't know them."

"I know them. I vouch for them. Or don't you trust me?"

"They can sleep at the Night Shelter. Tomorrow we can take them to social services."

"That is not happening", said Mr. Anarchy Tattoo.

"Look," said James, "the fact is I could call the police on all of you for trespassing and drug use." All the junkies were paying attention now. He pressed on, stammering: "Or you could come with me for a hot meal, a shower and a safe warm bed."

* * *

James compared packages of lasagna noodles. One would taste better, the other would be better for her. Why couldn't both just be both?

"Why are you getting those?" asked Jo-Marie.

"You love lasagna."

"You have no idea what I love."

"Then why don't you enlighten me?"

"McDonald's."

"Cheeseburgers?"

"No. McDonald's."

"We're not going to McDonald's. We're making cheeseburgers." Even that was most definitely a compromise.

"Fine. Whatevs." He bristled at this particular slang. She smiled to see it.

* * *

They came through the front door. "You can put your bag in the spare room. I'll get you a towel."

"You just want to see me naked."

"Your friends aren't here. You can quit with that particular act thank-you very much."

She scowled at him. James looked at her filthy hoodie and jeans. He didn't want any of that touching his furniture. "We can do your laundry too. I'm sure I have a spare house coat and…"

"I don't want you touching my underwear."

He wasn't excited about the prospect either. "Fine. You can do the honours. You remember how?"

"I'm not retarded."

"Please don't use that term in this house."

"Please don't act like I'm retarded anywhere."

James took out the laundry soap. He opened the hall closet. Handed her a towel. He took out a large bin filled with miscellaneous clothes. He soon rooted out a housecoat and handed it to her, then went back to rooting. "I think I have women's pajamas in here somewhere. We'll get you more clothes tomorrow." He found the pajamas, folded, at the bottom. Jo-Marie took them.

"Why do you have women's pajamas?"

He looked at her. She already knew the answer.

* * *

James was caramelizing onions when Jo-Marie came out of the shower, dressed in the pajamas and a beige housecoat.

"That smells horrible."

James took a good waft of the onions. They smelled wonderful to him.

Jo-Marie sat down on the couch. The photo album! He really had to stop reliving the past. Spotting it on his coffee table, she looked at him, at last softening her scowl.

"Do you remember?" James turned off the element. Put the onions on the burgers.

"I don't remember at all." The scowl had sharpened again.

"We had a good time." He put the burgers on the table next to the salad, made of mixed greens, sprouts and shredded beats, with pickled eggplants in oil for dressing.

"Mom was planning to leave you."

"I already knew that." Jo-Marie came to the table. James bowed his head in prayer. "Lord, bless us and this food to our use…"

"This is disgusting!"

"…for Christ's sake, Amen." James crossed himself.

"You ruined it with the onions." Despite her words and the various grimaces she made, she continued to eat voraciously. James had every confidence in himself as a cook. Jo-Marie's automatic rejection of everything he said or did was getting repetitive and predictable. She'd overplayed her hand. Ha!

James went to the cupboard, retrieving fish oil, zinc and vitamin D. (He was just like his mother.) He put the pills on Jo-Marie's plate.

"You trying to poison me?"

"These are vitamins. They're not drugs or…"

"What's that supposed to mean? You think I'm doing drugs? I'm not."

She probably was, he thought. Well, for tonight at least, she was safe. Still, he had a duty. "We should call your father to tell him you're all right."

"If you call him, I'm leaving."

"We'll have to call him eventually."

"We don't have to do anything."

"Did he do something to you?"

"None of your business."

"I want you to know you can always stay here."

"You should've thought of that before."

He had thought of that before. And many times since.

Chapter

12

Every creak of the house was a sound of escape. He was sure she was going to slip out the back door. Be rational, thought James. She has a free will. If she really wants to escape there's nothing you can do about it.

That was no comfort. Being stoic about political results or the Tony Awards was one thing, but how could he call himself human and yet be stoic about that little girl alone on the streets?

James heard a thud from outside. Was that her? Be rational. She's probably exhausted. Probably desperate for a good night's sleep. She probably feels safe and sound for the first time since Lord knows when. Even if she were angry with him, even if she hated him, wouldn't that sense of self-preservation trump everything else? She could always run away in the morning after breakfast. Why would anyone abandon a meal and a comfortable bed?

But maybe the bed would be too comfortable. Like for Jean Valjean. The cathedral bell woke him. James had a lot of antique clocks. Maybe she was tossing and turning right now. Not able to get dark thoughts out of her mind. James heard creaking from below. He ran downstairs. Turned on the kitchen light. Nothing was disturbed. He walked to her room. Put his ear to the door. The welcome sound of snoring.

He returned to the kitchen and took out a glass, pouring some sherry, thinking it might help him sleep. He took a sip. Looked at the bottle. Looked at all the bottles in his liquor cupboard. If she were to stay with him he'd have to put a lock on it.

James accompanied his sherry glass to bed where he took a final sip. He put his head to his pillow. Still his thoughts kept flowing. There was only one thing for it.

Neuf cent quatre-vingts dix-neuf nonilliard neuf cent quatre-vingts dix-neuf nonillion neuf cent quatre-vingts dix-neuf octilliard neuf cent quatre-vingts dix-neuf octillion neuf cent quatre-vingts dix-neuf septilliard neuf cent quatre-vingts dix-neuf septillion neuf cent quatre-vingts dix-neuf sextilliard neuf cent quatre-vingts dix-neuf sextillion neuf cent quatre-vingts dix-neuf quintilliard neuf cent quatre-vingts dix-neuf quintillion neuf cent quatre-vingts dix-neuf quadrilliard neuf cent quatre-vingts dix-neuf quadrillion neuf cent quatre-vingts dix-neuf trilliard neuf cent quatre-vingts dix-neuf trillion neuf cent quatre-vingts dix-neuf billiard neuf cent quatre-vingts dix-neuf billion neuf cent quatre-vingts dix-neuf milliard neuf cent quatre-vingts dix-neuf million neuf cent quatre-vingts dix-neuf mille neuf cent quatre-vingts dix-neuf.

Neuf cent quatre-vingts dix-neuf nonilliard neuf cent quatre-vingts dix-neuf nonillion neuf cent quatre-vingts dix-neuf octilliard neuf cent quatre-vingts dix-neuf octillion neuf cent quatre-vingts dix-neuf septilliard neuf cent quatre-vingts dix-neuf septillion neuf cent quatre-vingts dix-neuf sextilliard neuf cent quatre-vingts dix-neuf sextillion neuf cent quatre-vingts dix-neuf quintilliard neuf cent quatre-vingts dix-neuf quintillion neuf cent quatre-vingts dix-neuf quadrilliard neuf cent quatre-vingts dix-neuf quadrillion neuf cent quatre-vingts dix-neuf trilliard neuf cent quatre-vingts dix-neuf trillion neuf cent quatre-vingts dix-neuf billiard neuf cent quatre-vingts dix-neuf billion neuf cent quatre-vingts dix-neuf milliard neuf cent quatre-vingts dix-neuf million neuf cent quatre-vingts dix-neuf mille neuf cent quatre-vingts dix-huit.

Neuf cent quatre-vingts dix-neuf nonilliard neuf cent quatre-vingts dix-neuf nonillion neuf cent quatre-vingts dix-neuf octilliard neuf cent quatre-vingts dix... what was that?

Nothing. Get over it. Now where were you?

Neuf cent quatre-vingts dix-neuf nonilliard neuf cent quatre-vingts...

* * *

It was still dark when he awoke. 4:46. The small amount of sleep had him feeling hopeful. No loud noises in the night (and she'd probably want him to know that she was escaping). It boded well.

4:47. He wasn't going to be able to sleep anyway. Maybe he should get up early and make breakfast. James could think of nothing better than waking up to French toast with cinnamon. If she slept in he could always keep it warm in the oven. What a lovely aroma! His mom made that for him every birthday. Even when she was most sick she made it for him.

She had a special recipe. Different from any he'd ever tasted. Did he still have it? James snuck down to the kitchen. He took out the painted wooden chicken in which he kept his loose recipes. Flipped through. There it was on the index card, written in his mom's handwriting, filling him with melancholy joy.

Baked Orange French Toast
Ingredients:
¼ c salted butter
½ c maple syrup
¼ tsp cinnamon
1 orange rind (cut up in small pieces)
6 eggs
1 c orange juice
1 loaf of bread, sliced into pieces 2 inches thick.
Preheat oven to 400°F.
Melt butter to spread in pan. Add maple syrup and spread out evenly.
Sprinkle cinnamon and orange rind evenly in pan.
In mixing bowl beat eggs, slowly pouring in orange juice.
Dip bread slices in, letting them soak thoroughly.
Place bread slices in pan. Bake for 20–25 minutes

James followed the directions carefully, but doubled the amount of cinnamon, added slightly more than the half a cup of maple syrup, and did not use the whole orange rind. He also sliced up the orange, planning to use it as a garnish.

He checked his watch. 5:01. He would not set a timer. It might waken Jo-Marie. He could sense when twenty minutes were up.

He went to his couch and picked a Bible off his coffee table. He opened it to a passage from the Book of Daniel he had been re-reading a lot recently. "'If it be so, our God whom we serve is able to deliver us from the burning fiery furnace, and he will deliver us out of thine hand, O king. But if not, be it known unto thee, that we will not serve thy gods, nor worship the golden image which thou hast set up.'" It showed people doing right not for any reward but simply because it was right and because they had the strength of faith.

They could do it and so can you.

Then he spotted it: his safe open. How could he be so careless as not to lock it? Yeah right. Wishful thinking there reverend. It only took a quick glance to see which book was missing.

He rushed to her room. Knocked loudly. No answer. Burst through the door. Of course she was gone. He grabbed a flashlight from the drawer beside his fridge, threw a coat over his robe, slipped into his walking boots, and was out the door.

* * *

The uselessness of his search was soon evident. It was dark and would be for another hour. She could be anywhere in the city. She had he didn't know how much of a head start.

But he could at least walk Fernwood and environs. At least check some obvious places: around the school, beside the theatre. It was raining. She'd want to be in a covered area. Her hoodie wasn't even waterproof. Couldn't she have let him buy her a jacket before she ran away?

James shivered from feet to teeth. He should be keeping himself covered too, he thought. He would be better off with a car, warmer clothes, and a little bit more light. He might as well go home, change, and set out at dawn. He could call her father. The police too. It would increase the chances of finding her.

Once he'd finished checking the neighbourhood of course.

His flashlight conked out.

As he walked home, keeping his eyes peeled, he had decidedly mixed feelings about the matter. Obviously he was worried but he thought a normal person would also feel angry. He didn't in the least. The fact that she knew to take this particular book, that she'd remembered where he'd kept it and how important it was to him... well he'd be lying if he claimed not to find that touching. She'd even managed to figure out the combination. The girl knew him well.

However, knowing how much the book had meant to him she took it. Took it in order to hurt him. That was what stung the worst. Worse than any previous pain had led him to believe pain could be. Is this how God feels when we stray? Seven billion of us stinging Him like this at once. He did not envy God in the least.

He arrived back home. Called the police and told them she was missing. He didn't mention the 1717 copy of the BCP. No he wasn't her father. He'd found her on the street and let her stay. No he wasn't some cretin. He was her godfather. That meant he had certain responsibilities.

"Did you make her an offer she couldn't refuse?" James had heard this hilarious retort once or twice before.

"I am charged with her spiritual upbringing. Next to her father I am the person most responsible for the child."

"Nonetheless, you're not her father nor a family member."

"Could we not argue semantics? A little girl is missing."

"I hate to say this sir, but she's a streetkid. They're all missing."

"I hate for you to say that too." Stay composed. "Could you just call me if you find her?"

"We'll call her father. He can contact you if he wishes."

She could be anywhere. Any street. Any alley. She could have gone back to her father's, though he seriously doubted it. He called the bastard's. No answer. He left a message that he'd found her on the streets but that she'd run away again. If he saw her could he let James know she was safe?

He smelled something burning: the French toast! He opened the oven. Smoke everywhere. The detector going off. Maple syrup and egg baked carbon into his pan. No amount of soaking and scraping would ever get that off.

It had been a good idea at the time, he thought.

Chapter
13

At first light James headed towards the Church. She'd probably want to find her friends and that was where she'd left them. He had gotten dressed and made a list of people he might call. The folks at Food Bank and Night Shelter. All the night shelters in the city, if it came to that. Constable Pickett was an acquaintance. He'd be more help than the fool James had spoken to in the night.

He would call her father again of course. He would tell the Verger. Maybe the Street Priest would help. What was his name again? Was it James? He thought it might be James. That would be embarrassing not to know. He'd ask at the office.

He took a left onto Camosun, his head on a swivel, his eyes darting across the landscape. His heart lifted when he saw a girl with blonde hair, then fell again when he got a better view. At Cook Street he was splashed by a car driving too close to the curb. At the intersection of Vancouver and Mason four teenage boys told him that God is dead.

"I've read Nietzsche too."

"Who's Nietzsche?"

He walked around the perimeter of the church, before going down to Night Shelter in the crypt. No one had seen Jo-Marie or Ms. Piercings or Mr. Anarchy Tattoo. He walked through the alley where he witnessed a urinating homeless man who, upon spying James' clerical collar, shouted, "Where would Jesus pee?"

James considered wandering street to street again—checking every alcove and alleyway—but decided he should head to his office first. Her father would know to call him there. It would be easier if James had a cell phone.

James decided he must be too tired to be thinking straight. He bought a coffee at Wildfire and, after only two sips, spilled it all over himself when someone opened the back door of the Parish House unexpectedly. "Sorry James." It was the new Deacon.

"Don't worry about it", said James in a tone that said he should definitely worry about it.

* * *

"I left a message on your machine. If you had voice mail you could've checked from anywhere."

"You haven't seen her?"

"Not in weeks."

"Why didn't you tell me she was missing?"

"Because it's none of your damned business. You're not her father. You're not related to her."

"Anne stipulated that I be her godfather and…"

"Anne's dead. Her stipulations don't mean shit."

"This isn't getting us anywhere. We need to find her."

"You found her last night didn't you? And then didn't even bother telling her own dad."

"She told me she'd leave if I called you."

"Well as long as she didn't leave."

"I decided it would be best to call you in the morning. I thought it would be good for her to spend at least one night in safety."

"Staying by herself at the house of a middle aged priest. I wouldn't call that safe."

"Was that supposed to be funny?"

"I didn't mean it padre. I was just trying to lighten the mood."

"Pardon me, but the mood is most certainly not light. Nor should it be lightened. Your daughter is alone on the streets. She could be anywhere. I don't know about you, but I am terrified for her."

"You think I don't love my daughter, asshole? How could you even think that?"

Do you want a summary or my complete thesis?

"Fine. I'm sorry. We're getting off track. I've already alerted the police and the Night Shelter. I'll let the Street Priest and Food Bank know once they get in. Meanwhile, I'll continue searching on foot. Maybe you could drive around and…"

"They revoked my license, remember?"

"Then you search by foot, I'll drive."

"This is pointless, you know that? Even if you found her she'd run away again." At least she'd know I cared, thought James. "Hey, if you want to search for her that's great padre. Tell me when you find her. And if she comes home safe and sound I'll call you on your cell phone."

"I don't have a cell phone."

"Oh yeah. I forgot."

"I'll be purchasing one later today." As he spoke those words, he knew them to be true.

Crap.

* * *

James followed the sound of a vacuum cleaner to find the Verger, a balding middle-aged ex-pat Englishman. He knew the streetpeople better than any of the staff as he was the one responsible for chasing them off the property.

"Could you describe her?"

"She's thirteen. Not quite five feet. Blonde hair. Brown eyes. She's very angry with the world."

"Could you narrow it down?"

"Her name is Jo-Marie."

"They don't always go by their real names."

"She has in her possession a 1717 copy of the Book of Common Prayer, full calf gilt. Engraved by Sturt. Printed with permission of John Baskett."

"Is it valuable?"

"I've insured it for $2500."

"I'd pawn that if I were her."

* * *

As he headed for a pawnshop on Princess Street, James spotted a sleeping lump of Jo-Marie's size with blonde hair. It did look a bit matted and dirty. Could just one night on the street do that? Her face was obscured by the sleeping bag. But was it even her face?

"Hello?" She didn't wake up. "Hello", he said a bit louder. "Good morning", louder still. He didn't want to yell. Rubbing her back might waken her more subtly but Safer Churches had him worried and the sleeping bag looked positively foul. He had but one option, "HELLO! GOOD MORNING!" The sleeping lump awakened.

"What the fuck man?"

It was neither Jo-Marie, nor even a girl.

"I'm looking for my goddaughter. She's about thirteen, she has hair similar to yours."

"I was finally sleeping!"

James backed off. That hadn't done anybody any good.

* * *

The Verger had provided a list of pawnshops and their addresses. James went to each of them. He didn't find Jo-Marie (which would have been expecting too much luck) but asked the employees to let him know if they saw her. They wanted a picture for reference. "She's thirteen and would be selling a 1717 copy of the Book of Common Prayer. Certainly that can't happen every day."

They made a good point, though. He was terrible at describing people. All his pictures of her were at least three years out of date. He'd need to call her father back. Oy!

James returned to the church office to check his messages and ask about the Street Priest. (All James knew was that he operated independently out of the cottage on the far side of the parking lot.)

Stepping through the office door James stopped dead: Melissa sat in the corner, wearing a yellow sundress. She stood up when she saw him, smiling bashfully. James felt horrible for taking pleasure in this woman's beauty when that sweet girl was alone on the streets. But maybe it was meant to happen this way. Maybe Melissa would help him look. Maybe she'd find Jo-Marie and know how to talk to her so that she would come back and stay back, never running away again. Maybe they'd become a family. Maybe she was a sign from God that from now on things would be better.

Or maybe she was here to see someone else.

"Here he is", said the Receptionist. "Just the man you were looking for."

Don't let on how much this means to you. Just smile like you're trying to place her.

She smiled back at him. Her dimples! Her perfect dimples! Her uplifting smile!

"I'm so glad it's you", she said.

"It's me." Yes! Yes! Yes!

"I was worried it might be someone else."

"How do you mean?"

The washroom door opened. Out stepped a scruffy but handsome young man wearing jeans and a t-shirt. He shook James' hand.

"You must be the priest."

"They want to get married at St. Matthew's", said the Receptionist. "I told them you would officiate."

The young man kissed Melissa on the lips.

This is why you should never hope.

PART II

Proclamation of the Word

"'There is a bravery of the priest as well as the bravery of a colonel of dragoons—only', he added, 'ours must be tranquil.'"
—Bishop Myriel in Victor Hugo's *Les Miserables*

Chapter
14

The Street Priest was not in, but was named James.

The Receptionist re-scheduled Melissa and the Fiancé for the following Tuesday. As they left, James noticed that Melissa, if anything, was now more beautiful than ever. Fruit is tempting enough without being forbidden.

* * *

"Don't judge me, padre. I live my life. I don't document it."

James wanted to strangle the receiver. "What about school photos?"

"The school probably has them."

"Could you pick some up?"

"No."

"It could help us find her."

"Us? There is no us. Frankly, I think you've always confused her as to who her real father is. I think that's why we're having these problems now."

Really? You think *that's* the reason?

* * *

James came to the front door, inhaled long and slow, and then broke a vow he had made to himself and God when he was sixteen: he set foot again in his junior high school.

* * *

"You're not a relative?" asked the School Receptionist.

"I'm her godfather."

"Did you make her an offer she couldn't…"

"Her mother stipulated in her will that I have special access to the child."

"Do you have the will on you as well as a notary to verify that?"

"Could I talk to the principal?" A plaque on a blue door let him know that Mr. Bellis was still in charge. James had been one of the best students ever to attend the school. Surely that counted for something.

"He's at a conference."

* * *

James was at a loss. Hundreds of reviews—every single person seemed to hate both their plan and their carrier. Why couldn't there just be one good option rather than ten terrible ones?

A knock on his door.

"Yes?"

The Choir Master asked, "What's wrong?"

"Who said something was wrong?" The Receptionist! She was always spreading rumours. Oh he would be having a stern but polite conversation with her sometime soon.

"Something must be very wrong for you to be buying a cell phone."

"It's nothing." James hesitated. He only wanted people to know about Jo-Marie if necessary, but those people would undoubtedly tell more people. He might as well control the message. "My god-daughter seems to have gone missing, a bit, and..."

"I'm so sorry, James. How can I help?"

Within ten minutes the Choir Master had found a usable photo online, downloaded it, and printed off several copies for James. He'd also given James an old cell phone, suggested a very simple plan to go with it and helped James not yell too much as he set it up.

"There are some pluses to modern technology", smiled the Choir Master. "Good luck."

* * *

Returning from the crypt (the Food Bank team now had a picture of sweet Jo-Marie), James heard the unholy sound of Bono's voice echo through the church. The Rector and Deacon swayed as they listened, self satisfied smiles on their stupid little faces.

"James, we could really use your help with this."

"Could I talk to you privately for a second?"

"Reverend B should be included in any…"

"Privately. Please."

James noted that, at times of unbearable pain, he said "please" a lot more than usual.

* * *

He closed the sacristy door. "I need time off."

"Easter's coming up. It's the last month of the BCP services, which I thought you would have wanted to officiate. No, I'm afraid it's not possible."

"I just need a few days." Don't cry. Oh God. Don't cry. Hide your pain. Remember your English heritage. "Jo-Marie is missing."

"Is there anything I can do?"

"No", James reacted. The Rector had two grown boys and a nineteen-year-old daughter. They'd turned out well. "Thank-you though. Maybe at some point."

James headed back to his office. He didn't have to talk to Melissa and the Fiancé. He might not have to be involved with the U2charist. Too much good was coming from this tragedy… well not technically a tragedy.

Nor colloquially a tragedy.

He hoped.

* * *

James called through the whole Sewing Circle. He had to tell a couple of them, and the rest would get persnickety if they weren't personally informed too. Most could do little more than offer prayers but Zi-Wei lived in town and sometimes even had homeless people over for tea. Or maybe just bohemians. (They didn't shave, wore dirty clothes and reeked of patchouli and unwashed feet… maybe just New Democrats.) Zi-Wei was relentless and persuasive when his mind was set on something. James felt good knowing he was on the case.

Finally, James talked to the Old Man who assured him that all the food banks and night shelters in the Diocese would be made aware that Jo-Marie was missing. "But James," he said, "once you have done what you can, and it seems you're nearing that point, you're going to have to let it go. At least a little bit. You're going to have to leave this to God."

That's backwards, James thought. God's left me.

I mean God's left *this to* me.

Good cover there reverend.

* * *

Streetperson after streetperson gave James the finger if they gave him anything at all, but the Street Priest had arrived at the cottage and promised to put the word out regarding Jo-Marie. He warned that little would likely come of it, however: "They protect each other from the outside world."

"I suppose I need to give them something if I want something in return", said James.

"It's best not to want something in return", said the Street Priest. "Or at least not to seem like you do."

"How does one do that?"

"Just talk to them." James had been dreading that response. He was never a fan of being personable. "If you're too aggressive with your ministry you'll scare them off. But if you build up a relationship, your ministry will come naturally."

James was pretty sure that wasn't true. Things didn't tend to come naturally for him. And besides, he didn't want to start a ministry, he just wanted to find his goddaughter.

"What specifically can I give them?"

"Hope."

"What tangibly can I give them?"

"Purpose."

"Do you have business cards? Numbers they could call?"

The Street Priest gave him "info" on nurses, night shelters, and food banks. He gave him some hepatitis C pamphlets and also gave him a last piece of advice: "You must not be impatient or forceful but, on the other hand, you must not be too meek or they might walk right over you."

"You have to follow the middle way."

"Exactly. Though it takes time to figure out what that is."

James asked the Street Priest if he'd ever been attacked.

"A guy ran at me with a knife once. He was tripping out pretty bad."

"What does one do in such situations?"

"I took out my phone and said I had 9-1-1 on speed dial."

"That worked?"

"I'm still here."

"I think I'd freeze in terror if that happened to me", James admitted.

"It's surprising how you can be when necessity dictates."

As James was about to leave the cottage, in walked Mr. Anarchy Tattoo. James asked, "What happened to the girl I was with yesterday?"

"I ain't telling you shit."

James hated his stinky tattoos, his undoubted misunderstanding of what anarchy actually meant ("no rulers", not "no rules"), and that he was subjecting sweet Jo-Marie to danger through his dishonesty. "If you care about her at all, tell me."

"I'm outta here." James started a pursuit, but the Street Priest grabbed his shoulder, politely shaking his head.

Chapter

15

James had searched every street and every alley of the city proper. From Wharf Street to Foul Bay. From James Bay's Five Corners to the seven corners at Douglas and Gorge. He had driven through Hillside and even crossed the Blue Bridge into Vic West.

Mostly he stuck to the downtown core, distributing extra day olds the Food Bank had provided. When those were no longer sufficient, he acquired more from local bakeries, and began purchasing juice and water as well. It was too much for James to carry until the Verger produced a shopping cart he'd stored in his workshop. "I found it in the Well. Knew it would come in handy eventually."

He feared their germs. He was constantly checking for his cell phone in case someone lunged at him with raised knife. He wasn't sure if he was really even helping them. "We can always get food", one had told him, politely refusing a muffin. "But thanks all the same."

Instead of useful information, they provided their own sob stories. But, though he thought it was probably just a waste of time, he listened. James looked at them with (usually forced) compassion. Nodded occasionally. They told him conspiracy theories. How the world was out to get them. How society was out to get them. How businesses were out to get them. James did not think much of these theories—the world, society and businesses had provided the food they were eating after all—but he tried his best not to show judgment. He needed their trust.

In the 900 block of Pandora a gruesome giant (with a ring pierced through the middle of his nose like a Spanish bull!) took James' cell phone right out of his pocket.

"Excuse me. That's mine."

The man moved closer to James, providing far less personal space than the (barely) acceptable eighteen inches. His teeth were rotting. The stench was immense. "This ain't yours."

What to do? The 9-1-1 on speed dial line would be too much of a bluff without a phone. This man might kill him. Why should he respect James' life when he didn't even respect his own septum? But James couldn't back down. That wasn't the middle way.

"You will kindly return that to me." The man got even closer. James couldn't imagine anything worse than the rotting breath.

A beating. A beating would be worse.

"Bull!" shouted a bushy haired woman. "Give it back. That's Reverend J."

Reverend J? Ugh! Before James could ask her not to continue referring to him with that undignified epithet, "Bull" had handed back the phone. James returned to St. Matthew's so the Verger could industrially disinfect it.

* * *

He had not been to work in nineteen days except to view Facebook and feel his heart reshape itself as he vainly checked to see if Jo-Marie had responded. He had not performed a single service, had only thrice visited the elderly at the hospital, had twice rescheduled Melissa's wedding prep. His eyes were droopy. His face was weary.

The Old Man was worried about him: "You haven't slept."

"Sure I have. Lots." James had slept nearly thirty-seven hours over the nineteen days. He'd added it up.

"I think you should get back to your ministry."

"This is my ministry."

"But we need you to visit the old and infirm. Nobody performs that sort of pastoral care like you."

"That sounds like an exaggeration."

* * *

When Ashley showed up by his side, at Store Street and Fisgard, he knew the Old Man had sent for her.

James handed a muffin to Mr. Blond Dreadlocks.

"Thanks Reverend J!" Ashley noticed James bristling. He pushed his shopping cart forward.

"I'm impressed, James. I never thought you'd be the type for street ministry."

Two more streekids took their muffins, along with a bottle of water. James showed them Jo-Marie's picture. "We still haven't seen her. Good luck Reverend J!" They shook his hand, then headed towards Pandora.

James squirted disinfectant and wiped his hands cleanish. He whispered to Ashley, "I'm not doing this for them."

"I know. We all know. You're not fooling anyone."

"Hi Reverend J!"

"Except maybe them."

"I don't know what else to do", said James.

"A shower might be a good start."

He sniffed himself. He had to agree.

"It's good you're doing this", said Ashley. "It's beautiful in fact. But it's also obsessive."

"You think I'm not aware of that?"

"Even if you found her she'd run away again."

"At least she'd know I've looked. At least she'd know I cared." Stop showing your emotions. You're not a Frenchman.

"I bet you she already knows."

"Then why doesn't she come back?" Damn it.

"I don't know, James. But she knows where to find you. Sometimes all you can do is pray and have trust in God."

"Right. Him."

"Or Her."

"Right. Or Her."

James laughed for the first time in twenty-one days and seven hours, but Ashley was seeing through him.

"James... no. Never mind."

"What?"

"It's a stupid question."

"Not telling me will only make me want to know more. It's part of my fallen nature." Eat anything you like except the forbidden fruit of mystery: entrapment.

"It's just… do you believe in God?"

"I fear Him."

"But do you believe God has a plan for your life? That through faith and devotion you will find your path? That, should you earnestly follow this path, everything will turn out for the best?"

He still thought about God, pleaded with God, complained to God. But no, if he were honest, he did not feel God was an active force in his life. He did not see God at work in the world.

"That's personal."

"James, you can tell me anything. I will not judge. I will not spread it around. You know that." He did know that. Bugger.

"I used to. I used to be so close to God I felt His hand guiding every aspect of my being. But now I look to that same place, that place where I felt God and no, if I'm honest with myself, I do not believe in Him."

She touched his hand. Looked into his eyes.

"It's not that big a deal. I have no good reason not to believe in God. No good reason not to feel His presence in my life. It's gone and come back before."

"What if it doesn't?" Why was she asking him that? Why should he have to face it now? He had enough to face already.

"I'm a priest. It has to come back."

"But what if it doesn't?"

"It has to! I don't know how to be anything else."

She hugged him, stinky hairy mess though he was. He wouldn't have done the same for her. (Though that was mostly because he hated hugs.) She'd felt his burden. She'd sensed that he needed to tell her something he hadn't even found the courage to tell himself. Despite her laxness of liturgy, she was the better priest.

Bugger compassion! Reminding me I'm a failure.

Chapter
16

James awoke at 2:47 am, after two and a half hours of sleep. Just enough to no longer be tired enough to get enough. He had decided that two hours of searching a day, four tops, would be enough time to keep the word out for Jo-Marie, but not so much that his friends would worry about him. It was the *via media*.

But he couldn't stop imagining Jo-Marie in trouble. He'd hear her screams for help. He'd look at the hepatitis C pamphlets. It was easy to become infected, often asymptomatic, and could cause liver failure and death. The success rate of treatment was fifty-fifty, but exponentially higher if started immediately after infection. She might be getting infected at this very moment! She might already be infected and not even know. He had to get her to a hospital. He had to get her treated.

He had to find her first.

He tried prayer, but that just reminded him that his faith had faltered. God would know this. Maybe the Reformers were right. Maybe it was all predestined long ago: *sola gratia*. He wanted to believe. Desperately wanted to feel God's presence in his life again. Wanted to know He was real and watching over her. But James simply did not feel it. Maybe it was a sign.

Maybe he wasn't chosen.

He turned on his light. A scrap of paper softly fell from his night table to the floor. He picked it up: "πάντα χωρεῖ καὶ οὐδὲν μένει". He went to his dresser. Took out some sticky tack. Attached the scrap paper to his wall. This is as bad as the Receptionist's "Hang in there" poster, except that it's in Ancient Greek.

He needed such motivation. Tomorrow he would be back at work, taking Melissa and her Fiancé around the church.

Bugger bugger bugger bugger.

* * *

They were late.

"Give them a break", said the Choir Master. "You're the one that kept rescheduling."

"I had a bloody good reason."

"I know. I'm just saying."

The Choir Master apologized for not informing James that Melissa was getting married.

"Why should that bother me?"

"You two hit it off and everything. I thought she would have mentioned it at some point."

"Oh no. We didn't really hit it off. She was just interested in Ancient Greek. A lot of people are."

"Okay. Good."

"So they chose to get married here because they know you?"

"My working here is a happy coincidence", said the Choir Master. "This was Chris' church until he was twelve. His grandmother still goes here. What's her name? Hazel McAllister." James knew her well. He had visited her frequently after her hip operation. She was a cranky busybody, yet somehow she adored James.

"How are you holding up otherwise? Any leads on Jo-Marie?"

"No. None yet."

"Did you ever find your book?"

James said that the book was not the important thing right now.

"But if you find the book, maybe you could find her. It would be a lead anyway."

Before James could answer, Melissa stepped through the garden door, wearing a light checkered purple dress, revealing her beautiful sloping shoulders, her swan like neck, subtly hinting at the perfect line of her back. The Fiancé wore faded jeans and a t-shirt that said 'Relax'.

"Rodger, my man!" The Choir Master and the Fiancé embraced like Ben-Hur and Messala. Melissa hugged James, who accepted it awkwardly. James shook the Fiancé's hand.

"I'm sorry for all the delays."

"Did you get the matter sorted out?" asked Melissa.

"It's ongoing", said James. "Would you like to see the church?"

The Choir Master showed off the capabilities of the organ, a four-manual, fifty-five stop Casavant with full antiphonal—arguably the most impressive musical instrument on the entire island. James suggested a number of fine, traditional hymns that would take full advantage. Melissa seemed agreeable to them but the Fiancé shrugged and said, "We'll see."

The Choir Master went back to his office, leaving James alone with the happy couple. As he revealed that the foundation stone was laid in 1912, he noticed them holding hands. He heard them kiss as he showed them the stained glass windows of the baptistry. "These were the only windows to survive the fire of 1960. Note the heat fissures and the smoke stains on the brick."

"I know all this", said the Fiancé. "I used to be a server here."

The whole affair hurt much less than it might have if James' true thoughts hadn't been with Jo-Marie. Another advantage to her missing. James felt sick to his heart for even noting it.

In the bell tower the Fiancé asked if he could pull the rope. James, thinking he should be as magnanimous with the man as possible, relented. "You'll ring it when we come through the doors, eh?"

"The verger will ring it," said James, "if you wish."

He was doing his best not to dislike the Fiancé. He was making excuses for his dress (the Lord himself wore modest clothes). He was laughing off his sometimes boorish behaviour: "So can we have some alone time up here after the ceremony?"

But not disliking the man became nearly impossible when they returned to the nave. The Deacon had put his *U2* on again. Was writing notes. The Fiancé began to play air guitar.

"What's this for?"

"It's for the *U2*charist", said the Deacon.

"Is that just what it sounds like?"

"Absolutely."

"We have to go to that."

"It'll be this June", said the Deacon. "We have to have you."

James had hoped the matter would rest there. But the fires of the Fiancé's mind had been stoked. "Can we have rock music for our ceremony?"

"Of course you can", said the Deacon just as James was saying the exact opposite.

"It would be unusual", said James.

"You'd have to get the hymns…" (hymns!) "…approved but I've actually been to a few Rocktials. Christ is Lord: His is the power… chord! I'll get you some information."

As the Deacon and the Fiancé hit it off, Melissa noticed James kneading his brow.

"Don't worry", she said. "I'll talk some sense into him." As she squeezed electricity into his upper arm, James realized the whole affair was going to hurt on top of his pain for Jo-Marie, not dwarfed next to it.

* * *

Back in his office, James asked if they had set a date.

"The 2nd of July", said the Fiancé. "That means all of Canada will share in my bachelor party."

"Good. And you know you'll have to attend services for the three Sundays preceding that?"

"Why?"

"I am to publish the marriage banns."

"You are to publish the what?"

"'If any of you know cause or just impediment why these two persons should not be joined together in holy Matrimony…'"

"Is there any way you could waive that?"

"No." Actually there were many ways he could waive that. But James hated couples using the church like it was a community hall.

"He plays bass in a rock band, James. He's worried about getting up early the morning after a gig."

"This is a requirement if I am to wed you."

"We're paying and you have requirements of us?" asked the Fiancé.

"Your dad's paying", said Melissa.

"Okay. Fine. As long as we can have one of those Rocktials."

"I'd recommend you don't", said James.

"Why not?"

"It trivializes the ceremony."

"We can do what we like though. It is our ceremony after all."

"It's a communal event. It involves all present, including God."

"All this red tape just to make nanna happy."

"Okay. Great. Lastly, we're going to have a series of marriage preparation meetings like this one, where I give you a Christian understanding of this holy sacrament."

The Fiancé sized James up for good measure.

"You're going to give us relationship advice?"

"I would instruct you on what marriage means in a Christian context. It is a holy union. It must be able to withstand both prosperity and adversity. It must not be lightly undertaken."

"Have you ever even had sex? With a woman I mean."

Melissa glared at the Fiancé, who raised his arms in submission.

"It was a joke. Sorry. I love her. I want to marry her. That's the important stuff."

"It's still necessary that I educate you in..."

"Sure. Fine. Whatever's required."

"It is also my duty to ask if you know of any impediments to your union: something that would make it unwise or unlawful. If one of you were already married to someone else, for example."

"Or if we were related. Okay. Right. I know this one. I read it when I was a kid in one of those little purple books. You know it doesn't forbid cousin? Probably because the Queen married hers."

"Don't listen to him", Melissa said to James. "He does take this seriously. No, I don't know of any impediments."

"Neither do I", said the Fiancé.

"Are you both baptized?"

"He is. I'm not."

"Then I'll have to ask permission of the Bishop. That should only be a formality."

"Whatevs", said the Fiancé. "Say, not that you're not great and everything, but we could use that other priest if we wanted, right? I think he might be more on my wavelength."

"It would be unusual as he's only a deacon, but in special circumstances arrangements can be made."

"Great. Nothing against you. Nanna definitely sings your praises. I just want to know all the options."

After this, James very professionally inquired about their personal lives. Why had they decided to wed at this particular time? The Fiancé said he loved Melissa of course. He was finally settling down now that he'd reached thirty. "Though I suppose I'm young still. Thirty is the new twenty."

And forty is the new thirty and fifty is the new forty but dead is the same old dead.

"I'm quitting the band. I'm starting law school in September. Becoming a responsible adult."

"It is a very brave thing to do", said Melissa, squeezing encouragement into the Fiancé's hand.

D-Day was a very brave thing to do.

"I guess you reach a certain age you feel less and less bohemian and more like you just haven't grown up. Say, how old are you anyway?"

"I'm thirty-six", said James.

"Cool. You ever play *World of Warcraft*? It seems like it'd be your thing."

James didn't know what he was referring to and didn't care to find out.

* * *

None of it made any sense. How a woman so bright and intelligent could end up with that monstrosity. Oh James had tried to be fair to him. And he had been. He was being. Melissa apologized for the Fiancé while he went "to the can." (His words.)

"He's just acting up because both our families are making the wedding into a big thing. He never wanted it that way. He doesn't like the pressure."

A wedding is a big thing, thought James. You should feel pressure. He was ready, happily ready, to hand the whole affair over to the Deacon and thoroughly wash his hands of it when Melissa put her hand in his. Squeezed it, free and easy.

"Don't listen to him, though. I'm glad you're preparing us. It's comforting. I know we'll be taken care of."

"I c-c-couldn't think of a more lovely bride", James stammered. He could feel his hand shaking nervously in hers.

Bugger bugger bugger bugger.

Chapter
17

Stupid James was getting Melissa and Anne mixed up in his mind. They were both redheads, their facial features were incredibly similar, plus they both chose to settle with complete jerks. At least Melissa didn't have a child... that he knew about.

Anne had ended up going back to Joss and marrying him in a "civil" ceremony. (Joss had cleaned himself up. Had become a teacher at the local junior high school.) A month after the wedding she'd called James. They needed someone to sit with Jo-Marie. The nerve of it! "She kept asking about you. I thought you'd like to see her." Of course he'd like to see her!

Some people (Ashley!) called him a martyr. As if there were something wrong with that. Martyrs kept their integrity in the face of torture and death. James got paid five dollars an hour every Friday night for spending time with someone he loved. (Plus whatever he wanted out of the refrigerator.) And it gave him an excuse in case his male acquaintances told him he needed to come out to get shitfaced (their words).

There was only one real drawback. Every week he would watch Joss and Anne together. The couple in love. The hurt was indescribable, but it was his own fault. He'd known what he was getting himself into. Joss, Anne and Jo-Marie were the family. He was the intruder. He should have counseled reconciliation but instead he'd tried to fulfill his own happiness. Rather than do what was right he'd followed his instincts. Obeyed his emotions. Look where it had got him. You reap what you sow. He had learned his lesson. He would not make that same mistake again. He vowed it, before himself and God.

Remember that, reverend.

"He's a good guy", the Choir Master said, startling James from his funk. "You don't know him very well."

"He likes the U2charist."

"I know, and you think we should still face east and recite in Latin."

"Yes. It meant something. The priest faces outwards, leading the people in worship as they reach outwards toward God. As together we are transported away from the mundane to the spiritual. It has symbolic, theatrical, and spiritual elements all interwoven into one beautiful whole. It will never be replaced by the man who composed Spiderman the Musical!"

"You can't judge everyone by their choice of liturgy."

"I can and I will. You said you'd found something for me?"

"Yes, I did." The Choir Master leaned over James, typing on his keyboard. Clicking his mouse. James would have to spray and wipe all over again. "Is that your book?"

On James' monitor was a 1717 copy of the Book of Common Prayer. Published by John Sturt (engraver) with permission of John Baskett (printer). Full calf gilt. Some chips and rubbing but in generally good condition.

"It certainly sounds like my book."

"It's from a local pawnbroker."

Son of a preacher man, thought James.

* * *

Before James could get to his car the Deacon revved his way through the parking lot on his "hog". He steered it beside James. "Hey, are you going to do your street ministry?"

"No. Not right now."

"Next time you do, would you mind if I tagged along?"

Of course he'd mind.

"No. Not at all."

* * *

"Would I put it online if I thought it had been stolen?"

"I informed you this book had been stolen by a thirteen-year-old girl. I asked you to call me if she ever came in."

"Guess one of my employees bought it off her."

"You must have put the book into your inventory. You never made the connection?"

"Must have slipped my mind."

"Do you have any information on the girl?"

"Like I said, one of my employees…"

"Why do you keep saying that? It's obtuse. Are you implying you'd like a bribe?"

"This is a reputable institution."

"The other pawnbrokers were polite and helpful when we first spoke. You, even then, were rude and dismissive, reflecting poorly on your entire profession. Now do you or anyone you know have information about the girl?"

"Like I said. We're reputable and information of course comes free."

"I would expect no less."

"Once you pay for the book."

"You bought it from a minor and a runaway."

"There's no law against that."

"There are several laws against that. You have not legally acquired the book."

"Possession is nine tenths of the law."

"That's just an expression. I have the letter of authenticity. Rare book collectors are well aware it is in my possession and there is honour among us. Those who would know its value wouldn't be willing to purchase it from you." The last two sentences were pure bluff.

"I'll make a deal with you…"

"I'll make a deal with you. Give me back the book that was stolen from me and give me every bit of information you, or any of your employees, have on that girl and I will consider not calling the police." James made his best, most firm, stern priest scowl. He'd been working on it for years.

* * *

He walked out of the pawnshop, book in hand. Well, book in leather bound case in hand. It had been an exhilarating experience. Two times I've tried it and two times it's worked: threatening to call the police is fun and effective.

By the time he got to the car, however, his elation had deflated. The man knew very little about Jo-Marie. He'd only told James they had purchased the book three weeks ago. The lead was cold.

And it was just a stupid old book.

Chapter
18

Through the glass door to the courtyard James saw Mr. Anarchy Tattoo passing by with Ms. Piercings. He acknowledged them with a head nod. Mr. Anarchy Tattoo nodded in return. Ms. Piercings actually smiled at him. It had taken time, but they seemed, at long last, to be showing him some respect. Last time they'd spoken, he'd asked again if they'd seen Jo-Marie. Mr. Anarchy Tattoo had said, "No. Sorry."

It was almost polite! And it gave James some much needed hope. Much earned hope. This whole so-called ministry, he realized, was really for them. They knew Jo-Marie. He was sure they knew where she was. If he kept up this street priest charade, kept humiliating himself for their benefit, maybe, just maybe, he would find her. Better yet, they might judge him a good mug and convince her to stay with him. Peer pressure might, at long last, do the world some good.

James took a garbage bag filled with day old bread from the Food Bank donation box and placed it in his cart.

"You're going now?" the Deacon called from the main office. "Great. Let me get my coat."

* * *

The Deacon had an immediate rapport with the streetpeople. He even embraced some of them, Safer Churches and the Germ Theory of Disease be damned. Thankfully, at least some eyed the jerk with suspicion.

"Who's your friend, Reverend J?" Upon hearing James' nickname the Deacon actually clapped.

"Reverend J? I love that! The Reverend B helping the Reverend J."

Please don't follow that through to its mathematical conclusion.

* * *

The Deacon had very enthusiastically agreed to push James' cart up Cormorant Street.

"Did I ever tell you about my conversion experience?"

Did I ever ask?

"I used to be an athlete. I was both a basketball and hockey star. I had to give up basketball though since they're both winter sports." Fascinating. "My whole life was sport. School was this annoyance between practice." James remembered classmates like him. Not fondly. "I wasn't the greatest guy back then. I was a bully in fact. Not the worst, but I made life nasty for some kids. But what did I care about them? I was a top prospect, I had a full hockey scholarship to the University of Michigan. After that, the pros for sure."

And all the girls wanted you and all the boys envied you.

"But it all changed. I was going into the corner to get the puck. The whistle blew, then this guy came out of nowhere. Boarded me. You know what boarding is?"

"Not in this context."

"It's when a guy violently hits you into the boards. It can cause pretty severe injury. I broke my neck."

James was starting to like this story.

"When I got out of hospital I devoted myself to rehab. Day and night. I was going to make a full recovery, showing up all the so-called experts who'd told me otherwise. I was going to be better than ever. Sport's not about talent. It's about who wants it more. And my God did I want it more. Ten months later, ten excruciating months, I was on the ice again."

They rushed together across the six lanes of Blanshard.

"But I'd lost it. Sport *is* about talent. It's not all up to you. I just wasn't good anymore. Not pro level anyway. Not even college level."

They walked by the former needle exchange. A short lived experiment.

"It was awful not having sports. What was life even for then? Why'd that jerk have to hit me from behind? What was the point? I really started searching, you know? I tried everything. Yoga. Power cleanses. Buddhism."

James waved at Zi-Wei who was going into the corner store. Didn't see me.

"That's when I discovered the Alpha Course."

The Alpha Course had literally killed James' father. It happened at 3:15 pm on James' twenty-first birthday. Some people even called *that* a tragedy. It was not. The man was in his seventies and had led a full life. He died with all his wits about him. He'd had a heart attack mid-sentence during a critique of *Questions of Life* by Nicky Gumbel, the main figure behind this Alpha Course. The critique was quite a good one too. At St. Luke's Church Hall. The elder Biddle found the book to be superficial. A Christianity more interested in being entertaining than having a depth of spirit. "Light weight" were the last words to escape his lips. Then his heart went. He was dead before the ambulance arrived.

Some (Ashley!) lamented the fact that this had happened on his birthday. James mourned for his father, not his birthday. The only thing he'd ever liked about birthdays was the baked orange French toast. Otherwise they were too much recess, a reminder that he had almost no friends under sixty. On top of that, wrapping paper was wasteful (weren't we supposed to be saving the environment?) and gifts were a tribute to materialism. When his mom died he elected to cease the annual celebrations and his father thought enough of him to respect this. It was only recently that James began acknowledging his birthday again and then only because he had discovered there was such a thing as gelato cake. (It was even more delicious than it sounded!)

The Deacon was still blabbing when James started paying attention again.

"And I felt a real connection to the Creator."

Don't say "the Creator".

"I really felt the Creator enter my life."

How much marijuana do you have to smoke before "Creator" sounds "deep".

"I felt the Creator make a path for me."

Yahweh; Jehovah; Jah; YHWH; El; Elohim; Elyon; Ehyeh-Asher-Ehyeh; Allah; HaMakom; HaShem; Adoshem; Adonai; Tzevaot; Shekinah; Shaddai; Roi; God; God of Abraham and Isaac; The One True God; The Exalted One; The Holy One; The Holy Trinity; The Father, The Son and The Holy Ghost; The Lord; The Most High; The Lord Most High; The Lord God; He/Him; She/Her even: ANYTHING BUT "CREATOR"!

"And that's when I decided to become a priest."

James nodded as if he cared.

"What about you?"

"My father was a bishop. It was sort of the family business."

They walked towards the Well. James parked his cart at the top of the steps. This is where he always ended his daily rounds. He had to build up the courage to descend. To face not finding her yet again.

"So you always wanted to be a priest?"

James visualized himself going down.

"No. Not always."

A stench ascended from below. Wafted through every pore of his body. He could feel the smell.

"So you had a calling?"

"Of course."

James started the descent, bag of muffins in hand.

"Will you tell me about it?"

What will shut him up?

"It was because of a girl", said James, as if the experience was more than he wanted to share. (Which it was.)

Unfortunately it brought a new line of questions.

"So you've had *girl*friends?"

Doesn't he know when to leave people alone? Just give him a pat answer. Make it sound spiritual and priestly.

"Paul said it would be better if people could be chaste and unmarried."

"Paul also said women were to remain silent in public. We don't exactly follow that. He's not Gospel. He's epistle: 'I have no commandment of the Lord and yet I give my judgment.'"

Good point. Huh. Suppose it's part of the lefty evangelical tool kit. Be kind. Ashley's one of them. As were Newton and Wilberforce.

They reached the bottom of the steps. A half dozen streetpeople lined in a queue, each taking a muffin in turn. The Deacon handed out water bottles. He seemed to put them instantly at ease. He could actually be useful, thought James. He considered giving the Deacon the time of day.

For a moment.

James was handing a muffin to Mr. Anarchy Tattoo when the camera clicked. Walking down the steps was a photographer, a cameraman and four other people, two of them in suits.

"Who the fuck are they?"

"Good question", said James, aiming death eyes at the Deacon.

"The paper was curious about your ministry."

"How did they even know about my ministry?"

"Word gets around."

"I don't like fucking cameras!" Mr. Anarchy Tattoo left rapidly, telling James he could do all sorts of things that involved sticking things up and into other things. A month's worth of trust building ruined in a moment.

"Do you mind if we ask you a few questions?" said a reporter.

"Yes," James said, "I mind."

"He's just modest", said the Deacon.

"I can't believe you did this."

"People should know about the work you're doing."

"Why?"

"It might inspire them."

"I don't want to inspire people. I want to find Jo-Marie."

The reporter's ears perked up: "Who's Jo-Marie?"

Though James did not answer, the Deacon most certainly did. Always giving credit to James. Always emphasizing his great modesty. The struggles he had gone to in search of his goddaughter. How it had led him to start this ministry. It had the makings of a sweet special interest story.

"She might see herself in the paper", the Deacon told James.

"If she sees herself in the paper", said James, "it'll drive her away all the more."

Chapter
19

"Hosanna in the highest! Blessed is he who comes in the name of the Lord!"

Palm Sunday. James tried to savour the Eleven O'clock Service, tried to savour every beautiful word, every glorious gesture, but he just couldn't get into it. The Deacon had started a Facebook group to find Jo-Marie. It was his way of apologizing for the reporters and, in typical fashion, showed how little he understood why James was angry to begin with.

The paper refused to kill the story despite James' numerous pleas. His search would make a perfect addition to a series of feel good special interest pieces they were running. News about people's private lives. The paper was meeting Facebook half way, as desperate for readers as the church was for parishioners.

At least there would be a few days before it came out. Before the horsehair finally snapped, and the Sword of Damocles came crashing down.

* * *

James went back to his office after coffee hour, steeling himself for the scheduled meeting with Melissa and the Fiancé. He slowly unfolded his palm cross. Done this since I was a little kid. Like peeling the paper off a beverage bottle.

He looked at his watch. They were ten minutes late. He checked his work messages. Melissa's voice: "We need to reschedule the meeting for... well for June actually."

June? That was cutting it close.

* * *

That afternoon he spotted her at Paulo's, taking her first bite of nocciola.

"Some friends of his were going on tour. They needed a bass player."

"I see", said James.

"It's good for him. I think it's something he needs to do before he settles down."

"We all have our own paths." And your fiancé's path wends down jerk valley into the cave of asshole. "But what about the caterers, the guest list, the flowers?"

"We're doing it all via Skype." James looked as confused as he was. "An internet talking program. Chris suggested we do the prep meetings that way too."

"Absolutely not. We'll pick it up again in June."

"You think I should be angry with him don't you?" James shook his head, but very slowly. "It's his passion. He should do it. I'm just mad I'm not going. I was in a band once too you know but we never took off. Not that Chris took off either really. But he took off enough other bands pay him to play bass while I get stuck in a town where I hardly know anybody."

It was James' turn to order. He gave pistachio a shot.

* * *

They sat together on the northeast steps to the Belfry Theatre.

"You want to come to a concert with me?" asked Melissa.

"I doubt we have the same taste in music."

"I don't know which one of us you're vaguely insulting, but I have a wide range of taste. I know you'll like this band."

"I don't tend to like bands."

"Give them a shot."

"I don't like to give things a shot." Pistachio had been a mistake.

Melissa laughed at him. Touched his back. "I'll treat. Payback for your tip about the nocciola."

Why hadn't she told him she was getting married? Shouldn't that be the first thing out of people's mouths? Couldn't she have put it on her Facebook profile? That was Facebook's virtue: it prevented fools like James from being misled.

"I'm concerned it might be crossing boundaries. You see, I'm your priest and…"

"I don't really think of you as my priest. I'm not even baptized. We're only getting married at church to please Chris' nanna." A way out.

"That's really not a good enough reason. I don't know if I can, in good conscience, marry you."

Melissa took a last bite of nocciola. "If that's the case you can come to the concert."

* * *

James waited for her at the Tillicum Mall food court. He probably would end up marrying them. He'd recanted his refusal. (Refusing was unusual and would bring unwanted questions from the Rector.) Nonetheless, attending the concert still probably wasn't against Safer Churches. At least he couldn't remember a specific passage.

But why was he letting her pick out new clothes for him?

James spotted a teenaged girl with blonde hair in line at Orange Julius. Not Jo-Marie. Then another blonde sipping coffee. Not Jo-Marie. Another laughing with friends. Not Jo-Marie. He observed one of these not Jo-Maries actually handwriting a letter. She actually stuffed it into an actual envelope. Adhered an actual stamp.

He remembered receiving a crayon drawing in the mail from actual Jo-Marie. He'd gone away for the required three years of formal training at the Vancouver School of Theology. Yet they'd remained close. He saw her every Christmas. Every summer they would spend two weeks together while Joss and Anne went on vacation. After graduating VST, James made sure he got a posting in Victoria.

She was such a precocious child! Always asking him what he was reading: a lot of St. Augustine and Aquinas at the time. He explained their philosophies as best he could. She picked up so much of it! Her understanding of the "eternal present" was better than most of the clergy James knew. She asked him all about his vestments. Enjoyed playing dress up in them. He'd look after her most Saturday nights. On Sunday mornings the Receptionist would take her to the (ugh!) McDonald's up the street for breakfast while James celebrated Morning Prayer. During the Nine-Fifteen Jo-Marie attended Sunday school, though she found it at times to be trite and wishy washy (sigh). During the Eleven she closely observed every aspect of the ritual, asking James incredibly thoughtful questions when it was over.

Once a month Zi-Wei corralled James and Jo-Marie for lunch. She loved tripe, mistaking it for some sort of Chinese noodle. She could never figure out why none of the Sewing Circle would touch it. "It's cow stomach", laughed Zi-Wei. The thought made James' stomach churn, but Jo-Marie responded with a, "Cool", making the Sewing Circle erupt in hearty laughter. Zi-Wei still told the story whenever he introduced James to Chinese dignitaries.

James encouraged Anne to baptize her. Though Anne still believed in God, she had sworn never to set foot in a Catholic church again. James said there was always the Anglican one. Anne's mother objected, but James said they could make the service very Anglo Catholic. James became Jo-Marie's godfather and Anne's mother became godmother, but...

Before James could finish that thought Melissa entered the mall, wearing a sundress.

He'd always loved the sun.

* * *

"My mom owns a vintage clothing store in Toronto", she told him. James hated trying on the different pairs of jeans and shirts. It felt very undignified looking at himself stylishly dressed. "That looks amazing on you."

"It's $30", James said.

"I know", said Melissa. "Marked down from a hundred."

James knew places you could get jeans for $10, but didn't mention this fact.

Melissa had been complaining a lot about the Fiancé, revealing that, when they first started dating, he'd convinced her to have an open relationship.

"It's not open anymore."

"I should hope not", said James.

"I slept with another man. Chris didn't much like that. A lot more people think they're mature enough for an open relationship than actually are."

Who was this woman? Had he actually thought they were meant for each other? Idiot. There was no way anyone who had ever thought open relationships were "mature" would be compatible with him. Good. At last he could dismiss this stupid infatuation.

His entire body tingled when she touched his elbow. Damn it! Why couldn't he just turn it off?

"Are you trying to find a girl to pick up?"

"What?"

"You keep looking at girls going by."

More not Jo-Maries. He didn't consciously know he was doing it.

"Sorry. It's nothing."

"Are you okay?"

"Yes. I'm fine."

"You don't seem fine." She did some math in her head. "Does this have to do with the personal emergency?"

"Personal emergency?"

"When we first came to the church, you said you had a personal emergency."

"I like to keep my private life private."

"Okay. I understand." She pulled a shirt off a rack.

"I didn't mean from you specifically. Just anybody."

"I do understand. But know that you can tell me, if you want to."

Why did everybody think sharing things would help? It was going to be in the paper. They were going to get it all wrong. Everybody would know. Everybody would pity Jo-Marie and him but what help would any of it bring?

Melissa took a clean handkerchief out of her purse, handing it to James. Why had she done that? Why was everybody staring?

James felt hot tears smearing his cheeks: he was crying in public.

Chapter
20

His father had seen thousands die in Normandy. James never saw him cry about it once. Even when James asked directly about his service all his father would do was look wistfully into the imagined distance and say, "We made our objective." There was pride in his voice even though, as a pacifist, he'd been a medic, not a fighting soldier.

"I don't think any less of you." She handed James a drink. They were back at her place... her and the Fiancé's place. A handsome one-bedroom suite on the ground floor of a divided house just beyond the fringe of Cook Street Village. "I think it's good when men can show their emotions."

Achilles cried.

And Jesus wept.

"You shouldn't keep things bottled up so much", Melissa continued. "I'm the same way. That's how I know you shouldn't."

James looked at his watch. "We should get to the concert."

* * *

The seats were pews, a grim reminder of what happened to churches that could not replenish their congregations. The name of the band—*The Holy Trinity Bellwoods*—was a bit cute, and the lead singer's voice was a touch nasal, but their musicality was acceptable.

Though Melissa claimed that she completely understood James' unwillingness to share his story with her, she was obviously lying. But it wasn't her story to know. He wished he didn't know it.

Joss hadn't been drinking. Hadn't had anything to drink in weeks. He was driving Jo-Marie, Anne and her mother to the ferry.

They were going to visit Science World or some such thing. Joss and Anne got into a corker. He'd always had a short fuse and the absence of alcohol wasn't helping. He was in the middle of calling the love of his life a… James didn't even like to think the word (c-u-n-t). He was in the middle of calling her that word when the light changed.

The VW Rabbit should have gone through. Most cars would've gone through. But it was an old lady. Not one to risk accidents at dangerous intersections. She slowed down to stop. The distracted Joss did not. He tried to change lanes at the last moment. He half made it. Smashed the right side of the car into the old lady's bumper. Joss's car spun and spun before smashing into the median. Those on the right side—Anne and her mother—died on impact. Those on the left—Joss and Jo-Marie—walked away. The old lady lived too. Could've sued, but she was from a generation that didn't do that sort of thing to single fathers and their ten-year-old girls.

And Joss was nothing if not contrite. He asked James to hear his confession. Did Anglicans have confession? "Yes. We consider it one of the seven sacraments, but of lesser stature than Baptism and Communion."

"That's fascinating I guess. Will you hear mine?"

Joss seemed truly contrite about all the wrong he had done. He seemed to be committed to making things right for his daughter. Committed to make a better life from here onwards.

Of course, knowing how things turned out, James now suspected Joss had only told the confession to manipulate him. To keep him from trying to take Jo-Marie away. But back then, when family services asked for his opinion of Joss, James had stated that he'd definitely made mistakes in the past, but that he was committed to being a better person. That he truly loved his daughter. That he was a good father.

Jo-Marie thought otherwise. She first showed up on James' doorstep on a Saturday. She'd run away. James said she was welcome to stay as long as she liked, but they had to tell her father. She reluctantly agreed and, the next morning, Joss picked her up to take her back home.

Three weeks later, Jo-Marie was there again. James was disturbed that this had needed to happen twice. "Don't call him", Jo-Marie had pleaded.

"He'll know you're here either way", James said.

"Don't you want me here?"

"Of course I want you here", said James. "But a girl needs her father."

When Joss arrived James offered his services as mediator between them. He was trained in family counseling. Since Joss was willing to reform, James believed the chances for reconciliation were good. Joss said thanks, but they could figure things out on their own.

The third time Jo-Marie showed up she said, "You're just going to call my father, aren't you?"

"No," said James, "not this time. What's going on? Is there something I don't know about?"

Jo-Marie said nothing.

"Is he drinking?"

Again, nothing.

"Does he hit you?"

For a third time Jo-Marie did not answer. It was enough of an answer for James. Joss showed up (uninvited) asking for her, but James said she was in a bad way. He convinced Joss to give her a few days.

In those few days, James inquired about how he could get custody. He hated lawyers, and had sworn not to break up the family, but it was evident Joss did not a family make. James was godfather. That gave him certain responsibilities. Anne had even made a will where she expressly stated that, in the event of her death, James should take Jo-Marie into his care. Jo-Marie preferred being in his care. Nonetheless, the lawyers thought James' chances were less than good.

"But he hits her."

"Can you prove that?"

"She'll testify to that. I think."

"She hasn't told you?"

"She implied it. Sort of."

"Even if she says he's hit her, you'd still have to prove he would continue to do that in the future. You yourself stated he was resolved to be a good father."

"Now I state otherwise."

"Third party custody is hard to win."

"But Anne named me in her will."

"If both parents had died that might have been binding. But since Mr. Jones lived, full parental rights went to him." He killed her mother and got full rights. "He *is* the girl's father."

"But she wants to live with me. She keeps running away to me."

"Both those factors would be taken into consideration, but she's too young to decide for herself. I'm just being honest here. Your chances of winning are far from great." An honest lawyer: pah!

Jo-Marie refused to talk with a social worker about her father. "I just want to live with father James." No one could get her to talk. It wasn't their business. She should be able to live where she wanted and shouldn't have to say why. It was *her* life!

James was left with a dilemma. He could sue for custody in a case that he was not likely to win, put Jo-Marie through the agony of a legal battle, alienate himself from her father, and probably remove himself from her life altogether. Or he could try to reconcile that family into which he was the intruder. Just as he had sworn to do.

"Your father's here to take you home."

Jo-Marie said nothing. Went to get her things.

"I want to be part of her life", James told Joss. "I want her to have regular time here. Every weekend if possible."

"Probably not every weekend. But she'll see you."

"You have to be a better father to her. Otherwise she's going to keep running away."

"I know padre."

"And I want you to come to me for help, whenever your mood gets bad or you feel like hitting her…"

"I don't hit her. Is that what she told you?"

"No she didn't but…"

"Just speculating then padre, huh? You know, I've been through a lot. It's not right for you to stand there accusing me."

"I'm sorry." He was. But not to Joss and not for that. "I just want you to know I'm here as a resource."

"Yeah. Sure. Thanks."

James went to say good-bye to Jo-Marie, but she wouldn't talk to him. Though it was against his nature, he hugged her. "I love you. Always remember that."

But she wanted nothing to do with him.

In the following months she would always hang up when he called, actually speaking to him only once and then only to say, "Stop calling here! I don't want to talk to you! I never want to talk to you ever again!"

James made several anonymous calls to social services about possible child abuse at the Jones residence, but as far as he knew nothing had come of it. He'd even tried making a couple of surprise visits himself but, though he'd heard the television both times, no one had answered the door. He decided that he had no choice but to act sensibly. Do what everybody told him to do. Pray for Jo-Marie's well being, but let her go. Let Anne go. Let that whole episode of his life go.

Live in the now.

* * *

They were nearly in the lobby before Melissa finally asked him if he enjoyed the concert. He answered in the affirmative, and then they awkward-silently wandered towards the exit. Just as they were about to open the door the Choir Master appeared from behind.

"You guys came together? Isn't that against Safer Churches?" He punched James in the shoulder. James did not appreciate it.

Eve Smith, a pretty blonde seventeen-year-old chorister, came through a pair of double doors from the washrooms. "Fancy meeting you here", said the Choir Master. "It's a regular St. Matthew's get together."

Eve nodded hesitantly, saying, "I've got to catch up with friends." She headed outside.

"I don't suppose it's too cool to be caught with Church Staff", laughed the Choir Master. "Say, you keeping up with the election?"

"Election?" asked James before he could stop himself. He was normally a news and political junky, but had heard nothing about it.

"You have missed out on some hilarious stuff." The Choir Master took out his handheld computer phone and caught James up on the election campaign: a cacophony of unwarranted attack ads and misinformation. Robert Stanfield was undoubtedly rolling over in his grave. The fact that this vile change in political tactics was led by Stanfield's party, by James' party, by the Good Party, angered him. No matter who won it would be a loss for Canadian decency.

"I should get going", said Melissa.

"I'll give you a lift", said James, all too aware of the current sexual assault statistics.

"Don't forget Safer Churches", the Choir Master said, winking.

* * *

Walking west on Pandora, a number of streetpeople waved. "Hey Reverend J!" "Good to see you Reverend J!" "I'm sure you'll find her Reverend J!"

Melissa looked at them. Then looked at James. Then looked like she had completed a math problem.

* * *

James stopped his car in front of Melissa and her Fiancé's flat.

She kissed him on the cheek, whispering in his ear: "I'm sure you'll find her too, Reverend J. Whoever she is."

She looked at James like she pitied him.

Chapter
21

He slept so poorly that he almost slept in. He was the last person to enter the Rector's office for staff meeting.

"Here he is", exclaimed the Receptionist. "The big star!" A round of applause. James at first couldn't figure out why but then remembered reality. The bloody article had come out.

The Receptionist showed him the spread. Pictures of him and the homeless looking grumpy. A shot of the photogenic Deacon taking credit where it wasn't due. Then, to his horror, James spotted his new nickname: Monseigneur Bienvenu. How had that happened? How did they know? At last the nickname he had always secretly wanted but now had and did not deserve. He was not a monseigneur or even a monsignor. He wasn't doing it for the streetpeople. They would not be welcome in his home. He'd never be able to disinfect it enough.

"Congratulations James", said the Rector. "Though I do think you should have let me know there would be reporters at the church. It would've been good for all of us to be in that picture."

"I left a message for you", said the Deacon.

"Some warning next time."

The whole thing was a set up. It was probably the Rector's idea even if the Deacon thought it was his own. He's using my tragedy well not technically a tragedy for self-promotion. Unbelievable.

James was thankful that he could return to hating the Rector. It felt true and familiar.

* * *

"'Do not do your alms before men to be seen of them'", said the Venerable McCall.

"Yes. I know."

"'Do not sound a trumpet before thee as the hypocrites do in the synagogues and in the streets that they may have glory of men'", spoke the Reverend Doctor Leonard White.

"Yes. I understand."

"'Let not the left hand know what thy right hand is doing'", exclaimed Zi-Wei.

"Yeah. I get it."

They laughed good-naturedly at him. The Sewing Circle had met for lunch at Don Mee's restaurant, celebrating the Reverend Doctor Leonard White's eighty-first birthday, but all the talk was about James. (Just as he didn't like it.)

"It could help find Jo-Marie", said Canon Conroy seriously. "And it might bring in more parishioners."

"Even if it helped find her", said James, "it gives her reason to doubt the sincerity of my search. Even if she came back, this gives her reason to run away again. I wanted nothing to do with this, trust me."

They all did trust him. This was Welker's doing. James could not be held responsible.

"That Reverend B needs to be taught a thing or two about charity", said the Reverend Doctor Leonard White.

"And which clergy he can put his trust into", said the Venerable McCall.

"On top of everything the article mentioned the U2charist. Against my will I have spread the gospel of Bono." James felt his father's eyes judging down at him from a heaven he wasn't even sure existed.

* * *

He opened his e-mail to three hundred new messages. Mostly new friend requests or wall posts wishing him all the best. Delete. Delete. Delete. James accepted the friend requests (the more people looking the better he guessed) but the pure volume was maddening. Time consuming. And for every message he deleted two more popped up. Didn't they know it was Holy Week? The busiest week of a priest's year. All these messages were giving him less time to look for Jo-Marie. Idiots.

Joss had sent James an e-mail: "You think you're better than me? Think you care more about her than I do? Sincerely, Her Real Father."

The Choir Master had posted a link to a YouTube clip of a local television news story about James' search. It had 40 000 hits. 40 000 people knew of his private pain. How many of them would actually be helpful? There were 617 likes against only 7 dislikes. James wanted to add to the dislikes but it would involve signing up so he left it.

* * *

James, in knots getting credit for something he wasn't currently even doing, abandoned work to search for Jo-Marie. He was giving his usual round of muffins at Fisgard and Store Street when Mr. Anarchy Tattoo walked by and spat at him. James agreed with the sentiment, though Mr. Anarchy Tattoo was derided for acting that way to the beneficent Reverend J.

At the fountain in Centennial Square James attempted to give a bottle of water and a hepatitis C pamphlet to Bull, when a group of tourists pointed at them: "Look, it's Monseigneur Bienvenu!" They asked a clattering of questions neither James nor Bull cared to answer, topping it all off by requesting a picture "with the both of you".

* * *

Coming back to the office he saw Melissa waiting for him in her yellow dress. Having relived this experience many times in his mind he was not sure whether he was awake or asleep.

"The big star again", said the Receptionist.

"I have a present for you", said Melissa. "It's just a mix tape. How very 80s of me I know. Some of the songs are mine. I recorded them on GarageBand… computer music program. They're frivolous really but you inspired some of them. Not in a creepy way. Just listen to them. I know what you're going through, more or less, the constant pointless worry and, you know, anything to take your mind off it."

James looked at the encased cassette, now in his hand. Amongst the groups he'd never heard of were four songs by "M. Wembley". Inspired some of them? He should take this straight to the Rector. Bugger! He was already in the middle of a scandal and he hadn't even done anything. He couldn't deal with a scandal on top of everything else. It was very thoughtless of Melissa to do this to him.

Still, he'd *inspired* some of them.

Maybe he was just over thinking it. If the Receptionist thought a scandal was taking place before her very eyes she didn't let on. Instead she shredded paper. Yes, he was definitely just over thinking it. He'd been doing that the whole time. Mistaking pity for attraction.

And inspiration for attraction.

* * *

James listened to the mix tape in his office, ostensibly as he prepared the Eleven O'clock Service for Easter, but actually as he read Melissa's hand printed lettering on the case: *Heraklitos*. He listened to her voice sing out.

"River it flows
Day it goes
So too the night

"River it flows
Dark it goes
So too the light

"Astride a grave
Not yours to save
Nor you mine

"Success is change
Failure too
Lights they change
But you never do

"One constant is change.
But you don't change.
We don't change.

"A frozen river
Remains the same."

A frozen river isn't really a river anymore, James thought to himself. So her final point was a bit spurious not to mention depressing. Wasn't the whole point to cheer him up? Nor could he say he liked the twangy guitar accompaniment, though it was at a professional level for twangy guitar: a Maria von Trapp level. At least it wasn't a gushy love song like he'd feared. He doubted he was even the "you" in the song. He'd inspired her by introducing her to Heraklitos. A perfectly wholesome way to inspire someone. No need to go to the Rector.

He should write her a thank-you note. That was the appropriate response wasn't it? Her heart was in the right place, even if her mind wasn't. Or maybe a thank-you "shout out" on Facebook. Was that what people did? Was it too much? Would it escalate things somehow?

"Melissa's songwriting has really improved." The Choir Master took the case from James' hand. "Did she make you this, Monseigneur Bienvenu?"

"How did they know to call me that? No one at the paper is that literary."

"Mea culpa father. A reporter called for background on you. I told him about the book club we crashed. It seemed relevant. I thought you'd approved of the story."

"I did not", said James.

"No. Didn't seem like you in the end." The Choir Master read the case. "Did you enjoy the concert?"

"No", said James concisely.

The Choir Master smiled. Returned the case to its rightful owner. "Safer Churches, James."

"Priests get gifts all the time." (Usually bottles of wine in the $15-$30 range.)

The Choir Master patted James on the shoulder, before leaving the office.

Forget him. James befriended Melissa before he knew about the marriage. They were still allowed to be friends. He could go to a concert with her if he wanted. He could accept her gift and thank her for it in the socially acceptable way, whatever that was.

* * *

James thumbed through his more than one thousand albums. A mere thank-you note seemed too impersonal. He'd grown up in the 80s. He'd observed. People exchanged mix tapes with their friends. They didn't just receive them and then return thank-you notes.

Besides, if he gave her a mix tape then they would have made an exchange of mix tapes. Hers wouldn't be a gift anymore. He would actually be de-escalating the situation.

Sure. That sounds logical.

Was he supposed to put in stuff she'd like or stuff he liked? Or stuff he'd like her to like?

He was pretty sure polka was out. He loved classical music. Handel and Verdi. That couldn't be the whole thing. She'd hate that. Maybe he could pepper in a few show tunes. Schonberg, a little Sondheim and his favourite Rodgers and Hammerstein. Maybe even something from *The Sound of Music*. The masters had almost made the guitar a tolerable instrument in that show. It would be a sly compliment of Melissa's von Trapp level abilities.

No. Mix tapes were not him.

James looked at his watch. 9:36 pm. This whole mix tape business had in fact distracted him from his constant pointless worrisome thoughts about Jo-Marie.

Of course, the moment he noted that, he began to worry about her again.

* * *

James stared at the moonlight on his bedroom ceiling. He should just write Melissa a thank-you note, but a personal one.

Maybe it could include a sonnet.

Back when he was a teenager, reading Shakespeare voraciously, he had fancied himself something of the poet. He found the sonnet form wonderfully restrictive, yet not quite restrictive enough, so he had combined it with the acrostic. In doing so he had created a medium to satisfy the most fastidious of poetic tastes. He actually thought it might catch on. He wrote acrostic sonnets for several of his friends. By "friends", he meant the bookish girls who also studied in the library. Of course he never sent them. He hardly even talked to those girls. But this sonnet he could send. And Melissa wouldn't take it the wrong way. She was getting married to someone else, so obviously this wasn't a come on. If anyone questioned him, he could point to Shakespeare, who had himself written devotional sonnets, which were only meant in terms of friendship. It was common of Renaissance Humanist-style friendships. This was easily proven.

Right, reverend. It's the perfect crime.

Maybe just write it and don't send it. Just get it out of your system. James took out pen and paper. Sat down at his desk. The first thing he did was vertically print her name which was, conveniently, fourteen letters long. In a moment of inspiration he even filled the first line.

Meeting you struck my heart back to beating

E

L

I

S (T)

S (T)

A

W

Even so

M

B

L

E

Y

He followed the rhyming structure of Shakespeare rather than Petrarch as the latter would be hard to sustain given the difficulty of finding rhymes in the English language, at least compared to proto-modern Italian. As he gradually filled in the lines, writing in pencil, knowing he would rewrite them many times, a theme began to develop. Until, at last, he brought his sonnet into existence.

Meeting you struck my heart back to beating

Electrified my soul, my mind, my hands

Lightning through my limbs so quickly speeding.

Inside and outside my universe expands.

Speaking to you the earth again created

Striking life's spark to primordial clay.

Always your fiery red tresses fated:

World bathed in the light of your eternal day.

Even so I know not truly together.

My hopes for us can only ever sour.

Beating heart must still. Calm must be the weather.

Leave that be. Lose not her heavenly power:

Even if her glory must be kept distant

Yet it revives life in but an instant.

He looked at it and felt the feeling he was supposed to have after sex. Granted, the poem was effusive. But that was part of it being a Renaissance Humanist Devotional Friendship Sonnet. He reread it. And reread it. And reread it.

Enough with this schoolboy nonsense! Put away childish things. You're thirty-six going on thirty-seven. You're a man. Not one of these so called men who still play video-games and read Harry Potter and go to Pixar films and rock concerts and eat candy and popsicles and ice cream.

You eat gelato!

James scrunched the paper into a ball, which he threw into his recycling basket. He took a step towards his bed. Stopped. Looked at the basket. Retrieved the ball. Unscrunched it.

Folding it carefully, he put the childish thing away into a compartment at the back of his mom's old jewelry box.

* * *

"I dance with myself
Swaying with the wind
My father is the wind

"My mother the earth
Leap for the sky
To escape her

"Leap for the freedom
For the moment
Only a moment

"But I'm free"

James listened, utterly confused. He looked to the title for help: *Father Daughter Dance*. Hopefully he hadn't inspired this song. It had failed to inspire him: his many potential thank-you notes had all come out either too personal or too impersonal. He was desperate.

He still had to give her something. He didn't want to discourage her from being in his life. It was comforting to have a friend near his own age, even if she did have this need to share her music with him. He simply had to be careful not to imply he wanted something more.

Then, he found it. The exact right gift. The perfect Golden Mean.

* * *

James waited outside the Odeon Theatre. It was 7:01 pm on Good Friday. Not a day he should really be watching movies.

It wasn't the only thing he really shouldn't be doing.

"Monseigneur Bienvenu!" somebody shouted. James acknowledged with a Queen-of-England-like grimace before turning away, pretending to be in thrall with the latest movie poster.

Melissa took him by the elbow from his blind side.

"Was your Good Friday as solemn as you were hoping?"

"No, actually", said James.

* * *

The movie was over and done with. It had been four months since he'd watched one and he'd have been happy to skip the spring and summer seasons altogether, catching up with the art house pictures that clumped together in the fall.

He stopped his car in front of her place... her and her Fiancé's place.

"Did you get a chance to listen to the tape?"

"Yes", said James. "It was quite fine. You could be a von Trapp."

"I'll take that as a compliment."

"I meant it as a compliment", said James, taking the gift from his jacket pocket. "Actually, I have something for you." Should you give gifts on Good Friday? Seemed wrong.

"Exciting!" Melissa unwrapped the CD. "*St. Matthew's Church Choir Sings the Classics*." The church had recorded it five years previous. It wasn't bad. "Oh... Thank-you." She's hurt by it. She's given you something she created. Something she cared about no matter how twangy the guitar accompaniment. Now you're giving her this that means nothing.

"I sing tenor on a couple of the tracks."

She perked up a little. "I'll listen for you." She squeezed his hand and then left the vehicle.

Chapter
22

It had been a long time since the church was this packed. Ten after nine and people had to squeeze into the side pews that looked directly at the pillars and that was after they made extra room by moving the papier-mâché artwork display near the children's area at the back. Easter Sunday combined with the moderately popular news story had created a perfect storm.

The Deacon arrived at James' side. "It's all for you." He'd become even more ingratiating since the article.

"I think I should preach this one, William", said the Rector. "It's a lot of pressure to put on you for your first Easter."

"I think James should preach", said the Deacon. "He's why they're here."

"Do you have anything prepared?" the Rector asked doubtfully.

"No", said James, displeased with the Rector's presumptiveness.

"Maybe James could preach at the Eleven", said Canon Conroy.

"Good idea!" exclaimed the Deacon.

"That's still not enough time to prepare", worried James.

"Yes", agreed the Rector. It angered James how quickly.

"It's Easter", said Canon Conroy. "You must have a few sermons in the archives." Actually the Rector had never let James preach on Easter. Not even once.

"James can't miss the Nine-Fifteen", said the Rector. "They're here to see the big star."

"Okay," said James, "I'll come up with something."

* * *

Why had he volunteered to do this? Was it to help the Eleven or to spite the Rector? To spite the Nine-Fifteen? To spite his "fans"? A sermon written out of spite. What was wrong with him?

James had nothing. Correction: he had too much. Death and Resurrection were pretty big topics. There was a lot James could say. But he wanted to do something focused and he felt a need to make his "fans" properly understand his search for Jo-Marie. (If they were going to pity him, it should at least be for theologically sound reasons.) But how could he talk about Jo-Marie without exploiting Jo-Marie?

Aaargh!

James put the mix tape on absentmindedly. Melissa's voice blared *Heraklitos* out of the speakers. James turned down the volume. Feverishly began to type.

* * *

"The service is about to start", said the Deacon. "Canon Welker said it's okay if you don't have anything. He's happy with what he preached for the Nine-Fifteen."

James took his sermon off the printer. "Ready", he said.

It was more wishful thinking than the truth.

* * *

James stood up before the people, considering his options. Maybe he could just pretend to faint and see where that led.

No. He had a duty to God, to His people, and to His proper liturgy. Time to go.

"'Nothing is constant. Everything changes.' 'This too shall pass away.'

"I have been searching. I have been searching and not finding. And I am not sure sometimes if it is for my goddaughter or my God. People often tell me that after a point my efforts to find my goddaughter are useless. Even if I found her, I can't make her stay. She has a mind of her own. She could always run away again. For my efforts to be worthwhile at all, she must find me or at least want to be found. And yet that mind of her own, like any mind, is constantly flowing. Constantly changing. So while I may find her again and for a moment be happy, I should not be so foolish as to call it a happy ending. It doesn't end. It is not constant. Nothing is constant. Everything changes. This too shall pass away."

A camera flash! Another damned reporter? James looked out at many damned reporters for the damned Facebook news: a mass of smart phones and cameras pointed at him. Had they no respect for sacred time spent in a sacred space? That would have to be his next sermon. For now James looked back to his notes.

"Our relationship with God is much the same. He cannot find us. We must find Him. We must want to be found. I've been found before. I've had absolute faith. I have felt God the Father's love. It is wonderful to be a child of God and yet, it's not so simple as that sometimes. All we need is a mustard seed of faith and yet there are times when I have truly, sincerely searched my heart, the Bible, literature, Rodgers and Hammerstein and everywhere I can think of looking and yet not found Him. Nothing is constant. Everything changes. This too shall pass away.

"I take great comfort from the Cross not just because I'm morose…" (people laughed at this) "…but because it is on the Cross that Jesus was most human. 'My God! My God! Why have you abandoned me?' Even God Himself, made human, knew what it was like to lose faith, to lose hope, to feel that He had lost the love of God. Jesus did not feel the love of God and He is God." (An underscore of clacks, beeps and buzzings. James, seeing members of the congregation typing on their smart phones, wanted to stop everything to give them each a thorough scowl, but considered it unfair to those few who actually were listening to him.) "If that could happen to God Himself how can we expect to be steadfast in faith? Nothing is constant. Everything changes. This too shall pass away.

"I take comfort because the Cross was not the ending. Death was not constant. Jesus rose again. That is what we celebrate today.

Jesus conquered death. He also conquered this constant change, because he gave us eternal life. 'Eternal' doesn't mean 'forever'. It means 'outside of time'. 'Timeless'. If there is no time, there can be no change. God is eternal. Our lives, through Jesus, are eternal. This is the one constant we can cling to. The one hope we have that will not pass away.

"But I leave you with this: never take faith for granted and never be proud to have it. Never lord it over others. Never have pride that others are lost while you are found. For even Jesus knew what it was like to lose faith and even God the Father knows what it is like to lose a child. But when you are lost, seek. Seek and have faith… have faith that eventually you shall find Him…"

"Or Her", James heard the Deacon whisper from his prayer desk.

"…and then for all eternity. In the name of the Father, the Son, and the Holy Ghost."

As James stepped down from the pulpit he endured applause from half the congregation. More than half of the other half were nose deep into their smart phones. Why? What were they smart phoning about?

The Deacon leaned over to James, whispering a cryptic answer: "Dude. You're trending."

James' next sermon now had a title.

* * *

He shook two hundred and ninety-eight hands. All covered in germs. Each and every mouth attached to those hands congratulated him for the sermon. Canon Conroy said it was both heartfelt and Neo-Platonic. He had always been quite the flatterer. Melissa had been in the line too. "Good job", she said painfully. Did she mean it? She seemed distant. He was sure she must have hated the CD. At least she hadn't told him that his sermon had changed her life. A lot of people said that. Were they trying to be funny?

James, for his part, felt sick. He'd meant the sermon. Or at least he'd meant to mean it. But it felt utterly wrong and false. He'd exposed too much about his feelings for Jo-Marie, recorded by too many camera phones and "posted" on too many "walls". Misery should not have a fan club. And his faith hadn't magically come rushing back. Nor was he sure there really was eternal life. It felt right for the sermon. It sounded right. But was it right?

Oh well, he thought, I guess I might have helped the Eleven.

Chapter

23

He watched the Verger stack purple book after purple book into boxes. James picked one up, flipping through. He'd made sure all the elderly at the hospital got a copy, as well as the last few parishioners from the now defunct Eleven. He'd managed to give away a few copies to residents of St. Matthew's Court, the low-income senior's apartment complex next door. He'd directed some copies to St. Barnabas' and the Cathedral. Those books would have good homes. The rest would be stored in boxes at the back of the choir loft behind the Christmas decorations.

James returned the BCP to the box. He wondered how many years it would be before another human opened that book and read its pages. He looked at his watch. Twenty-eighth of April. He'd almost forgot about the Royal Wedding. He bet they got to use the BCP.

* * *

A "Spotted Jo-Marie" message from Facebook. Briefly James' heart elevated, though he did his best to tamp it back down. He clicked on the link, first having to go through a useless Facebook survey that asked for his age and gender and cell phone number.

Finally he got to the message. A young public servant had spotted someone at Fort and Douglas that looked a lot like Jo-Marie.

A lot of people, it turned out, looked a lot like Jo-Marie. Fort and Douglas was one of the busiest intersections in the city. The sighting meant absolutely nothing. A thousand and twelve friends giving him false hope, false concern, false friendship.

The cell phone had helped even less. The Deacon would call to ask useless questions about the details of his sermons: "Do you think

I should say 'for the Father' or 'of the Father'?" The Receptionist would call if someone came to the office looking for James. The phone was for Jo-Marie related emergencies only. He'd been very clear about that. He would get harassing text messages from Joss and, great, just got spammed: "Great to have a sense of humour, but don't go overboard with the jokes or it might be a turn off." Might it? Nothing in this world comes without spam. Vanity of vanities, saith the Preacher, all is vanity.

* * *

James chopped the eggplant into half-inch cubes, which he threw into the pan. He listened intently to them crackling in hot oil, adding three cloves of minced garlic, savouring the smell. He shook the pan, mixing the flavours, then turned down the heat and went over to his couch. He picked up the sonnet. He didn't like the way "World bathed in the light of your eternal day" flowed so he erased it and wrote "With bathing the world in your eternal day" in its place. He put it back down, then returned to the stove, shaking the pan again. He had a sip of wine.

There was a knock at his door. He assumed it was another stupid campaigner for the federal election. Half of him didn't want to answer. The other half couldn't wait to be rude.

The falling sun streamed in, sanctified by the auburn haired beauty, holding a bottle of wine.

"I don't think the tape was good enough."

"I don't think the CD was good enough."

"What are you talking about?"

"What are *you* talking about?"

"I want to tell you something. It's private. I don't like to share it and I don't want you sharing it. But I believe it might make you feel better about your situation. And I think, maybe, I know it sounds stupid, but I think maybe I was meant to tell you."

Oh great, sharing. He knew the sermon had been too personal.

"What were you meant to tell me?"

"I used to live on the street."

* * *

Melissa sat forward on his couch, a few drinks in. She swallowed another gulp of wine, then began. "I'd grown up on a farm until I was fourteen with my older brother and parents. A hobby farm. Just north of Toronto. So anyway, my dad was a neurologist but he got it in his head he needed to do real good for the world so he left to be doctor of a very poor village in Vanuatu."

"That was good of him."

"Yeah but he left us. Gave everything to us, but left us. My mom hated him for it but I think she was relieved too. She was a city girl. She sold the farm and used the money to buy her store and a small house in the Annex. So anyway, now I go from being a farm kid, looking after chickens and a couple of cows, to living in the big city and I didn't fit in. I started eating nervously to cope so then I was fat and didn't fit in."

She poured another glass of wine. Okanagan Falls Shiraz. He knew it well. It was maybe the most common "vintage" gifted by grateful parishioners. Retail value of $17.95, at least the last time he'd checked.

"So anyway, there's this gang of girls that liked the fashion at my mom's store, and hey, I had some of the merchandise right there. First they stole my bag from my locker. Then a necklace of mine they took at knifepoint. One time they pushed me into an alley and took my clothes right off me. I walked home crying in my underwear."

"You didn't alert the authorities?"

"You know how snitches get treated at school." (He did, and proudly.) "Life at home wasn't exactly fun either. I used to write songs to get through it. I wrote the lyrics on my bedroom walls along with little sayings I thought were beautiful. Things to encourage me that I would get through all right. I walked into my room one time to find my brother, who'd been fitting in great mind you, I find him displaying the writing on my wall to his new friends. Word about this gets out. Like I wasn't enough of a freak before. I painted over all those words. All those beautiful words."

She took a sip of wine. Composed herself.

"Everybody says it was teen angst and maybe it was but I was seriously thinking about killing myself. I told my mom I was having troubles. She said maybe I'd feel better if I lost a little weight. I said okay, I will ignore the world around me and pour myself into schoolwork…"

Good strategy, thought James.

"So at least I get that validation… sort of. I said, 'Mom, I got straight A's…'"

At least they gave out A's, thought James.

"And she congratulates me with a belt."

"She beat you?"

"No. It was a nice belt. But it was too small for me: she was giving me a weight loss goal. I just handed it to the gang of girls. I missed my dad. He was the one I got on with, so anyway, this guy Grey took pity on me. Let me hang with his friends. They were all ravers. I don't think they really liked me, but he made them be nice to me. So anyway then his dad moved to Hamilton. So I asked Grey if I could come too. He said sure so I packed a bag and took the GO train. I stayed out of the way. For the first few days it was all fine. Then his dad walked in on us…"

James didn't want to think about this part.

"…having a bump of Special K."

What that sex act could involve literally boggled James' mind.

"You were a couple?"

"No. What? We were doing drugs."

"Oh."

"Yeah, the other problem was that Grey was holding hands with his new boyfriend. So yeah Grey got kicked out which kind of made me kicked out too. Grey's boyfriend didn't have room at his parents' place and neither me or Grey knew anyone else in Hamilton so yeah, luckily it was springtime. I didn't get beaten or robbed or raped or anything…" (If Melissa thought this was making him feel better about Jo-Marie, she was mistaken.) "…but Grey got the shit beat out of him." (Very mistaken.) "I screamed and screamed but there were three of them. I couldn't have stopped one of them. So yeah, he begged his dad to let him stay there again, which it turned out his dad was legally obligated to let him do. But he wasn't obligated to let me stay. So I went back to my mom's."

"She must have been glad to see you."

"She hadn't noticed I was gone."

Melissa took a deep sigh but she did not tear up. "She's not a bad woman. Just oblivious. So anyway, my point is, I've turned out all right. I've got a degree. I've got work. I'm making music again. I'm going to get married. You can do the wrong things—run away, do drugs, live on the streets even—and still end up okay."

Her informal confession was a little melodramatic, obviously, and had actually backfired about some of his Jo-Marie related worries, but it was, he had to admit, more comforting than not. James didn't even correct her about the fact that two nights on the street was not even close to the same thing as several months. Melissa squeezed encouragement into his hand. Her eyes caught his eyes. Her perfect eyes were tearing up.

He desperately wanted to kiss her. She wanted it too. Her eyes were saying it.

Oh God. What should he do? He was supposed to be her priest, but he didn't want to be her priest and he didn't think she should be getting married at least not in a church and certainly not to that fool of a fiancé but it's not like he wasn't biased but he did meet her before he knew she was getting married and it's not like she'd attended any services or was even Christian and they were only getting married to please the Fiancé's grandmother and family and the Fiancé takes her for granted but still he should counsel reconciliation of course it didn't work that last time but it would create a scandal if it got out and the Choir Master had seen them and did he really like her yes she was very kind to share her story to comfort him but was it really for his sake or was she just one of those people that got off on sharing her pain and that was why she wanted him to hear her songs too probably and she was also once an illicit drug user and how could he take pleasure in Melissa's beauty while Jo-Marie was quite possibly quite currently in danger and did Melissa really even like him or was he just projecting and if she did like him might it not be because she was having doubts about her getting married and he was just a fling maybe just a bump in the road before she fully committed herself to someone else and my God she truly is the most beautiful part of all creation and you could just kiss her, just kiss her...

Just kiss her.

"Please excuse me." James stood up. "I have something to attend to in the washroom."

* * *

James stared at himself in the mirror. He could have pursued his passion, but instead did the right thing. That's what integrity is all about. It's not enough to do the right thing if you'd do the wrong thing given the opportunity. No, by St. Augustine, it was not. He had been tested. He had passed. Now believe it. Believe that you do not want her.

It's the easiest thing in the world.

Something gnawed at the back of James' mind. What was it? Something he'd forgotten. What had he forgotten?

He had a sudden vision of his living room. Directly in front of Melissa, underneath her bottle of wine, sitting on the coffee table, spelling her name, hand printed, there was a sonnet.

Maybe she'd think it was poorly written. Maybe it would scare her off. Send her running back to the Fiancé with open arms. On the off chance she did appreciate it James could always say it was a Renaissance Humanist Devotional Friendship Sonnet. He could show her other examples. She'd believe that.

Definitely.

* * *

James tried not to stare at the scrap paper. He was sure she hadn't read it. Who reads all the scrap paper on a stranger's coffee table? As long as he didn't draw attention to the fact that it was there everything would be fine. She hadn't mentioned it. Obviously she would have mentioned it if she'd read it. But she hadn't asked to go either. He would have if he'd just shared a very personal story and someone responded by going to the washroom. But maybe, in her bohemian, guitar laden, open relationship addled world, staring at someone sadly then leaving the room was perfectly appropriate.

She emptied the bottle. Only a quarter glass left. She put the bottle on the coffee table itself. The paper was exposed. She could read it now if she wanted. She could focus her eyes on her name.

She turned. He went to grab it. She turned back. He quickly sat back in his chair.

"I love your house." She'd reverted to small talk. He was terrible at small talk. She'd want to go soon, barring incident. "The whole way it's laid out. Did you get a designer?"

"No", said James.

"It was very sensibly done."

"Thank-you." Maybe if he distracted her he could grab it. "I know the artist that painted that." Just as she was turning her head she put the glass back down on the sonnet. Bugger!

"It's beautiful."

"He's a parishioner. He'd be glad to know you like it."

She picked up her glass. He lunged, but she put the glass back down without even taking a sip. Was she trying to torture him? She picked it back up again. Now came the sip. The last sip. James had a flash of brilliance.

"Let me get you some more." James picked up the glass and the paper in one swoop. She didn't even notice. Just laid her head on the armrest.

He knelt down at his liquor cupboard. He wasn't in her sightline. He folded the paper and slipped it in his wallet. He selected and opened a new bottle. The third of this "vintage" they'd opened. He filled the two glasses. "Here you are."

Her eyes were closed.

"Melissa?"

James looked at the empty bottles of wine. He'd consumed two glasses, maybe.

* * *

He could have called her a cab. He supposed that would have been a sensible thing to do, but she was quite drunk and he hadn't trusted cab drivers since his last vacation to Greece.

She half awakened as he stumbled with her to the spare bedroom, but fell asleep again the moment she hit the bed. Remembering an info session on alcohol from his university days, he was sure to lay her on her side, resting her head on her hands. That way she wouldn't choke on her own vomit.

Instead she'd vomit all over his second best quilt!

He rolled her off the bed, waking her again.

"I'm drunk, aren't I?"

"Very much so."

He removed the quilt, then helped her back onto the bed. He tucked her in under some generic blue sheets and an old ratty blanket. "Make sure you sleep on your side, resting your head on your hands", said James.

"Thank-you", she smiled. He smiled back, sitting down in a chair nearby. He felt creepy watching her fall asleep but, he reasoned, he'd feel more creepy if he didn't follow the proper steps (ensuring 12-20 breaths per minute) and the next morning had to explain about the corpse in his spare bed. Okay she probably wasn't that drunk, but caution was his favourite side to err on and yes, he admitted, her tired face was pleasant to look at.

Botticelli never painted such an angel.

The angel started snoring. Sixteen snores in one minute. Very reassuring. He fetched her a glass of water, bottle of aspirin, towel, still packaged toothbrush, toothpaste, housecoat and pajamas for when she awoke, then put himself to bed.

* * *

He turned on his side. He'd thought if he'd made the right choice then that would be that. A one-time thing and then you get on with your life. But here he was feeling as bad as before. Worse.

Well, maybe she hadn't wanted a kiss. Maybe she just stared at him because she was embarrassed and drunk. He had a talent for misreading people. But she'd made him a mix tape filled with songs he'd inspired, invited herself over with wine, and truly did look him deeply in the eyes. That must have meant something.

Idiot.

He could hear her snoring loudly not ten feet from him (vertically speaking). So close was that woman he maybe even loved and who seemingly felt something for him and he'd sabotaged the whole thing.

Idiot.

No. He had shown both honour and moral integrity.

Idiot.

* * *

He tiptoed down the stairs, needing to dull his nerves. A sip of sherry should do it, or maybe port.

As he passed by his front door he heard faint tapping. He listened closely. It wasn't a knock but it was distinct. Like a tree branch swaying against the house. But there wasn't a tree close enough. There wasn't a wind strong enough.

James opened his door. There, in the dark and the mild drizzle, stood Jo-Marie. Alive, if not well.

PART III

The Thanksgiving

"'When the gods created man they alloted to him death, but life they retained in their own keeping. As for you, Gilgamesh, fill your belly with good things; day and night, night and day, dance and be merry, feast and rejoice. Let your clothes be fresh, bathe yourself in water, cherish the little child that holds your hand, and make your wife happy in your embrace; for this too is the lot of man.'"

–Siduri's Advice, *The Epic of Gilgamesh*

Chapter
24

She didn't say anything. He didn't need her to. Wordless he let her into the house. Wordless he gave her a towel. Both her pajamas and housecoat were in the spare room, so he fetched her an old bathrobe and some sweats that he never wore anyway. She had a shower upstairs while he slowly warmed milk and cocoa and gathered necessaries for a cheeseburger. He was frying the patties when she descended the stairs.

"I'd like lasagna", were the first words out of her mouth, whispered to suit the nighttime. The sweats were far too big for her, as was the robe. She looked cozy.

The patties were easily split into tiny pieces but otherwise he was undersupplied. He chopped up tomatoes, adding salsa and left over eggplant to make up for the lack of sauce. James' cottage cheese had given rise to a civilization of mold so he substituted with ricotta and sour cream. He substituted onion with shallots and garlic. But James simply did not have enough noodles, even if he made half a layer with reginette.

"Use spaghetti", she whispered.

"Don't be absurd", he whispered. "They invented the lasagna noodle for a reason."

"How do you know unless you try?"

"Fine. But if it turns out terrible you can't blame me."

"I can and I will."

James poured her hot cocoa from the saucepan into a mug, adding a pinch of sea salt before serving. He would boil the spaghetti until it was just past al dente, drain, then layer. James looked at his watch.

"It'll be 4:00 before this is ready you know."

"Since when did you ever sleep?"

James glanced up at her, then back to the garlic he was chopping. So many questions to ask, but best to wait.

"You probably want to call my father don't you?"

"I promised to. But no, I don't want to."

"I don't want him to know."

"He'll figure it out eventually."

"I told you. Don't call him."

"Not from me. But with the Facebook group and the news reports…"

"You made a Facebook group and called the newspapers?"

"Of course not. I was just so worried looking for you word got out and people, fools really, overstepped their bounds and…"

"I already knew about it father James." He had missed her winsome grin.

"Oh. Good. But I don't think we could stop your father from knowing you're here."

"I'll call him tomorrow. I'll tell him I'll run away again if he tries to come get me."

"You're welcome here as long as you'd like." James smiled at her, hoping it didn't look awkward.

"Good." She turned away from his smile. "If you want your book back, I don't have it. I've spent the money too."

"Don't worry about that. I got it back free of charge."

"How?" Jo-Marie looked rather impressed.

"I have secret strength no one gives me credit for."

"I'm sorry for taking it but you were holding me against my will."

"I accept your apology but not your reasoning."

"I won't take anything this time since I want to stay. That would be stealing."

"It was stealing the first time."

"Right. But it would be wrong this time."

"It was wrong the first time." James was exasperated but simply incapable of anger. He dumped the chopped garlic and shallots into a pan to sear them.

"I'd like to keep *On the Road* though."

James looked to his shelf. Sure enough there was a vacant spot in the "K" section. Huh, he thought. "How do we ask?"

"I'm not five anymore father James."

"Then you should know how to ask."

She rolled her eyes. "May I keep your copy of *On the Road* please?"

"Yes you may."

"Thank-you."

"You're welcome." James was concerned she might become one of those newfangled beatniks but at least she was reading an actual physical book. Jo-Marie giggled to herself quietly.

"What?" asked James.

"Why are we whispering?" She raised her voice to a normal conversation level. "People are ridiculous sometimes."

"Yes, well…" James stammered at a continued whisper.

"What? Do you have a woman here?" She was only teasing. She thought it was a completely ridiculous notion. But James looked as if he'd been caught at something. Then she noticed the open bottles of wine. The wine glasses. Lipstick on one of them. Looked at the sweats and the bathrobe she herself was wearing. "Oh God! I'm sorry!" She backed away towards the door, wretchedly embarrassed. "I should go."

James nearly spilled the frying shallots and garlic, rushing as he did towards Jo-Marie. "No no no no! God. Sweetie. You never have to go. It's not what it looks like."

Melissa, squinting through thin eyes that still hated the light, trundled out of the spare room, wearing Anne's old housecoat. James was terrified. She must look like a ghost to her, he thought.

Jo-Marie, for her part, was frozen.

"Oh my God! You must be Jo-Marie!" Anne he meant Melissa rushed to Jo-Marie and gave her a big loving hug. Jo-Marie stiffened in as anti-social a manner as she could muster. "I'm sorry. That was crossing several boundaries. I've just heard so much about you. James was so worried about you and…"

"Who the hell is she?"

"Jo-Marie, meet Melissa. She's a friend."

"You guys were fucking."

"What a thing to say! No. You maybe didn't notice that she came out of the spare room."

"You were doing it on my bed?"

"I was in my room. She was sleeping down here. Nothing untoward happened between us."

Jo-Marie breathed again. "Okay." She went back to the kitchen and sat down. Her face went sour. "You better not have been doing it on my bed."

"We weren't", said Melissa. She could not take her eyes off of Jo-Marie. She could not contain her smile.

"Stop staring at me."

"Sorry. It's just such a blessing you're back."

"I'm a person, okay? I'm not anyone's blessing. It's tough enough getting by without the added pressure of being a blessing."

"She didn't mean anything by it, Joanne Marie", said James. "You will kindly be more polite. She's our guest." He took the pan off the heat. He added the fried shallots and garlic to the meat sauce. Stirred.

"I'm sorry", said Jo-Marie like she didn't entirely mean it but partly wanted to.

"I completely understand", said Melissa. "I should probably just leave you two to catch up."

"No. It's okay", said Jo-Marie, forcing out a smile. "Please. Sit down. We're making lasagna."

"Where exactly is the 'we' in this?" asked James, spreading out a layer of meat sauce.

"I suggested the spaghetti noodles. Without that suggestion you would never have become what you are today."

James tried to hide a smile as he added ricotta and sour cream. Jo-Marie turned to Melissa. "So, where are you visiting from?"

"From?"

"You're from out of town aren't you?"

Melissa's brain had barely overcome its inebriation. It looked to James for guidance.

"She lives near Cook Street Village."

"Cook Street Village? Like a half hour walk from here?"

"She was… She'd been… I didn't want her to walk at night."

"Ten bucks for a cab."

"I had the room anyway and we were both tired and how do you know how much it is for a cab?"

"Something is going on then."

"James is prepping me for marriage", said Melissa.

"What does that mean?!" asked Jo-Marie.

"He will be the priest for my wedding. But my fiancé's out of town so…" Melissa shook her head at herself.

"What's going on?"

"Nothing", said Melissa.

"I am her priest. She came over to…" Was it his place to share? Would Jo-Marie want to hear it? "…she came over in that capacity." James spread some cheddar.

"For wedding advice?"

"Yes," said Melissa, "that's right. And I had a fair amount to drink…" Melissa shook her head again.

"Nothing happened", blurted James.

"So I can tell anybody about this", said Jo-Marie. "That would be fine?"

"Look, whatever crazy things you're thinking…"

"What crazy things am I thinking?"

"That we had…" James paused. Said more quietly, "…congress on your bed. I would never consider using that bed for such purposes. Trust me. But if others became aware that Melissa slept over, well that would start rather unfortunate rumours. Were you to start those rumours I would never again make you lasagna."

"Yes you would", said Jo-Marie. "You really didn't do anything?"

"Nothing untoward", said James. Melissa nodded in support.

A moderately sadistic smile crept across Jo-Marie's face. She clapped. "But I can still blackmail you."

"If you wish." James wasn't too worried. He put the lasagna in the oven. He set the timer, went to the couch and collapsed down.

"What problems are you having with your man?"

"We're not going to talk about that." Melissa sat down on the stool next to Jo-Marie.

"Fine then. Where is your man?"

"He's touring Ontario."

"Touring? Like he's in a band?"

"He plays bass guitar."

"Father James is cutting in on a rock star's wife!"

"Nothing untoward." James smiled. Jo-Marie had so much energy!

"What group is he in?"

"Right now he's touring with *The NikNaks*", said Melissa.

"No way!"

"But he's normally in *The Fissures*…"

"I love them! I lost all their songs when I got my iPod stolen."

"That sucks! I dropped mine in a storm drain once."

They'll get on, thought James. They fit together. Jo-Marie actually just laughed at Anne's joke. I mean Melissa's joke. Better not make that mistake out loud. I wouldn't. The resemblance isn't what I think it is. She and Anne could be sisters maybe. Not twins or anything. Maybe sororal.

James' brain considered these worries to be venial at worst. Jo-Marie was safe and sound. Was with someone he trusted. He didn't understand the words they were saying. Probably talking about some band or being beatniks or something.

He'd been very satisfied when he purchased this couch. Firm yet comfortable. Maybe he could just close his eyes. Just to rest them. Just close them for a moment so that he'd have energy for serving the lasagna. An extended blink really. I think the Royal Wedding starts soon. We could all watch it together.

He fell into the first real sleep he'd had in months.

Chapter
25

Orange mixed with cinnamon mixed with maple mixed with sugar. It was perfectly caramelized. He could tell by the smell. Caramelized. Was there a more lovely word? When was this? He must have been ten or eleven. What a wonderful memory. It was so vivid. Even the smells. James opened his eyes. Anne was part of the dream. No, Melissa. Jo-Marie was there too. He began to worry that maybe last night was a dream. Maybe Jo-Marie was still missing. He sat up, knocking over an empty wine bottle. That part had been real at least.

"Morning sleepy head", said Melissa, her voice high pitched and exhausted.

"What time is it?"

"I'm not sure. Eleven or twelve."

James was suddenly very awake. "I'm supposed to be at work. It's Friday Meditation." He looked at his watch. "They should've called me."

"I left a message last night", said Jo-Marie. "They know I'm back and that you're sleeping." She set the table with napkins, knives and forks.

"That was very thoughtful of you", said James, glancing at Melissa. She winked at him as the timer beeped. She rushed into the kitchen and took a pan filled with baked orange French toast from the oven. The divine smell sextupled in strength.

Why did he choose "sextupled" of all the options?

"How did you know to make this?"

"Jo-Marie found the recipe."

"I've decided today will be your birthday", said Jo-Marie.

Gelato cake, thought James. And Lent was over.

Melissa took a spatula and freed the pieces of toast from the sticky pan. Her messy hair fell over her eyes. She smiled at him. There must be a loving God to make someone so beautiful. Blech! He was glad he hadn't put that in the poem.

Still... Wow!

"Did you sleep?"

"A little", said Melissa, rubbing her no doubt pounding skull. "She took your bed. She wanted to keep our scandal from getting worse."

"I expect payment for this."

"You already took my book", smiled James.

Water in a pot came to a boil. Melissa opened the container marked "tea". "Is all of it loose leafed?"

"Sit down, lady." Jo-Marie took the container out of her hand. Put it on the counter. As if part of a ceremony, she poured a splash of boiling water into the teapot, swayed it gently, warming it. She poured out this water, eyed what remained boiling and measured out six spoons of tea. She then poured in the boiling water, put the lid on the teapot. She opened a drawer, she knew which one, and put a cozy over top. "Let it steep five minutes."

James tried his best not to see her as a blessing.

* * *

They should have used more cinnamon but the French toast was delicious. Granted it could have used a garnish too, but the presentation was decent. They'd taken crust off the bread and dropped it in chunks around the pieces proper, soaking up the syrup and melted butter. It was a brilliant touch.

James mentioned that it was brilliant out loud. Made no mention of how the toast could've been improved. He did not complain of how gauche it was to be served on the same plate as cold lasagna that, he had to admit and did admit loudly and with praise, turned out better than he had expected. He made much conversation about how well he'd slept and how wonderful the whole morning now afternoon was. He repeated the word "thankful" multiple times, usually accompanied with a "how" or a "so". He could tell this was getting old, however, and neither of the ladies added anything substantive to stoke the conversation. Nothing that kept it going. He was thankful. That point was made. Thankful for the breakfast. Thankful that Jo-Marie was back home. Thankful for the spaghetti noodle suggestion. Thankful. Thankful. Thankful.

But where had she been? Could he ask that now? Was he supposed to ask that now? Would she be offended if he asked? Would she be offended if he didn't? When was the appropriate time? It was a fair thing to ask after what she'd put him through. Just do it casually. No need to make a big deal about it. Maybe come at it from an angle.

"So how have you been?" Good. Brilliant maneuver.

"Good."

"Really?" Oops.

"Yes, father James. I was doing so well I came to your house in desperation at two in the morning to make you breakfast and tell you how good I was doing!"

"Maybe we could talk about something else", said Melissa.

"Good idea", said James. Jo-Marie said nothing. The three of them sat silent.

It was better when I kept repeating "thankful", thought James.

Melissa and Jo-Marie tried to speak at the same time. "After you", said Melissa.

"No, what were you going to say?"

"Just that it's been a chilly spring."

"It sure has", said Jo-Marie. Has she slept outside all this time?

"It's La Nina", said Melissa. "Ocean currents cause weather patterns to get locked in. That's why there's been drought in some places but record cold and rain in others."

"I see."

More silence.

"You were going to ask something Jo-Marie", said Melissa.

"I was just going to ask father James who he was going to vote for."

She wants to rile me, thought James. "I haven't decided yet."

"Yes you have."

"Not so."

"Conservative."

"Not necessarily."

"You should vote Green."

"No." She definitely wants me to lose my cool. I won't do it.

"You shouldn't be so dismissive."

"I'm not being dismissive. They're a one issue party."

"It's an important issue."

"So's health care. I wouldn't vote for a party that called itself 'The Health Care Party' either. It's typical self-righteous liberal…" Damn it.

Jo-Marie grinned wide. She'd won this round. "Let's get gelato cake", she said.

* * *

As James was putting together what clothes to wear he saw a pile of pamphlets he'd gathered for the streetpeople. About nurses. About basic health requirements. About not feeling lost and alone. I will not think about that today, thought James. I will cherish today. But then he saw the Street Nurse's pamphlet for hepatitis C. "The quicker it is dealt with the better." "Don't delay." Bugger, thought James.

* * *

Jo-Marie's clothes were dry. Her hoodie was stain covered but clean. James wore the stylish shirt and jeans he had bought with Melissa's help.

Jo-Marie took one look at him and burst out laughing.

I've already used my one stupid question, thought James. I bring this up too it's going to ruin everything. But it was her health. It was her life. Every minute counted. But that was if you had just been lanced. Even if she'd been lanced yesterday it would be a little late to take her now. Today or tomorrow probably didn't make much difference at this point. Or did it? How long before it became chronic? The pamphlet always led to such dark thoughts, he'd never properly studied it.

Radiant Melissa emerged from the spare room in the same white with red flowers dress she'd worn the night before. She probably knew about hepatitis C too. Why did he have to be the one that worried? Things were going well now. Why couldn't he just enjoy it?

* * *

They were out of the nocciola coconut combination James was hoping for but nocciola hazelnut wasn't exactly a shabby back up. As they were paying, a random middle-aged gentleman vainly trying to look youthful with his fitted t-shirt and spiky brown hair exclaimed, "Is this Jo-Marie?"

"Uhhmm", said James.

"You've found her at last! That's so wonderful!" Jo-Marie squirmed under the man's gaze.

"Thank-you", said James, pulling Jo-Marie towards the exit.

"You should put that up on Facebook. A lot of people are worried."

"Right", said James.

As they left the store, Jo-Marie glowered at the world, back in a nasty mood. He could kill the Deacon, pacifist or not. Maim him at least. How could James bring up hepatitis C now?

* * *

While Melissa was cutting the cake and Jo-Marie was in the washroom, James had the exceptional idea of simply leaving the hepatitis C pamphlet amongst other papers on the coffee table. It was well known he'd been working with the streetkids. It was perfectly reasonable he'd have the pamphlet. Jo-Marie had found his photo album there when he hadn't meant her to. Only his quick thinking had prevented Melissa from finding the sonnet. Time to take advantage of this town crier of a coffee table.

He was putting the pamphlet in place when Jo-Marie sat down on the couch.

"What's that?"

"What's what?"

"Shouldn't you be taking stuff off the coffee table, not putting more on?"

"That's what I was doing", said James. Jo-Marie grabbed the pamphlet from his hand.

"You think I have hep C?"

"I... no... You've jumped to several conclusions."

"Good."

"Although, since you mentioned it, it would be a good idea to get checked out. The sooner you get to these things the better." It wasn't what he'd just said so much as how he'd just said it: like the weakest actor in an after school special talking directly to camera. He'd never been capable of any form of subterfuge.

"I can't believe you!" Jo-Marie had slammed the door to the spare room before James could take the breath necessary to object.

"What did you do?"

"I didn't do anything. I was just... The sooner you get to it the better and..."

Melissa took the pamphlet from James. She shook her head at him. "I'll go talk to her."

It was several minutes of pleading before Jo-Marie opened her door and then, it seemed, more to show that James specifically wasn't allowed in than that Melissa specifically was. Jo-Marie slammed the door behind her.

James put the melting gelato cake pieces back in the box and the box into the freezer.

"Some fake birthday", he said to the freezer door.

* * *

"I hate him", said Jo-Marie's voice.

"You don't hate him", responded Melissa's.

James sat beside the vent in his en suite washroom. He had a scrub brush in his hand in case he looked suspicious. Jo-Marie wasn't aware, but anything said in the spare room could be heard through the vent.

"He's probably eavesdropping by the vent", said Jo-Marie's voice.

"Then I'll tell a story he already knows."

Melissa told the same story as the night before. James listened for discrepancies from what she'd told him but found none of interest until after the end: "My mom didn't notice I was gone. James did notice. James noticed so much half the town ended up searching for you." Five per cent at most, thought James. It was still a lot of people. "Think how much he cares about you. He cares more about you than anything else on earth. He's going to make mistakes, but remember that you are lucky to have someone like him in your life."

Melissa then lowered her voice so it was inaudible. Jo-Marie did the same. I might as well return to the kitchen, thought James. Make it look like I wasn't eavesdropping.

The top step creaked. They all creaked. He tiptoed along the side. One step at a time. No, this was more incriminating. He should just walk at normal speed.

"I'd like you to take me to the clinic, father James."

"I'll get my coat", replied James, mid tiptoe, toilet brush still in hand.

* * *

A long wait.

Two more random people were happy to know about Jo-Marie. They too thought he should update the Facebook group. They asked James who the red haired woman beside him was. "She's been helping with Jo-Marie", said James, hoping that didn't sound suspicious. Jo-Marie came out with the doctor. "Excuse me", said James to his "fans". The test results would be back in a couple of days. Unexpectedly, shockingly in fact, Jo-Marie gave Melissa a hug. Then, pretending she was going to hug James too, she instead took his car keys and ran.

As they headed to the exit, Melissa told James, "You're the only two people I've ever told that story to." James didn't say anything in response, but his face certainly did: Melissa was an absolute Godsend.

And he still wasn't sure if he believed in God.

Chapter
26

The phone tree angered James more than normal and it normally angered him. He looked over the bill again. The usual overcharging for set up fees and the like. But the biggest fee was for something called data messages: $220 plus taxes.

Oh great. Another junk text: "Did you know the giraffe has the longest neck in the animal kingdom?" Yes. I didn't think it was information worth sharing.

During his ten minutes on hold he got to hear advertising for the company he had already signed with and wanted to yell at.

He looked at Jo-Marie who looked up from her book just long enough to smirk at him. He had tried to arrange quality time for the two of them and now he was wasting it with this phone crap. He'd used the Jo-Marie Facebook group to thank people sincerely for their help but also to ask that they respect her privacy. He'd used his wits to argue against attending the new Ten-Thirty service with the new but not improved congregation. "People will be expecting you", the Rector had replied. "They'll be wanting another sermon."

"I'm sure you can come up with something."

"That's true", the falsely modest Rector had admitted.

Both James and Jo-Marie would have been delighted to spend their quality time with Melissa but the Godsend couldn't rearrange her shift at work.

The advertising ceased. The call might be recorded for training purposes.

"Hello my name is Chad." (Chad? Seriously?) "Thank-you for choosing T*lus. How can I help you today?"

"I signed up for a $30 plan and my bill is for more than $200."

"Set up fees are a necessary…"

"What's data messaging and why does it cost $4 per…"

"Those would be text messages you signed up for."

"I've been receiving spam messages, unasked for."

"You would have signed up for them."

"Why would I sign up for spam?"

"Maybe an ad on Facebook? You gave them your number."

"Never", said James searching his memory. Was it the survey?

"It might have been a fake survey. We've received complaints about that but it has nothing to do with us."

"It's on your bill."

"We act as a third party. We pay on your behalf."

"Don't pay on my behalf. It's a scam."

"It doesn't work like that sir."

"Yes it does."

"I'm afraid not."

"I'm afraid it does."

"Not so."

This exchange went on for a while.

"I'm not paying!" Chad from T*lus said he would have to talk to his manager about that, putting James on hold for another ten minutes.

"Sorry about the wait, James. We'll take it off your bill as a one time courtesy."

"You won't help someone rob me as a courtesy?"

"I recommend you text 'stop' to this company and don't go to strange websites in future."

"I never went to a strange website in the past. I can assure you I will never pay for something I don't want and didn't sign up for."

"That's not the way capitalism works sir."

"Capitalism? How dare you invoke that name? Capitalism is when you pay an agreed upon price for something you want. You charge for something I don't want…"

"It wasn't us sir."

"…and you overcharge for something I do." It sickened James that this would actually add to GDP.

The call then dropped. "Bugger modernity!"

Jo-Marie looked up from her book. "Can I have a cell phone?" James was shaking his head before she finished asking. "I'll text you wherever I go. That way you won't have to worry about me."

"I'll worry about you either way." He attempted to text "Stop!!!" but the phone kept trying to guess what he wanted to say and wouldn't let him just type in the letters: "Saw" "State" "Story" "Ssttrrpp".

"Let me try." After several minutes she said, "You need a newer phone."

* * *

The Choir Master talked James through the text. He assured James it wasn't Facebook's fault. "People try to hack them constantly."

"It's the death of true capitalism. It's neo-capitalism." James pronounced the prefix "neo" as if it were worse than excrement.

"But hey, e-mail is useful and it's free", said the Choir Master.

There's no correlation between price and worth. This was a major cause of the world economic meltdown. Neo-capitalism and neo-conservatism and neo-liberalism can all jump off a bridge together.

* * *

James and Jo-Marie spent their quality time with books. She read *On the Road*. He read Ovid's *Metamorphoses* in the original Latin.

"I suppose you should vote tomorrow."

"I suppose I should. Would you like to talk to the principal about schoolwork while we're there?" The polling station was at the junior high school gym.

"I'd forgotten about school."

"You don't have to right away."

"Might as well get it over with", she said.

A knock.

"Do you think it's Melissa?" asked Jo-Marie as James answered the door.

"Where's my daughter?" Joss tried to step past James, who blocked his path.

"Get away", yelled Jo-Marie. "I don't want to talk to you!"

"Sweetie! Please don't be like that. You know I love you. You're all I have left to love." He pushed James aside like he was nothing.

"Excuse me. This is my home. I have not given you permission to enter."

"That's my daughter."

"Go to your room Jo-Marie." Joss reached for Jo-Marie but James held on to his right arm.

"Get off me!" James was no match for Joss, but enough of a distraction that Jo-Marie made it past.

"Touch me and I'll bite you! Take me and I'll run away again!" Jo-Marie slammed her door.

Joss twisted until James fell from his arm.

"Pussy."

"I'm not a pussy", said James, standing. "I'm a pacifist."

"Like I said."

"My father served in Normandy."

"So? You ready to admit I was right?"

"About what?"

"Your searching didn't find her. Just like I said it wouldn't. Nothing you did brought her to you. You made yourself sick with worry, made a spectacle of yourself quite frankly, and for nothing. She came to you when she good and chose to."

"That's right. She came to *me*."

"She's my daughter. She's your nothing."

"She's my goddaughter."

"Like I said."

"It appears that she disagrees with your assessment."

"Don't look at me with those fucking judgmental eyes. You taught that look to Jo-Marie didn't you?" I did, thought James proudly. "Life hasn't been easy for me you know."

"Life hasn't been easy for anyone." Probably for some people.

"You've accused me of struggling with alcohol. Well my old man didn't struggle. He just drank. You see this tooth? This tooth ain't real see? You know how that happened? I was a kid. Twelve or thirteen. Younger than Jo-Marie. I was watching television. My old man came through pissed out of his skull. All my life I knew don't cross him when he's pissed. You had to walk on fucking eggshells of eggshells. I'd get so nervous. You understand nervous don't you? Well like that but for a real reason. Okay so then this time he looks at me. Stares me down. His breath stank." Joss' breath stank too. It made it easy to imagine. "What little hair he had was sticking up from his balding head. His body odour like rancid goat cheese." Joss' was more like aged parmesan. "And I think, how did this man ever get laid? And I feel this laugh coming up and I say to myself Joseph don't you dare let it out. I dug my fingernails into my palms. I bit my cheek. But the more I tried to stop it, the stronger it wanted to come. And my old man kept staring. He says, 'Something you wanna tell me champ?' I got a good strong whiff of his breath and I lost it. I just burst out laughing. I didn't even feel the first hit. The laughing numbed it maybe. But Christ did I feel the second and third and fourth and fifth and you get the idea. He was a big dude my old man. So yeah, I struggle to be a good dad sometimes but Jo-Marie's never lost a tooth. I have bad days. I have days when I'm not altogether there for her but who the fuck was ever there for me? Answer me that padre."

"You've told me stories like this before. Remember? When you confessed. I vouched for you to family services. I offered you my help. You didn't take it."

"Like I wanted help from my dead wife's ex-lover."

"There are a lot of sob stories out there. Yours isn't even the worst I've heard this week. You're over forty. You have a daughter. It's not about you anymore."

"I know. It's about Jo-Marie. Her happiness is all that matters to me. But she's never going to find that unless she makes things up with her old man. I know it. I never made things up with mine."

James struggled not to feel compassion. "That's up to her."

Joss stood up straight, leaning into James. This intimidation technique used to work, but now it just seemed ridiculous. Joss was big, but many of the streetpeople had been bigger. He was unstable, but they were more unstable. He smelled horrible. But they smelled worse. And there was only one of him. James remained calm. In control.

"If Jo-Marie agrees to see you I will give you a call."

"What if I just called the police on you now?"

James never liked to be in wrong with the authorities. The idea of having them called on him, perhaps for a technically legitimate reason, made his hand desperately want to shake. But he held it steady. Held his moral high ground. Something from deep inside told him the right words to say. "Call the police and I will sue you for custody. We're going to sign her back up at school tomorrow."

"I don't want to go back there." Joss had taught English until they'd fired him.

"We'll probably need you to sign some forms. You'll help with that. You'll clean yourself up. Then, if Jo-Marie wishes, we'll talk about attempting some sort of reconciliation."

"What if I don't want to do any of that?"

"You can have your personal life judged in a court of law."

"Yours will be judged too."

"I've already been judged", said James. "I'm Monseigneur Bienvenu."

Joss faked a punch, but James calmly held the bastard's gaze. Joss bumped James as he walked past him to the entranceway.

"This ain't over." He slammed the door. James locked it. Took a breath.

Jo-Marie emerged. She looked at James' right hand as it shook vigorously.

"Now can I have a cell phone?"

Chapter

27

James had a decision to make. In its heyday the Good Party almost always lost, but it had been the party that stood by its principles. Even though he never became Prime Minister, Canada could rightly be called the country of Stanfield because, back in those long forgotten days, it was a country where politicians won or lost on ideas. In their way, Stanfield and Clark did far more to make Canada what it was than Trudeau or Mulroney or Chrétien or any of those "personalities".

Prime Minister Attack Ads frightened him. He played Beatles tunes for goodness sake. James could think of only four other heads of government quite so intent on entertaining their own populace: Henry VIII, Kim Jong Il, Emperor Nero and Bill Clinton.

But vote Liberal? He would never be able to wash himself clean afterwards. NDP? Green? No thank-you. Not vote at all? His father hadn't served in Normandy only for his son to betray the very nature of democracy. Why couldn't there be one party to vote for, rather than four to vote against?

James looked at his options on the ticket. "You have to mark an 'x' or a 'check' or it's a spoiled ballot", the Elections lady had told him, as if he didn't already know. He could think of only two names he wanted to check beside (the 'x' seemed a bit pornographic). With clear, crisp letters he wrote and checked the one he'd never been able to vote for (but had always wanted to): "ROBERT STANFIELD".

James came out of the voting booth, mildly disgusted with himself. Would this impress the beatniks? Would it impress Mr.

Anarchy Tattoo? Would he have to start smoking boo and talking about his art projects now?

* * *

Mr. Bellis thought Jo-Marie should be held back a year. James didn't like that option, but he was concerned too much school all at once would be stressful. He wondered if there was some middle way. Maybe she could be held back half a year.

"I don't want to be held back at all", said Jo-Marie.

"You have a number of assignments you've missed. Experiments you haven't done. Math you haven't done. Books you haven't read."

"I've read the books", said Jo-Marie. "Assignments are pointless busy work. Give me the English final today. I'll ace it." Such confidence in herself! "Father James can teach me French and social studies." Such confidence in me!

"That's true", said James. "I'd just need the text books."

"You'd challenge all the finals?"

"I'll do math and science in summer school. Anything. Just don't hold me back."

"What do you think James?"

"If she wants to do all that work I don't want to stop her."

"We'll need parental consent of course."

"Yes. Joseph is a bit… indisposed."

Mr. Bellis read into those words just as James hoped he would. He had been the one to fire that drunk.

"Are there forms he could sign?" asked James.

"I'll make arrangements", said Mr. Bellis.

As they left the office, Jo-Marie whispered to James, "We'll forge his signature. Good idea."

"He'll sign them."

Two hoodlums passed them in the foyer. "Hey look it's the freak!" James was sure they were talking about him until he caught sight of Jo-Marie's scowl. Hopefully she'd be over it by the time she reached thirty-six or at least would never have occasion to return to junior high.

"Your dad's a drunk. You're a streetkid freak. What's your kid going to be like?" The hoodlums continued on their way.

"Don't worry", said James. "People called me a freak too."

"I'd already guessed that", said Jo-Marie.

* * *

Melissa looked at her old cell phone. "It's ancient."

"Newer than father James'." Jo-Marie hit the buttons as if to text. Two plans he'd be paying. James let out an audible sigh.

Jo-Marie asked, "What?"

James held up his cell phone. "This is what you've done to me."

"Get over yourself", said Jo-Marie. Melissa gave her a look that seemed to change her tune. "Do you want to go to the park?"

Of course he did. "You have schoolwork to do. I'm sure Melissa has her own life."

Jo-Marie raised her eyebrows at Melissa, who said she could use a day in the park. "Put this botany degree to good use."

* * *

A salty breeze swept through a field of blue flowers. She bent down with Jo-Marie to examine a single plant. "Do you know what this is?"

"A flower."

"It's camas. The Songhees used to cultivate it. It was a staple of their diet. That's why there's so much here. This was a communal farm."

"They ate flowers?"

"The bulbs. They'd harvest them in the spring and fall." She caressed a white flower. "But they were careful to dig up and discard these white flowers. Can you guess why?"

Jo-Marie thought for a moment. "They were weeds."

"Not bad. This is death camas."

"Cool!"

"The bulbs look just like the camas bulbs, but they're poisonous. They had to dig them up while the flowers were still in bloom so the bulbs wouldn't get mixed up and make them sick."

"Awesome!"

"Don't get any ideas", smiled James, trying to act normal. Why did Jo-Marie want to come here? Was she trying to relive that day? Did she even remember it? Was she doing it for him? Was she trying to replace her mother with Anne he meant Melissa?

* * *

The kites at Clover Point were in full bloom. A paraglider took off from the cliff in front of them, gliding over the ocean. Kite surfers in binding wet suits bounded through the waves.

Jo-Marie led the way down to the rocky beach. A couple of teenagers were making out on a surf washed sea log. Otherwise it was quiet for May.

Election day. Weekday. Chilly day.

"I want to tell you what happened."

"Okay", said James, acting cool.

"You can hear too", she said to Melissa.

"Thank-you."

"Okay." Jo-Marie paused. "I've been having problems with my dad."

"What sort of problems?" asked James.

"That's between me and him", said Jo-Marie.

"It's important."

"Do you want me to tell you or not?" James kept his mouth shut, stumbling on a smooth stone. A clatter of clacking as he steadied himself. "The kids at school called me freak. You saw that. My dad had come to classes drunk sometimes. They still remember. The only ones that didn't call me freak were the other freaks. They let me hang with them." She probably started smoking, thought James. "So I made close friends with this girl Sal. I told her I was having trouble. She let me crash on her couch." This sounds a bit like Melissa I mean Melissa's story. "But then her dad thought I'd been there too long. He wanted me out. Sal had introduced me to this guy Davie. He had his own place."

"How old was Davie?"

"Seventeen. He'd emancipated. He let me stay on his couch. There were a bunch of us staying there. But then he was short on rent and his landlord was pissed at him even if he was just seventeen. No one had enough money." Where had Davie got his money before this? Didn't the government subsidize that sort of thing? "I remembered your book. I thought I could grift..." Where did she learn "grift"? "...you of your book so I pretended to be sleeping on the streets at the church so you'd find me but you remember that." James nodded. "I'm sorry but we were desperate."

"You could have just asked for some money."

"You would have asked a lot of questions. You wouldn't have let me stay there." Excuse me for giving a damn. "It got us enough to make rent. But when rent time came again Davie asked if I could get more money out of you. I told him I couldn't do that to you again. Not with you searching everywhere for me and everything. Davie accused me of not pulling my weight. We got in a big fight. He took away my key. Kicked me out. I didn't want to sleep on the street. I didn't want to go back to my dad, so I came back to you." Jo-Marie paused. "You know the rest."

"Thank-you for being honest with me."

"Now I want a milkshake." Just as James was about to correct her she added, "Please."

"We'll swing back that way", said James.

"I'll get us started", Jo-Marie ran off ahead.

James slowed his pace until Jo-Marie was out of earshot. Melissa stared at the horizon, fascinated by the ocean.

"She's lying isn't she?" James asked.

"I don't know."

"If she was staying in an apartment why was she so dirty? They would've had a shower. She could've washed her clothes. Mr. Anarchy Tat... the kids I saw her with... I saw them sleeping on the street. They were always on the street. I saw her sleeping at the lych gate. I don't think she faked that. I don't think she told us the truth."

"Maybe not. Not the whole truth anyway. But I doubt you'd want to know the whole truth."

"You think she was sleeping with the seventeen-year-old? You think he's actually older?"

"I think your imagination is getting overactive. She's safe now. Focus on that."

"What should I do?"

"Buy her a milkshake."

"But she'll think she can lie to me and get away with it."

"If she's lying, it's to test you", said Melissa. "I think you should pass the test."

"How do I do that?"

"You know how."

"No I don't. That's why I'm asking you."

"Just be yourself."

"Myself wants to interrogate her."

"Be your better, less suspicious self. Buy a milkshake. Enjoy it. See where your instincts lead you from there." "Instincts"? "Be yourself"? The Godsend was giving some wishy-washy parenting advice. Weren't there specific rules you could just follow and then things would work out? "You were worried sick about her. Praying that you'd find her. Instead she found you. She's safe and sound. Be thankful for that." She held the back of his neck, affectionate. Was she coming on to him? Or was this something people who weren't like him just did?

Melissa he meant Melissa really wasn't so much like Anne. Their hair colour was more or less the same but they could not be more different. Both were beautiful, granted, but each in her own way. Melissa's features were soft. Anne's had been sharp. Melissa was voluptuous. Anne had been petite. Both were damaged to be sure. But Anne had used it as an excuse. It wasn't nice to say but it was true. She turned her pain inward and then lashed out. Melissa turned her pain into compassion. (And into earnest guitar songs he wished he liked more. But mostly compassion.)

And then, without willing it, without needing to, James stopped thinking about Anne or pain or what really happened to Jo-Marie or the Melissa questions or any of that. He simply enjoyed the day. He enjoyed climbing back up the cliff. Enjoyed every step. Enjoyed how he had to stop to catch his breath. He enjoyed walking by the world's tallest totem pole (depending on whom you asked). Jo-Marie of all people telling Melissa all about its restoration and resurrection. He enjoyed his milkshake at the Drive-In. Enjoyed seeing Jo-Marie smile. Enjoyed walking by the petting zoo as the peacocks strutted, spreading out their feathers. Enjoyed watching the mini-golf, the waterfowl, the cricket. Enjoyed getting the bocce set from his trunk, then coming in third to Jo-Marie and Melissa both games. Enjoyed the cold fried chicken and potato salad Melissa had thought to pick up at Thrifty's. Even enjoyed the random strangers who just wanted to say a quick hello, disobeying the Facebook request to respect Jo-Marie's privacy.

He had let his worry submerge into his subconscious. He'd let his thankfulness submerge too. Let all his meta-mind submerge.

And then he just was.

Chapter

28

Happy.

There was no other word for it.

Euphoric. Thrilled. Glad. Delighted. Content. Contented. Pleased. Pleasant. Cheery. Cheered. Cheerful. Jubilant. Jovial. Joyful. Elated. Elevated. Exulted. Exultant. Ecstatic. Head in the clouds. And over heels. Over the moon. Overjoyed. Overwhelmed. Bliss. Blissed. Blissful. Beautiful. Beatific.

Social studies was one of his favourite subjects.

Jo-Marie was a very receptive student.

James had gone to Joss' apartment. Joss again tried physical intimidation again to no avail. He'd signed the forms. Pushed them back at James. Then slammed the door.

"What's a Tory?" asked Jo-Marie.

"Originally they were the British parliamentarians unwilling to exclude James II's right of succession simply because he was Roman Catholic, the term coming from an Irish word for 'bandit' as Irish guerillas had earlier sided with Royalists against Cromwell during the War of the Three Kingdoms. In nineteenth century Canada they were those who adhered to our British traditions rather than strengthening ties to the United States. Nowadays, a good Tory will believe in the common good, balanced with fiscal responsibility, guided by prudent, sensible decision making when faced with an evolving world."

"You could have just said 'Conservative'. Or 'The Tories won the election last week.'"

"Those aren't real Tories. They're undignified and greedy extremists, neither sensible nor prudent nor do they practice noblesse oblige." The No Longer Good Party with a majority. The Lefty Loonies in opposition. Two extremes. Two vices. Whatever happened to the halcyon days of Centre Right vs. Centre Left? You had real choice then.

It was a thing indifferent—James again had people for whom to make dinner and for whom to clean: he had a family.

Yes, it was part illusion. Melissa was getting married to someone who would be back in a few short weeks. Yes, it gnawed on the back of his mind that Jo-Marie hadn't told him the whole truth. But she seemed happy now. Things weren't over with Joss. But they were for now. Now is the Golden Mean between the future and the past. He took a breath, letting the worries submerge again.

Melissa was around nearly every day. She'd waited with Jo-Marie for the test results: a clean bill of health. She helped with the tutoring sometimes and sometimes she even looked after Jo-Marie's dinner when James had a late meeting or appointment. Sometimes she just puttered in the garden, quietly working wonders, a greener thumb even than his father had been. "We don't have garden access", she said. "This is inspirational." Sometimes Melissa would sit in the garden, working on songs.

> "She can measure time
> And meter her rhyme
> And observe the earth
> From its death to birth
>
> "She can long shore drift.
> In sand she can sift
> As in fields she digs
> Amassing fields of Higgs.
>
> "But all I know is no one knows
> From whence we rose
> No man nor woman neither
> Can say whether nor why there
> Is you and I. Is you and I.
>
> "For she's tested doubt
> Washed, repeated it out

And it changes if you shout
Or even just look about.

"That damned double slit
Damn thing changes it.
Just ask Schrodinger's cat.
In the box not in the hat.

"For all I know is no one knows
From whence we rose
No man nor woman neither
Can say whether nor why there
Ain't you nor I. Ain't you nor I."

"What do you think?"

"The musicality was exceptional." Melissa didn't look satisfied. "The lyrics were interesting. On theme." (As far as he knew. He hadn't understood most of the references.)

"You hated it."

"I loved it", said Jo-Marie. "Very sciency but Eastern mystical too in a way. The music's got a great freak folky quality." Melissa and Jo-Marie shared a smile. "Don't worry about father James. Him not liking your music is a good sign. I think you should record it properly and release it online."

"Really? You think it's that good?"

"I already said. Now you're just fishing." Jo-Marie yanked off a pea pod and then headed back inside.

"What do you think I should do?" asked Melissa. James felt an affinity with deer in headlights everywhere.

"You know what to do."

"Now where have I heard that before?"

"I'm serious. Your heart: it knows."

Melissa nodded significantly. "You're right. You're terrible at bullshitting, but you're right."

James could not remember ever talking like a wishy washy liberal before. It frightened him how much he enjoyed it: passing the buck was absolutely marvelous.

* * *

Days had flown by. James' initial worry that Jo-Marie might run away when he was at work had been replaced by exasperation over the mess she always made of the place. She did weird things. One day James and Melissa came home to find her mixing iced tea crystals with a grape freezie. She crunched it all together. Took a generous bite.

"That is one of the most disgusting things I've ever witnessed", said James.

"Get over it", said Jo-Marie. "Ice tea's brown. I think brown sugar's one of the ingredients."

"I'm almost positive that's not true, but even if it were, so what?"

"Brown is healthy."

It was a good thing someone else would be teaching her science.

* * *

One night, just before turning in, he saw it on his bedroom wall: "πάντα χωρεῖ καὶ οὐδὲν μένει". He ripped it down. Was prepared to tear it up but the Godsend had written it. He had first taught it to her.

He submerged it in his dresser drawer.

* * *

The Sewing Circle doted on Jo-Marie. Zi-Wei gave her Chinese candies, which she also claimed to be healthy. "Oh yes. Yes. Smart girl."

"Don't encourage her", said James.

The Old Man made an appearance through the Pandora Street entrance.

"Haven't seen you in a while", said the Venerable McCall.

"Glad you could make time for your old friends", said James.

"I thought you would be wearing your mitre", smiled Zi-Wei.

"How can you let them cancel the Eleven?" asked Canon Conroy.

"I do not micromanage individual parishes. If Canon Welker thinks it will help bring more people into his parish then I hope he's right."

"It was James who brought in more people", said the Venerable McCall. "They're still coming thanks to that beautiful sermon."

James and Jo-Marie locked discomforted eyes. The youngish reverend was about to change the subject when the Old Man jumped in.

"Give poor Welker a break. He's not selling doves or money changing. He's finding new ways to reach out to the people."

This did the opposite of quiet the Circle, so the Old Man changed tactics.

"Let me say hello to sweet Jo-Marie." She smiled wide. The wider her smile the more treats they insist on giving her. She'd learned that young.

* * *

"I found a typewriter at the back of my closet", Jo-Marie had said over their Sunday afternoon cuppa.

"It's hard to find ribbons for it anymore. You have to order them special."

"Can I use it?"

"I thought you were an English expert."

"What does that have to… Oh… May I use it, please?"

"Yes you may."

Hours on end he'd hear her clack away in her room. Though it pleased him immensely (he'd make a Luddite of her yet!), it also kept him awake, so he put a curfew on it between 10:00 pm and 7:00 am.

"What do you write in there so feverishly?"

"It's just practice. I'm learning how to write like Kerouac."

Oh no! She was turning into a beatnik.

"You're liking *On the Road* I take it."

"I finished that ages ago. I just read *The Dharma Bums*. I'm really getting into expansive philosophy and Eastern religion."

God help us, thought James. Please don't start quoting *Siddhartha* and *Le Petit Prince*.

"It makes so much more sense. You get to live over and over again until you get it right. The world is billions of years old. You should become a Hindu."

"You ever heard of the caste system?"

"Right. Okay, but Buddhism…"

"…has a history and not an entirely pleasant one. Every faith does. Christianity is perfectly beautiful if you removed its history. If you just quoted the best parts. Ignored what is ugly. 'The Kingdom of God is within you.' That's beautiful by any standard. The Beatitudes are beautiful. You just have to gloss over about half of the Gospel of John… but not all of John. Some of the most beautiful stuff is in John."

"Kerouac was Catholic and a Buddhist."

"At times."

"He said 'Beat' comes from 'beatitude' and 'beatific'." Thank-you! "He just took the most beautiful parts."

"He tried to", said James. "When he was young he was an idealist, but don't forget he died a bitter alcoholic conservative."

"A Tory."

"Not a Tory. Just bitter. A similar thing happened to Wordsworth, to Plato, to pretty much all the hippies. Idealism crushed by the cruel weight of reality."

The world will sooner change the man than the man will change the world.

"I'm not an idealist", said Jo-Marie. "Even if I was, shouldn't you want me to keep my ideals?"

"I don't want you to lose them, assuming they're good ones. Not when you're all of thirteen."

"You'd want me to lose them later?"

"Of course not. But it happens to the best of us." Late twenties to mid thirties seemed about standard. "Just promise me you won't become one of those hipster beatniks."

"Hipsters aren't the same as beatniks. Hipsters dress weird and talk funny; beatniks dress weird and talk funny and have something to say."

"Fine. But if ever someone asks you to join a drum circle, leave immediately."

"I don't even like the drums."

Melissa came through the front door with a guitar. "Ready for your first lesson?"

James kneaded his brow. Had he really called her a Godsend?

Melissa began tuning. Strummed the low E string. Twisted the knob until it was in (a sort of) tune. Jo-Marie matched the note.

Melissa looked at James. She'd heard it too. Melissa plucked the B string. Jo-Marie responded with better pitch than any guitar could generate.

* * *

The Choir Master played a note on the piano. Jo-Marie hit it perfectly. Beautifully. Sustained it.

"She's fantastic."

"Of course I am", said Jo-Marie.

"I don't want her to be a spectacle with all those Facebook people and such", said James.

"That's died down", said the Choir Master. "You can't keep her hidden forever."

"I haven't kept her hidden. We've gone on several outings…"

"It might help ease her back into school", said Melissa. "I imagine church kids are nicer."

"Not necessarily", said James, remembering. "What do you think, Jo-Marie?"

"Whatevs. I guess it would be cool to learn singing on top of guitar—I could start a band like Melissa did way back when." James attempted to stifle his shuddering. "Who's that?" Jo-Marie asked, looking at the Deacon, who was entering from the garden door.

"Nobody."

"You must be Jo-Marie." The Deacon was about to give her a hug but, probably remembering Safer Churches, instead just shook her hand, warmly enclosing it in a handwich.

"Yes", was all she could muster, her face beet red.

"He's the reason you ended up in the paper", said James.

"I was worried", said the Deacon. "I thought it might help."

"Yup," said Jo-Marie, "it did."

"Anyways, I'll come back later. I don't want to interrupt."

"It's okay", said Jo-Marie.

"I just wanted to talk to Rodger about some hymns."

"Hymns for what?"

* * *

She'd put a *U2* poster up in her room. She must be trying to irk him. There's no way she was that shallow. She'd been through too much. She wanted to be a writer. She liked Melissa's folky music and those weird hipster beatnik bands. She was incredibly bright. She was an idealist. She was very complex.

She was a thirteen-year-old girl.

Chapter
29

"Bono is a lot like Gandhi."

"Bono is nothing like Gandhi."

"Gandhi would've supported the UN's Millennium Development Goals."

James had never considered this one way or the other. "What do you even know about Gandhi?"

"He like invented non-violent resistance."

"He took inspiration from Tolstoy. Tolstoy took it from Jesus. 'To him who smites your right cheek offer your other also.'"

"So Bono's a lot like Jesus."

"You're over doing your little act, just so you know."

"It's not an act."

"Uh huh."

"So Gandhi really gave your beloved British Empire a run."

"Don't knock the British. If they had been complete villains they would simply have fired on him." (Of course, by that logic, they had been villains at Amritsar. Well, Dyer had at least.)

James actually admired much about the East Indians. They still knew the importance of family, hard work and discipline. Westerners could learn a lot from them. But not the things they think they could learn.

Melissa came through the door. Just like every time, James half expected her to kiss him hello. Instead they'd hug or shake hands, usually doing an awkward dance trying to figure out which.

"Ready?"

"Yup." Jo-Marie ran to the door to put on her shoes.

"Where are you two going?" asked James.

"I need some Sunday bests if I'm going to be singing in the choir don't I?"

"None of the other kids have Sunday bests. You wear a choir gown over the whole thing." Why was he discouraging proper church-wear?

"There's still coffee hour."

Melissa smiled at James knowingly.

* * *

He was updating his notes on Erasmus' *Μωρίας Εγκώμιον*. Frankly, he wasn't really even into it. He glanced up at the clock. It was a half hour later than the latest they said they might be late. Stay calm. Stay calm. There are plenty of perfectly logical explanations. He'd always worry when his mom didn't come home on time. Worry that she'd died. Then she did die. He would be terrified that something bad had happened to Anne and Jo-Marie. It was years later, but something bad did happen. Worrying hadn't stopped any of it.

So stay the bugger calm.

They could have been in a mild fender bender. Then why hadn't Jo-Marie texted him? Isn't this why he allowed her a phone to begin with? Why hadn't Melissa told her to text him? She was normally so thoughtful about this sort of thing.

Calming breath. Calming breath.

But what if he just called Jo-Marie? He was allowed. He was paying for her cell phone plan. He was allowed to call her if he was worried.

But she'd accuse him of being overprotective. There wasn't a predicament she could be in where calling her would solve it. It wouldn't help her. It would only reassure him. Shouldn't he be putting her needs first? Maybe they were having a great time. Maybe he'd ruin it by reminding her of his worries and tribulations. She should be learning to enjoy life. No doubt it had been hard on the street, which no doubt made for a lot of bad memories. It was high time for her to make some good ones.

What if she was in an accident like before? He should call to check.

Cell phones cause accidents. They don't prevent them.
Calming breath. Calming breath.

* * *

They finally returned, fifty-seven minutes late.

"Sorry," said Melissa, "we got caught on the wrong side of a parade."

"No worries", said James. Melissa gave him a look that said he'd failed to fool her. She was wearing a green dress, successfully. The first woman on earth to truly pull that off.

"Do you notice anything different?"

"You're wearing a green dress and got a minor trim of your bangs."

"I meant about Jo-Marie."

Her change was more obvious. No more hoodie and jeans. Now a black dress with blue leggings. She was growing up. He didn't like it.

"You look beautiful."

"My mom's store carries some accessories that would just make that outfit", said Melissa.

"Cool", said Jo-Marie.

Accessories? Since when did she care about accessories?

"She has a crush", said Melissa while Jo-Marie was in the washroom. "I think it's sweet."

"Mmh", James half snorted.

Melissa smiled at him. Squeezed his hand, injecting him with life. Her eyes met his. He turned away and faked a cough. She rubbed his back. Why couldn't he just kiss her?

Because he was her priest.

Because she was betrothed to another.

Because he was charged with that betrothal.

Because he had taken a sacred oath.

Because he had made a vow.

Because following his own selfish desires had already stung him once.

Because he defined himself by his moral choices.

Because it would be against his moral duty.

Because it would be against his moral integrity.

Because he believed in always doing what was right, not what would make him happy.

Because he would be trampling on conservative ideals that were too often trampled on.

Because he was not a savage beast.

Because he was not soothed by her music.

Because he was incapable of subterfuge.

Because he never got away with anything.

Because word would undoubtedly spread.

Because the scandal would ruin his career.

Because the scandal would ruin his church.

Because he had signed a form against doing this exact thing.

James had more, but decided his point had been made.

He looked to her again to say a silent "thank-you" for the back rub. Grimaced his face, not committing to a smile. She held his gaze. Silently they just looked at each other for more than a usual amount of time. Couldn't dismiss this on alcohol like before. Maybe they should talk about it. Maybe this was talking about it in a manner of speaking that didn't happen to involve speaking.

"Are you going to dump your man or what?" Jo-Marie started mixing one of her freezie iced tea crystal concoctions.

"Excuse me?"

"It's obvious you like father James."

"Joanne Marie, this is not up for discussion. Melissa is already in a relationship with a man" (yeah, right, "man") "with whom she has chosen to spend her life."

"Then where is he? If he wants to spend his life with her, why isn't he doing that? If you're counseling them on marriage, shouldn't you counsel that that's a bad freakin' sign?"

"I've respected your privacy, Jo-Marie. Please respect mine." Melissa's tone was very defensive. A definite sign. And Jo-Marie was right. It was James' duty to counsel Melissa regarding the Fiancé's less than acceptable behaviour.

Careful there, reverend. Be very careful.

Chapter
30

James read through his "Safer Churches" agreement. It was written in essentially incomprehensible legal jargon but one thing was clear: even the whiff of a pursuit of Melissa would be grounds for dismissal. What had he been expecting to find? A clause stating, "But if you really like each other go ahead and risk the future of your church by acting like a couple of dirty modern self-centred left wing neo New Age hippies because the twenty-first century is morals optional"?

Yes, actually.

He had no choice but to marry them. It was time to get that into his thick head with a BANG!

He'd hit his head against his desk. It failed to produce any positive results.

BANG!

Harder this time.

BANG!

"You busy?" asked the Deacon from James' door. Before James could answer, the Deacon had pulled up a chair. James turned over the Safer Churches form to the equally incriminating other side.

"Watcha reading?"

"It's confidential", said James, burying the paper. "What do you want?"

"Here's my order of service. I was wondering if you could give it a perusal. Catch any spelling mistakes. Make any liturgical suggestions." James did not throw up in his own mouth, but he did get a waft of stomach acid. "You are our liturgical expert after all."

"Thank-you", said James. "Not on my CV. But thank-you. Yes. I do care about liturgical grace and will happily give you a couple of pointers."

The Deacon whipped out his notepad like an intrepid reporter. Clicked his pen. "Shoot."

"Firstly, as a church service is an offering of devotion to God and not actually a rock concert you should ask people to hold their applause until, I don't know... ever."

"No applause. Got it."

"Secondly, no phones. Or at very least get people to turn them off or at very even less than least get them to put them on vibrate and refrain from texting or talking or other distracting behaviour so long as they are in the sacred space itself. You know, give church— God's house—the same respect you would give the local cineplex."

"When you put it that way I see where you're coming from."

"Thirdly, that also means banning cameras and other recording devices. Banning frivolous and completely unsacred words including, but not limited to 'trending', 'blog', 'upload', 'post', 'Facebook', 'tweet' and most especially religious puns that make jocular the part of the service in which we ritually give thanks for the miraculous sacrifice God Himself made for us by dying in the most humiliating and painful manner then available."

"What part of the service is that? The...?"

"Eucharist."

"But our service is called the... oh."

The Deacon clicked his pen, taking the order of service back from James. "I suppose I ought to get someone else to proof this." He managed to stand up while keeping his head down, slumping out of the room.

Proper liturgy was victorious! Its enemy hanging his head in shame. At last James was on the winning side.

It didn't feel quite as wonderful as he'd imagined.

* * *

James knocked on the Deacon's office door. "Can I come in?"

"Isn't it 'May I'?"

"Yes. Right. May I come in?"

"Of course."

"I was just curious about which charity will benefit from this event."

"We're helping build a village school in Uganda. It's what that male Irish manatee…"

"Male Irish banshee."

"It's the sort of thing he likes."

"No matter what one's opinion of paternalistic self-righteous liberal Western charity propping up corrupt regimes in Africa and perpetuating the stereotype of Africans as victims, there's no denying the importance of education, provided the act of charity is done with humility and a sense of duty because of our good fortune, not taking credit as if it were we alone responsible for our greater material wealth and political stability."

"You lost me somewhere."

"Obviously I don't approve of this service from a liturgical perspective but…" James managed to keep his teeth from clenching just enough to get the words out "…I'd like to help out nonetheless. Give it the best grace I know how."

"I don't understand."

"Despite your numerous faults, you are part of my church. I have taken much good from its community. I must also take the…" ('bad' seemed right, but sounded wrong) "…obnoxious."

"Thank-you?"

"You're welcome", smiled James with a grimace. Socrates used similar logic before taking the hemlock. Officiating a *U2*charist paled in comparison.

"Could you help me find a *U2* tribute band?" Or maybe it was the hemlock that paled.

"I don't know any bands."

"Ask that Chris guy. He's in a band isn't he?"

"Right", said James.

Definitely the hemlock.

* * *

The Sewing Circle made him almost do it.

"You are performing this U2charist?" Zi-Wei had asked.

"What has become of you?" Canon Conroy had asked.

"You're giving it legitimacy", the Venerable McCall had said.

James' black and tan had tasted especially bitter and he had liked it that way. "It's ugly. It's tacky. It's superficial. It's stupid. It's a microcosm of everything wrong with the church today. But ultimately it is a thing indifferent."

"Would you lead an Alpha Course then too?" Canon Conroy had asked.

"Now you're just being petty."

"I'd hate ever to celebrate a U2charist", the Reverend Doctor Leonard White had said.

Of course James hated the prospect too. But soon he would have to live with things like it and without people like them. He would have to live on with this brave new generation and probably another brave new generation after that. He didn't have the luxury of dying soon.

But, if it was right to change to his disadvantage, why not to his advantage too? The Fiancé obviously wasn't even in love with her, abandoning her just before their wedding. Just like her father had abandoned her.

Nice insight. Good job.

This wouldn't be like before. He wouldn't be breaking up a family. He would be fighting to keep a family together: she was the perfect mother for Jo-Marie, even if she did insist on teaching her guitar. Why should Safer Churches trump that? Why should moral integrity?

What had moral integrity ever done for him anyway?

They should at least talk about it. It didn't have to be a disaster. If Melissa didn't choose to be with him then that would be the end of it. He'd be heartbroken, but that would pass... diffuse at least. If she did choose to be with him, James could explain the situation to the Old Man who, as his bishop, could instruct him on the best course of action. Certainly James would be reprimanded, but not necessarily defrocked. He had even managed to find a Safer Churches loophole: should Melissa quit being part of the congregation (a moot point really), and should she and James wait a full two years, they would then be permitted to start dating.

Two YEARS. "Loophole" was perhaps the wrong term. But he'd made it ten years hadn't he? Patience was his most familiar virtue.

He picked up his phone. How to broach the subject? He should tell her that Jo-Marie would be singing solo, an amazing feat for someone with so little training. "A lot of the girls are really jealous", Jo Marie had exclaimed, delighted by their pettiness.

James was sure Melissa would be delighted too. Then it was a simple, if not easy, segue into talking about the whole relationship situation. His hand shook while he dialled.

No answer.

Great. For the best actually. It would give him time for sober second thought.

Five minutes of tortuous second thoughts later she texted: "I don't have time to talk. I'll call you back in a few." Why was she busy? She should've been back from work by now. Why'd she text rather than call? Was she okay?

An hour and twenty minutes went by. James tried to think of a reason why "a few" should turn into an hour and twenty minutes. Had she been kidnapped? Should he text her? How would that help? She'd text him if she'd been kidnapped and still had access to her phone. But maybe they didn't know she had a phone. His text would alert them. She might lose her phone. Her one chance... Wait. These thoughts are totally crazy.

Chapter
31

He was in his office working on a sermon when she rang him the next day. "Sorry for taking so long to return your call."

"No problem", said James in a tone that said it had definitely been a problem.

"Chris is back."

"I thought he wasn't due back until next week."

"They found another bass player. He missed me."

"I see", said James. "You must be happy to see him."

"Yes. Absolutely. Yes."

"And things are okay between you?"

"Yeah. Things are really good."

"Great. Okay. Great. Let me know when you two want another meeting."

"Will do, James. Thanks."

They exchanged goodbyes. He hung up.

Idiot.

His "fling" with Melissa had abruptly ended. Their "family" one fewer.

Why couldn't he have a life, rather than a "life"?

Nothing to be done. Sounded like Melissa and the Fiancé could definitely reconcile any problems that they may or may not have been having.

James was happy for them. He was. It was lucky it had happened this way, actually. To think he'd almost been so cavalier with his own integrity and for what? For a silly little infatuation. He deserved to participate in a *U2charist*.

Now, stiff upper lip and all that. Back to the sermon. Work. Work. Bury yourself in work.

After a bit of time outside.

Definitely there's this overwhelming need to be outside and also to scream... but let's just do the outside thing.

* * *

James felt guilty walking the streets but not helping the homeless. Maybe he had just been performing the street ministry to find Jo-Marie but when the streetpeople waved at him or called out "Reverend J" it stung more than expected. So he got the Verger to help bring up the old cart from the basement. Food Bank provided a (clean) garbage bag full of day olds. James purchased cookies and juice boxes.

He was back at it, proud to be making the most of things, proud to have turned a negative into a positive. He would do that from now on.

That was how he would change himself—from this moment on he would be an optimistic, positive man.

* * *

It was the worst thing in the world. He was not exaggerating.

Okay, obviously he was exaggerating. But not by as much as you might think.

James had found himself handing out muffins on Store Street, looking up at the old Blue Bridge, the one and only twin-spanned Strauss bascule bridge in the whole wide world. One of the city's true landmarks. Of course the populace had voted to replace it. It's what populaces do to blue bridges and to purple books.

He turned himself around. Pushed his cart towards Swift Street where he saw Jo-Marie, wearing her hoodie and ripped (not stylishly) jeans, walking with Mr. Anarchy Tattoo and Ms. Piercings.

"Jo-Marie."

She looked like she'd been caught at something. "What?!"

"I thought you were at home studying."

"I have to do schoolwork all the time? I can't hang out with my friends?"

Chapter 31 • 185

"You said you'd always text me where you were." Jo-Marie took out her cell phone. Started texting. "Very funny."

"I'll be home for dinner. Isn't that enough for you?"

"You have choir practice tonight."

"Choir practice?" Ms. Piercings found this hilarious.

"Thanks", Jo-Marie said to James before walking up Store Street, away from him.

"Where are you going?"

"Nowhere in particular."

"I'll make sure she's back for choir practice", said Ms. Piercings.

"I'd like to know where you're going", said James.

"Just back off", said Jo-Marie. "Let me live my fucking life."

She and her two so called friends continued up the street.

"Hey Reverend J," said Mr. Pockmarks, "I've found Jo-Marie. She's right there."

James left his cart with Mr. Pockmarks and asked him to distribute the muffins. He rushed after Jo-Marie. She hooked a right onto Herald Street.

He lost her for a moment. Couldn't tell where she'd gone. Wasn't up the street. She could have gone into the art supply store. He rushed up the block. Maybe they'd slipped behind a parked car or van? He looked left and saw her with her friends descending the stairs that led to Chatham Street. "Jo-Marie!"

"Quit following me. I know how to handle myself."

"Not according to your story."

"I could run away again any time if I wanted. I got by fine without you."

"Excuse us please", James said to her friends.

"We ain't leaving", said Mr. Anarchy Tattoo.

"You don't need to leave. Just continue on your way another twenty feet. Give us two minutes. Thank-you."

Ms. Piercings pulled Mr. Anarchy Tattoo down the steps. James thought he should use his authoritative voice more often.

"What?" asked Jo-Marie.

"Do not talk to me like that again in future."

"You can't tell me what to do. You're not my dad."

"Isn't that a good thing?"

"Don't judge him. You don't know him. He's had a rough life."

"Are you saying you want to live with him again?"

"No. He's an asshole."

"Joanne Marie, you know I care about you. You know what I've been through for you. Or at least you have an inkling. Look at me. Please treat me with respect."

"Fine", she said in a tone unbecoming a singer. "May I talk to my friends now?" She'd used "may", at least.

"I'm not so sure they're a good influence."

"You get to hang out with streetkids but I can't?"

"An act of charity should not be mistaken for…"

"They're not charity cases. They're people."

James looked at them. They might pull her back to the streets. But what would forbidding her do? She'd shown before that she'd never obey.

"You all can help me. I would really appreciate it."

"We'd love to help", Ms. Piercings called up from the steps.

* * *

He could hear Jo-Marie's voice lift up from the rehearsal room below his office. Her "friends" had only helped out for thirty-seven minutes. They'd been very enthusiastic for the first ten. Sought people out. Knew of secret alleyways and other hidden places to find people. But the charity game soon got boring so they ditched. Jo-Marie stayed with James, scowling all the way back to the car. Scowling all the way back to the house to pick up her "Sunday bests". Scowling all the way back to the church offices.

James was too worried to do much good for his sermon. He picked up his receiver, dialling cautiously. He needed consultation and no one else understood Jo-Marie like she did. "Hi James."

"Hi. Are you busy?"

"Yes. What's up?"

"I need your help with Jo-Marie."

"Is she okay?"

"She's fine. I think. I don't know."

"It's not urgent?"

"I guess not but…"

"If it's not urgent then I think it's best I don't get involved."

"Right."

"Listen, James…" (nothing good had ever started with those words) "I really am sorry to brush you guys off like this but the wedding is suddenly here. You know what I mean? I have my final fitting. I have to confirm with the caterers. Chris' cousins said they can make it to the reception now so we're not sure if there's enough seating. All that stuff."

"Right. Of course." He and his heart had already been through this. "Sorry to bother you."

James hung up. Idiot. It was good things were ending before they went too far. He'd already seriously considered talking about his feelings with her. What other crazy things would he have seriously considered doing if she'd become even more entrenched in their lives?

Now it was time to move on. Now it was time to tie up his bootstraps and figure out Jo-Marie on his own.

Calming breath. Good. Relax. Good.

RING! RING! RING!

"Yes?"

"Sorry, James, I just wanted to say briefly, you know, just to mention…"

"What?"

"I miss you."

"I miss you as well."

"I gotta go."

Chapter
32

Hope compels inaction. If he had no hope that his faith would come back he would have no choice but to get on with his life and find a new vocation. But no matter how many days and nights of doubt he felt, there was some small part of him that still believed he could again believe. That he might feel that love again. But no matter how hard he prayed or pushed or pulled to make this hope grow stronger so that his faith would grow stronger, it disobeyed. You don't choose. God chooses you.

James wished that He'd make up His mind.

Needless to say God wasn't the only holy being James felt impatient with. Why had Melissa called back to say, "I miss you"? It was just cruel.

"You have to fight for her." Jo-Marie was cranking the mechanical mixers. James had electric ones but she insisted on doing it by hand for sake of the environment. "You stood up to my dad. You have to do something like that for her."

"You assume a lot."

"It's obvious you're in love with her."

"No it's not." The timer went off. James turned on the oven light. The cake had risen. He took a mitt from its hanger.

"You're a terrible liar father James." James opened the oven and removed the cake pan. Turned it over. "You have to make the grand romantic gesture so she'll know you care."

"What grand romantic gesture?" He let the cake fall onto the cooling rack.

"Any grand romantic gesture." He turned the oven down twenty-five degrees.

"That doesn't sound like me." He put in the spaghetti lasagna.

"Then maybe you should change you." He set the timer for thirty minutes.

"I've done that too much already." A knock on the door. Jo-Marie answered. In clambered Mr. Anarchy Tattoo and Ms. Piercings.

"Hello", James said. "Welcome."

* * *

They took turns showering. Part of the arrangement was that they'd each get a new change of clothes for the dinner. Jo-Marie picked them out, successfully finding clean carbon copies of what they always wore. James himself dressed down for the occasion, wearing ten-dollar jeans and his least favourite blue shirt. Jo-Marie wore the black and white dress Melissa had bought for her. "They'll have to get used to the new me", Jo-Marie explained.

James was expecting everything to go wrong but, for the longest time, it didn't. The actual dinner went okay. The street urchins weren't big on conversation but said their pleases and thank-yous when asking for garlic bread or butter or salad dressing, Jo-Marie having informed them that this was important. She told them all about the U2charist and the project to construct a primary school in Uganda.

"What about the poor here?" asked Mr. Anarchy Tattoo.

"They can already get primary education", said Ms. Pier... no. Tru. Her real fake name was Tru.

James had bought them each a sleeping bag. He'd even purchased a couple of small air mattresses and moved his town crier of a coffee table out of the way so they'd have room. (Jo-Marie slept on the couch.) He could hear them laughing and whispering incomprehensibly through half the night.

* * *

"Where are they?" The baked orange French toast would go to waste. Not waste. It would be nice to have extra for himself and Jo-Marie. But still.

"They were gone when I woke up."

"That's odd", said James.

"Not really", said Jo-Marie. She began to roll up the sleeping bags.

"We should wash those first", said James. Jo-Marie scowled at him.

"You have to get over that."

"I don't know what you're talking about", said James, who knew exactly what she was talking about. "But certainly used sleeping bags need to get washed."

After breakfast James thoroughly cleaned everything Ink and Tru might have contacted. He sprayed and wiped his mom's old jewelry box then lifted it so he could spray and wipe underneath. It was definitely lighter than it should have been.

* * *

"You don't know they stole it."

"All the jewelry was there when I cleaned yesterday. They had plenty of time upstairs alone." He knew being his better less suspicious self would eventually backfire.

"It's just stuff."

"It was my mom's stuff."

"Then it became your stuff. Now it's someone else's stuff. It's still just stuff."

"Actually it's your stuff. I was planning to give it to you."

"They can have it then", said Jo-Marie. "I give it to them… if they even took it."

"That's generous", said James, "but…"

"Bishop Myriel gave the silverware to Jean Valjean."

"This is different."

"No it's not."

"He bought Valjean's soul with it. He really laid the guilt on thick."

"I'll be sure to do that next time I see them", said Jo-Marie.

I can probably get it back from that pawnbroker, thought James.

"What's this?" Jo-Marie picked a folded sheet off the floor.

"An old shopping list probably." He casually swiped for it. Jo-Marie stepped away.

"It's a sonnet."

"A sonnet?" It must have fallen out when they'd stolen the jewelry.

PS: Fuck!

I just swore. In my brain: doesn't count.

"In your handwriting."

"Is it?" Fuck! Fuck! Fuck! Fuck! Fuck! Fuck! Fuck! Fuck! Fuck!

PS: Must stop brain swearing.

"It's sickening."

"It's effusive", James countered. "That's the proper style."

"I know. That's why I hate sonnets. It's about Melissa, isn't it?"

"Nonsense. It was a grade 9 English assignment."

"It spells her name."

"Does it?"

"You totally are in love with her."

"You're judging it by modern standards. By Renaissance Humanist standards it..."

"'Bathing in the light of your eternal day.' Are you kidding me?"

"You will kindly hand that over."

"You should invite her to Clover Point."

"Please explain your reasoning." James lunged for the paper, but Jo-Marie was too spry for the likes of him.

"Part of your grand romantic gesture. You should say she has to come or you won't let them get married..."

"A: I don't have that power. B: I've never been a fan of declaring love via extortion."

"Just get her there. Say you wanted to fly a kite and then on the kite you should have the sonnet written. As she's reading it, you should tell her that you've noticed how many great songs she has now and that she shouldn't be afraid to share them. Mention the parable of the talents if you want to sound priestly." (Jo-Marie remembered her Gospel!) "Tell her that you shared your talent with your sermon and it's not that hard. Then say you bought her studio time to properly record her album. Bam: grand romantic gesture." She let him grab the paper.

James tore it up, throwing its pieces into his recycling basket. "Marriage is a sacrament. It wouldn't be right."

"Maybe what's right is what makes you happy."

That'll be the day.

"I know the mores of this era glorify selfishness, but I am a priest. I have a sacred duty."

Jo-Marie shook her head at James as she started towards the door. "Excuse me. I have to take a sacred doodie."

Chapter
33

"I hated the tour", said the Fiancé, parishioners trickling in around him. "I thought I needed to do it one more time just to get it out of my system but the moment I got off the plane in Toronto I knew I'd made a mistake. I wasn't where I needed to be. I wasn't with who…" (whom!) "…I needed to be with. Nothing felt real or right or good because it didn't happen with her." He looked at Melissa with loving eyes. Held her hand tenderly.

"That's wonderful", James said.

"When I was here before I acted very rude and like I didn't take this seriously. I apologize for that. Nothing is more important to me than Melissa."

"I'm sure Melissa is glad to hear that."

"Of course", she smiled. The Fiancé gave her a loving kiss. Held her in his arms.

The Catholic Church had recently redefined hell as a place where you know you could have true and everlasting love, but don't. It was quite controversial. Some people actually preferred that hell be fire and brimstone. James considered those people to be a bunch of sentimental jerks who should just move on with their lives.

* * *

Though she looked a bit nervous and slouched in a way that would no doubt cause her back problems in the future, Jo-Marie sang beautifully. No one could deny it. James did overhear Eve say to another choirgirl that she was flat on her high notes and sharp on her low notes but that was obviously just the petty jealousy Jo-Marie had mentioned. He was so proud. He caught sight of Melissa's eyes. They seemed proud too.

"'I publish the Banns of Marriage between Melissa Jane Wembley and Christopher Philip Knowles. If any of you know cause or just impediment why these two persons should not be joined together in Holy Matrimony, you are to declare it.'"

I'm allowed to wait right? That wouldn't be suspicious or anything. You really should give it some time. Most priests just say it and then go on, not giving a chance for someone to speak. Jo-Marie looked at James. Will the sweet girl pipe up?

I could beat her to it and declare my love myself. My whole life could change in this moment. Everything I was would be gone. My priesthood gone. My reputation gone. My quiet and discreet way of doing things loudly and indiscreetly bulldozed. By me. By the new me. Everything I am to become would be born, delivered by a bold grand romantic gesture before my church, my friends, my community and, if He exists, my God.

"'This is the first time of asking.'"

Or not.

* * *

"You did a wonderful job singing", said Melissa as she took a sip of coffee in the courtyard.

"Thank-you, *Melissa*." Jo-Marie was sure to emphasize the name.

"You know each other?" asked the Fiancé.

"I got left behind in a city I just moved to", said Melissa, "and yes I actually did get to know some people, including our priest and his goddaughter."

"Okay. Okay. Point taken."

"Here he is", said the Deacon, shaking the Fiancé's hand. "Do you have any suggestions for my band?"

"Band for what?" asked the Fiancé.

"Our *U2* tribute band fell through so I'm scrambling. James was supposed to ask you about it."

"Melissa could play", said Jo-Marie.

"She's more an acoustic musician", said the Fiancé before Melissa could speak. "But I'd love to do it."

"Do you have time for that?" asked James.

"It won't take long to figure out the songs", said the Fiancé. "We've got what—just under two weeks?"

"We do indeed", said the Deacon.

"Great. One question though: can we publish one of those marriage banns at the U2charist? That would be kick ass."

* * *

Jo-Marie didn't open her mouth until she shut the car door (way too hard like she always did). "Isn't it your sacred duty to mention cause and just impediment when you are cause and just impediment?"

"Do you always have to slam the door?"

"I'm mad at you."

James started the engine. "You do it when you're happy. You do it when you're indifferent."

"Don't nitpick me. I'm trying to berate you."

* * *

Ten minutes of berating later, they turned onto Vining street.

"Stop being a martyr."

"There's nothing wrong with being a martyr." That sounded wrong out loud. "I mean I'm not being a martyr."

James pulled into the driveway—about to go into a long discourse on Socrates' moral integrity in the face of societal opposition—when Jo-Marie yelled out: "Fucking asshole!" That hardly seemed fair. "Run him over!"

Joss was sitting on the front steps.

"Stay in the car Jo-Marie." James turned off the ignition. Got out.

Joss raised his hands, palms outward. "I was just dropping off some clothes. Okay? Just saying hello."

"Good-bye", said Jo-Marie.

"I've cleaned myself up, sweetie."

"Bullshit!"

"Roll up the window", said James.

"Get her to talk to me. You promised you would."

"You should have called first so she could have time to prepare."

"Prepare her now then. I can wait." Joss plopped down on the front steps.

"Joseph, please. You know that's not what I meant."

"I ain't leaving until you make good and I talk to her. Alone."

James turned to Jo-Marie, who shook her head, pleadingly. Turning back, he took out his cell phone.

"I have 9-1-1 on speed dial."

* * *

The buzzer had gone off for the shepherd's pie at the same time that the doorbell rang. He took the pie out of the oven then headed for the spy-hole. He peeped through, frightened Joss might have returned. That it was Melissa and the Fiancé struck him as a relief, just not a very good one. He opened the door.

"Did you write this?" The Fiancé held James' sonnet, taped at the tears.

James briefly glanced to Jo-Marie, who looked to the ceiling, pursing her lips as if to whistle.

"You did, didn't you?"

"No."

"Yes he did", Jo-Marie piped up. "I sent it. But he wrote it."

Uh oh. Think fast. "It's merely a Renaissance Humanist Devotional Friendship Sonnet."

"A what?" asked the Fiancé.

"Shakespeare wrote them for Mr. W.H. All Happinesse and Erasmus wrote several letters to Servatius Rogerius that were effusive but are generally interpreted as youthful exuberance for a new friendship."

"It was very sweet", said Melissa.

"Don't tell him it was sweet", said the Fiancé. "He's our priest and he's macking on you. God, you priests are all the same. I mean that U2charist guy's cool, but the rest of you... You act all holy, telling people they're all going to hell, but you're nothing but a bunch of letches and pedophiles."

"You're a prick", said Jo-Marie.

"Language", said James.

"You think everyone should worship you 'cause you're in a band but you're just the bass player. I mean c'mon."

"Paul played bass", said the Fiancé, "but that doesn't matter…"

"Paul also wrote or co-wrote most of the songs", said Jo-Marie.

"We collaborate on our music, but that doesn't matter."

"Melissa's a better songwriter than you."

"That doesn't matter", said the Fiancé. Jo-Marie turned her smirking face to Melissa. "I had doubts. She's had doubts too. But we love each other and we want to spend the rest of our lives together." He turned back to Melissa and, with undeniable reticence, asked, "Don't we?"

For probably hardly any time at all—but still, not for absolutely no time—Melissa paused, before answering: "I want to be with you. Of course I do."

"Thank God!" He kissed her with the passion of relief.

"He doesn't appreciate you", said Jo-Marie. "You're making a mistake."

"She's not", said James. "Though I did not intend to, I have obviously overstepped my bounds. I think it's best if I quietly hand this service off to the deacon."

"No", said the Fiancé. "Nanna has been very insistent about you. She's paying for our honeymoon. It's going to be you."

"I don't know", said Melissa.

"It's fine", James said. "Whatever you prefer."

Chapter
34

James was savouring the silence of a very quiet dinner up until the point that Jo-Marie spoke. "You tore it in barely even eight pieces and then put it on the top of recycling. You wanted me to tape it up and send it to her."

"I honestly didn't."

"But I can't be the one to fight for her. You have to. *Carpe diem et cetera.*"

"*Quam minimum credula postero.*"

"She's meant to be with you."

"There is no 'meant to' in the real world, Jo-Marie. It's a fantasy. I know you're young. I know you still believe certain things about love and life that, as an adult..."

"Shut up!"

"Excuse me?"

"I know about the ugly things in life better than you. But, when you find something beautiful, you have to fight for it. If you don't... if you just let things happen... then what good are you?"

She slammed down her knife and fork, before slamming the door to her room.

At least dinner would be quiet again.

RING! RING! RING!

"Hello?"

"James?" It was the Rector.

"Yes."

"We need you to come in immediately. We're having a Safer Churches meeting."

* * *

James was using his travel time to come up with counterarguments. Churchmen would know all about Renaissance Humanist Friendship wouldn't they?

Why was this happening? He didn't deserve it. He'd just let the woman he loved get away without fighting for her and was feeling unbearably miserable about it. A sure sign that he'd done the right thing. But apparently the Fiancé had changed his mind and decided to make a stink anyway. Wasn't victory enough for that man? Did he have to rub it in James' face?

* * *

"Everyone's here", said the Rector. "Time to begin." The Rector, the Deacon, the Parish Administrator, the Verger, the Receptionist and of course James all sat around the Rector's coffee table; but the Choir Master, James' only real ally at the office, was missing. "As some of you are no doubt already aware," the Rector continued, "two of the choristers have come forward about Rodger's sexual misconduct."

"What?" said James before he could stop himself.

"Both Samantha Caruthers and Eve Smith have come forward with similar stories. As both are over sixteen this is not a criminal matter. However, if true, it is a breach of power and trust, and against the Safer Churches form Rodger had signed. I have decided, therefore, to suspend him immediately. Mrs. Mathers…" (both deaf and tone deaf) "…will take over organist and choirmaster duties until this matter has come to its conclusion. This will of course cost us another musician for the U2charist but nonetheless we have decided to continue with the service as planned."

* * *

James called Jo-Marie from his office.

"Are you okay?"

"I'm still a bit pissed at you but I'll get over it."

"The Choir Master didn't do anything to you, did he?"

"Do anything what?"

"Anything untoward."

"Do you need me to show you on the bear?"

"How was a bear involved?"

"It was a joke. What's going on?"

"He's been suspended for alleged misconduct."

"I knew it! He called me pretty like all the time and would touch the small of my back when he wanted me to stand straighter rather than just telling me to stand straighter."

"Did he do anything else?"

"No."

"You'd tell me if he had?"

"Sure. Who's he boinking anyway? Is it Eve? I bet it's Eve. She's a total slut."

"Don't use that term. I have to go."

* * *

The Choir Master lived in a ground floor suite just off Oak Bay Avenue. James knocked viciously on the door.

"I guess you heard."

James entered. What a gaudy paint job: Pompeian red and grass green. He was glad he'd never visited before. "This scandal will sink us."

"I fell for her."

"She's seventeen."

"She's legal… in this country."

"How could you?"

"I love her, man."

"What about Eve?" James remembered the way she'd rushed out from that concert.

"She was a mistake."

"Seventeen. You're nearly thirty."

"Don't most scholars think Mary was fourteen and Joseph in his thirties? Jesus himself came from that union."

"Joseph wasn't Jesus' father."

"Oh right. It was God. He was even older."

"Don't make light of this. Samantha is a lovely young woman."

"'Lovely young woman.' She's hot man. You think it too. Millions of years of evolution made us this way. A few hours of Safer Churches can't change that."

"What about human decency?"

"What about you man? Chris told me he found your sonnet."

"It was a Renaissance Humanist Friendship Sonnet."

"You didn't even fuck her did you? Don't lecture me man. At least I got some fun out of the deal."

"I have kept my integrity."

"Congratulations. I got laid by two hot seventeen-year-olds."

"Stop talking about them like that."

"I'm happy. You're not. So don't preach, preacher. I didn't break any laws."

"Do you look at Jo-Marie that way?"

"What do you want me to say? She's pretty James. Anyone can see it. She's getting older. She's going to be hot. You're going to have to get used to letches leering at her."

James had never before been violent. He was easy to frustrate, but slow to anger. Certainly he agreed that "love is not easily provoked", but hearing this cad speak of sweet Jo-Marie like she was a piece of meat was too much by the width of a duck's breath. Before he could think to stop himself he had punched the Choir Master in the face, knocking him to the ground.

The next moment of James' life had two very distinct halves.

Half one: seeing a man on the ground that he had put there, a man who deserved to be put there, gave him a feeling of exhilaration, of triumph, of pure euphoric joy. I knocked that bastard down, he exclaimed to himself.

Half two: he's getting back up.

Yes, James had never before been violent, and there were several good reasons for that. The Choir Master hit back. A vain man, he definitely went to the gym. But he wouldn't want to hit again. His fingers were so thin and precious to a musician's tr… never mind. The Choir Master pummeled James with blows. Guess he's not thinking rationally right now, thought James. There must be some way to defend this. He screamed a primal scream. This distracted the Choir Master long enough for James to wrap himself around the git, pinning his arms.

202 • Part III

"That's no way to fight. Let go of me you freakin' pussy."

"I don't care what names you call me", said James. "I'm an adult."
He squealed with delight as he held on to his grip.

The Choir Master was not that strong after all. He wriggled. He
wobbled. But he could not break free. "Truce", he finally said.

"Most certainly not. But I'll let go."

James released the Choir Master from his grip.

"I'm a musician. I never pretended to be holy."

* * *

James looked in his rearview mirror, assessing the damage to his
face. His nose was bleeding. His eye was already puffing up. His
glasses miraculously didn't break, but did give him a cut above his
right eyebrow. Nothing too serious. If he only ever fought church
musicians he might do okay.

His cell phone rang: Jo-Marie. "Hey sweetie!"

"You coulda been raped and it would have been that freak's
fault!" The voice was in the background.

"Father James?"

"What's going on?"

"He came to the house. He knew about the choirmaster." Gossip
is the sound that can travel faster than light. "I was in the garden
studying. He dragged me away."

"Where are you now?"

"His house. I locked myself in my old room."

James heard pounding on her door.

"I just want to talk to you."

"Hang tight sweetie", said James.

"You're a manipulative little bitch sometimes you know that?"

James hung up. Dialled 9-1-1. Thank God for his cell phone. The
dispatcher connected him with the police.

"My goddaughter's been kidnapped."

"Did you witness this?"

"She called me for help. It's her biological father. He's acting
violent and irrational."

"She told you this?"

"Yes."

"At what address?" What was it? He knew how to drive there. C'mon. You always remember numbers.

"Uhhmm… 29** Shakespeare Street."

"We'll send someone right away. What's your name sir?"

"Monseigneur Bienvenu!"

There was a brief pause.

"How do you spell that?"

"My actual name's James Biddle. Two 'd's."

* * *

James wasn't about to just wait for the police officers.

He sped. He didn't usually speed. He ran amber lights. He didn't usually run amber lights. He weaved in and out of lanes. Heard many a honk from many a concerned citizen. Every light seemed to be with him. Amber after amber. He came to Hillside Avenue. Three minutes from the Choir Master's to here? He didn't think an ambulance could have made it that fast. The light turned green as he arrived in the turning lane. He didn't even have to stop. Missing the turn onto Myrtle wouldn't cost him any time.

One more minute and he would be…

SMASH!

Everything in slow motion spinning spinning on and on, silently spinning, endlessly spinning.

And then darkness.

PART IV

After Communion

"Jesus Christ is the same yesterday, and today, and for ever."
—Hebrews 13:8

"You can never step in the same river twice."
—attributed to Heraklitos

Chapter
35

Light. Light. Too much light!

He closed his eyes again.

"James?"

"Mmh."

"Or should I say Monseigneur Bienvenu?"

He could feel his face reddening. Slowly his senses formed themselves like a balloon filling with agony. Sharp stings to the right eye twitching. His chest outraged at every breath he took. Elbow shooting lightning knives.

"I need more drugs", James said.

"You need less broken bones." Beautiful smiling face: Ashley.

"Where am I?"

"The Jubilee."

"What am I dying of?"

"You broke your elbow. You have a gash above your right eye. Two cracked ribs. A lot of bruising. You'll live. Your car, not so much."

Reality came flooding back.

"Jo-Marie!"

"She came by earlier with her dad but you were unconscious so he took her home."

"She needs me."

"She said not to worry about her. She's safe at her father's."

"She's not safe. He kidnapped her."

"You can't kidnap your own child."

"Yes you can. It's a common form of kidnapping."

"Not when you're the only legal guardian."

"But…"

"Joss convinced them it was a simple misunderstanding."

"And they believed him?"

"Jo-Marie backed him up."

"Why would she do that?"

"Maybe she's afraid of getting her own father in trouble with the police."

"He's horrible."

"He's still her dad."

"He beats her." James started to get up out of the bed. Ashley held him down.

"I'll swing by to make sure she's okay. You're in no condition."

"I have to go." James nearly screamed in pain. Bugger elbow!

"You're not in a state to do that."

"I have to fight for her."

"You have James. I know you'll continue to, but not today."

James lay back down. "Make sure you talk to her in private. She won't speak freely if he's watching over her shoulder."

"Okay." Ashley hesitated with something.

"What?"

"Melissa came by."

James could not hold back his smile though it hurt like needles in his eyebrow. "Is she here now?"

"She didn't stay long."

"Oh." The needles stopped pricking.

"She came against her fiancé's wishes."

"Oh. Huh. Good for her."

Ashley breathed through her teeth.

"What?"

"It wasn't so good for you. Her husband…"

"Fiancé."

"It angered him." She touched her magic computer phone, showing James his Facebook profile. The Fiancé had posted the sonnet to James' wall. Hundreds of people had commented on it, at first supportive of its form and technique. No one had suspected he might write poetry. They were curious about this woman for whom he had such feelings.

But comment twenty-seven marked a change, initiated by the Fiancé. "Yeah, but he wrote it for my future wife (he's supposed to marry us!) after she spent the night at his place, in his bed." This wasn't exactly true, but that didn't stop the vitriol from starting. The "shame on yous". Post after post expressing disappointment and disgust over his actions. (Inactions. He'd never actually pursued her.) And just what's his interest with this thirteen-year-old girl he's not even related to? (The same that it was when you were all so impressed with me.) He certainly spent a lot of time with that dirty choirmaster. (He was my co-worker.)

He'd peaked at 1697 friends, but was now down to 234. This is what it is to take a stand nowadays? This is how people express their moral superiority? But it was fair, in its way. He wasn't the saint they projected him to be, nor was he the devil. Their wrong opinions averaged out about right. The Golden Mean. *Via media.*

"Is there any good news?"

"Yes James: He is risen." She smirked.

"For me specifically."

"You're not liable for the accident. They caught the guy on the red light camera."

Chapter
36

Lawyers tell lies, create misery and, for this service to the world, bill $200 an hour. James would need a good lawyer.

He found such a thing (as opposed to "person") in the Venerable McCall's grandnephew. His reputation was impeccable. He specialized in child custody. Before becoming a lawyer he had been a theatre director, folk musician, and social worker who for years served at risk youth in the Greater Toronto Area.

But there was something sinister about his smile. And he had hair plugs. His office was ridiculous. A fake ficus plant. A fake oak desk. A lot of paintings of boats.

"We're a bit backed up but since you suspect abuse I'm going to rush this through."

"Every minute counts", said James authoritatively. It was hard to pull this off as every breath felt like a hatchet to the chest.

"Would you like to lie down?" The "Good" Lawyer pointed to a couch in the corner. Was he a psychiatrist too?

"I'm fine, thank-you. I just want to get Jo-Marie back."

The "Good" Lawyer explained that James' chances had improved from three years ago. Though not officially law, judges almost always followed the wishes of children fourteen and older. So obviously thirteen was borderline. But it was all about the child's well being: if Jo-Marie testified that Joss had a history of abusing her then he could be deemed unfit.

"She's always guarded that fact. He did definitely hit the mom."

"I recommend you file for interim custody as well. A moot point without her I know but I think you'd have a decent shot."

"Okay. Good."

"I take it this is the second time she's run away from her father's care?"

"More times than that. She texted me that she's okay, but that she'll be laying low since she doesn't want anyone to send her back to Joss."

"We should use that text as evidence."

"Text messages in a court case? Brave new world."

"You don't want to use it?"

"Of course I want to use it."

* * *

He wanted to be outside. He wanted to be searching for her again no matter how injured he was. It didn't matter that his cell phone was a better connection to her than any streetperson. He wanted to be anywhere but sitting in the wicker chair in the Rector's office.

"He was always very clear about Safer Churches", said Melissa, smiling encouragement at James. The Fiancé rolled his eyes, or so James assumed.

"We still have a scandal on our hands", said the Rector. "Especially in the wake of what happened with Rodger."

"But James didn't do anything", said Melissa. "You can't just fire him based on perception. That's not Christian."

"I've forgiven him online", said the Fiancé. It had done little to temper the interweb's fury. Simply made the Fiancé look good. "Who am I to judge? I left her here where she didn't know anyone. She made friends with a lonely man who developed a crush. It's adorable really." No one had called James "adorable" since Anne. He'd found it much less condescending back then.

"Obviously you can't officiate the wedding", said the Rector.

"Obviously not."

"Nanna will be pissed," said the Fiancé, "but I don't care who officiates. It's not going to change anything." The Fiancé put his hand in Melissa's. She squeezed it.

* * *

James lay on his back perfectly still. If he didn't move any muscle and breathed with the utmost care, the hurt was almost bearable. He had no reason to move at this moment anyway.

His doorbell rang.

"Come in", yelled James.

"It's locked." It was Melissa's voice.

James slowly raised himself with his left arm. Ow! Ow! Broken bones jostling. His ribs shooting pain. He unlocked the door. She was wearing that damned yellow dress, holding a fancy black shopping bag. His heart pounded, punching his ribs from the inside: it literally hurt to see her.

"Come in." James slowly walked towards his kitchen. Shuffling. Stiff. Constantly correcting his movements trying to find any comfort. "Would you like something to drink?"

"I'll get it", said Melissa. "You should just sit down."

"Don't fuss", said James. "I'll be all right."

James filled a pot with water. Slowly moved it with his left arm towards the stove, sloshing several small splashes to the floor. He turned the element on.

"They didn't reprimand you. That's good."

"Very good."

"You'll still be able to provide for Jo-Marie when that gets sorted out. And it will for the best."

"Where's your fiancé?"

"He's rehearsing for the U2charist."

"I'm supposed to be there." I can't have you. Why are you making me look at you?

"I'm sure they'll understand."

"Definitely." Fuck it. Fuck everything. That's right, I'm brain swearing yet again and I don't even care. "What's up?"

"I wanted to see how you're feeling about Jo-Marie and all that."

"I don't know. Hopeful…-ish."

"And I brought her a present for when she comes back. Because I know she's going to come back to you." Melissa opened her shopping bag. She took out a bracelet, a handbag and a belt. "It's in her size and everything."

Just like the belt from her story. Well so what? It was probably just some sort of emotional manipulation so he'd forgive her for marrying that jackass. Or maybe a call for him to make the grand romantic gesture they both knew he'd never make. Or maybe there was symbolism he missed because he didn't have any interest in pop culture after 1965. It was passive aggressive behaviour really.

Still, it was a nice belt.

"Thank-you", said James. "I'm sure Jo-Marie will appreciate it."

"I also brought my demo." Melissa reached into her bag for a cassette, handing it to James. "She texted me that you wanted to hear it."

"I would like to hear it", said James.

"She said you loved my songs but you have trouble with spontaneous compliments. You better express yourself in secret poems or sermons."

"That's very true."

"I'm not sure I believe either of you", said Melissa. "You were always very enthusiastic about gelato. But I hope you like the new songs more than you did the other ones." She squeezed his hand. She held his gaze silently. This again. He wanted not to feel anything. Wanted simply to be moving past it. But every pound his heart beat into his chest exclaimed that he felt it now more than ever. It would be so much to his advantage if he could turn it off. Why couldn't he just turn it off?

She moved in towards him, never closing those striking blue eyes. Closer. Closer. So close he could feel her breath on his lips, could almost taste it, sweet with nocciola.

Ow! Ow! Heart beating faster. Ow! Ow!

They held the moment so long James started to like that pain. Held it so long that their lips finally touching was not a separate thing. There was no beginning to their kiss. It was as if it had always been—something like eternity. She kissed him so soft so sweet so slow. When he awakened from eternity he realized another sort of eternity had finally ended. The colloquial hyperbolic eternity: ten years. Ten years since he'd kissed a woman. Ten years since a woman, a beautiful woman, a woman that could have had so many other men, could have kissed so many other lips, chose his lips for this moment. This beautiful, holy, blessed moment.

Her cell phone rang.

"Hey sweetie. Yeah. Just delivered the present. Yes. I managed not to jump him. We just said good-bye actually. " That was good-bye? "Okay. See you soon." She hung up her phone. "I should go."

No! No! No! I need more than a moment.

"You should."

"See you at the *U2*charist I guess."

"I guess", said James.

Chapter
37

He arrived home, back from the "Good" Lawyer's, to find that the bathroom towels were disturbed. Food was missing. The freezie and iced tea mixture was in a bowl on the counter, liquid but still cold. He called her name in vain, wincing from the pressure it put on his ribs. He called her phone. It went to her message service. "You should just stay", he told it. He went to her room. Chafed at the *U2* poster—she'd managed to rile him up even when she wasn't here. It was comforting.

She'd been reading his paper, curious about the awful mess in Vancouver. Mr. Anarchy Tattoo was probably pleased. Spectator sports had always been trouble. The world should have learned its lesson after the Nika riots in Byzantium. What truly terrified James about Vancouver was that so many well-groomed youths, seemingly from good homes, had so gleefully joined in. Called it being part of history. Their grandparents and great grandparents had become part of history risking their lives to protect their cities, this accursed new generation to destroy.

He received a text: "My father would try to take me back." More evidence they could submit to court.

His cassette player was on her shelf. James pressed play. Melissa's voice sang out about rivers flowing and changing time. It wasn't such bad music really. Maybe he could make himself like it. Maybe if she recorded it properly. It might help take the twang out of the guitar.

On Jo-Marie's desk was two thirds of the missing jewelry with a note—"Sorry Revrend J"—signed by both Ink and Tru.

There was an eight and a half by fourteen inches sheet in her typewriter, both sides covered. She'd forbidden him to read her writing. It would be very intrusive to do so.

James unspooled the paper.

write write type type clickity clack holding nothing back like young Jack Kerouac my fellow French Canadien though he was also American and also I'm only half and don't speak a lick of it but I am young JM Jones sounds literary like a novelists name like a poets name so I shall call myself JM Jones from the here on in on out bring me more stout what's stout I think it's an alcohol and I don't even think I've ever had that but I've had a few extra sensory perceptives if you know my drift what I mean you catch

(Drugs! What might you catch? Are we going to have to do more tests?)

but that road leads to death all roads lead to death some quicker some slower go slower go slower go slower stop stop stop stop that road leads its own way I don't want to go that way today bring me more happiness bring me more time less time flows time goes time goes the world away I sleep on the sidewalk on flattend cardboard it is not soft but without it you get jabbed with little rocks I think they might rip the bag and then I don't sleep but sometimes yr so tired you just sleep as if you were in a bed I have slept on cardboard and in a bed or on a bed I have slept in an apartment with ten others no one bathes enough soap costs too much yet they all buy lottery tix and candy and they give sope free with shampoo at food banks you'd think you'd get used to the smell but you only just accept the smell I have slept in shelters where the smell is worse I have slept unsheltered where it depends where sometimes a worse stench sometimes the beautiful smell of warm bread I have lost many pairs of shoes I have found many pairs of shoes I have walked barefoot on the pavement and in the park I have kept a smile on my face a sunny disposition in my heart this gets you more spare change than honesty they think I'm older but look younger but I am young as I look I was young I will be young I will die young I will live young I will die young even if I live to be a hundred so young will I live my hole life all my days clack away clack the pages hit those keys so hard so hard hit those keys open slap those keys then its only discipline if you punch the keys its much worse you dn't even know what it's like so don't start crying you baby you never lost a tooth you baby tooth you don't even know I'm sorry I'm sorry but you don't even know not really just open slap the keys until they cry stupid keys shut up keys shut up

keys shut up keys useless keys stupid keys I hate the keys can't
stand the site I mean sight of those keys damn keys live keys die
keys what does it matter keys what is the keys to life what are
the keys to life slap those keys don't punch those keys well a little
I suppose but not too much but that's too much yet I feel for him
sorry for him sad for I do even know stupid don't go that way
again don't fear that way don't hold back this is for no one to read
but yrself father J will probably find it here you go father J I know
yr reading this one day from now or one decade I know you spy
don't spy don't dare spy don't eavesdrop through the vent don't
you dare read this father J you can't read this father J

(I can and I will.)

but I do respect you father J but do respect me father J

(I worry for you, thought James. Worry trumps respect.)

dont read this father J don't read this and think you know me
nobody knows me nobody knows anybody for everybody changes
everybody projecting their needs on people and projecting
themselves to people like they think people need them to be
want them to be like with God there can be no God for people
project what they need to exist on the universe and call it God
and project themselves to the universe like they're not and call
themselves good becuase they need an anchor in the khaos sea
they make up stories for their lives out of khaos because they
need an anchor and when the stories don't make sense cause
anchors are no good cause life is a landless bottomless khaos sea
they change their stories rather than their minds but in the end
its why nobody knows life nor knows themselves nobody knows
and I am wiser that I know nobody knows you taught me that
socraties taught that he was the justust man not named Jesustice
so since its just us for justice i I mean I care I care I do care if
you live or die or breathe or don't breathe I do care that you
care but I'm not going there except for literary purposes except
for the greater glory of my pen my typewriter I am a fourth
generation or fifth generation beat the generation goes on as does
the beat it will never die if we keep it alive in our hearts how
long has christianity lived and we don't even have his writings
i I mean I will keep it alive with my experience my personal
experience my personal purpose make me alone make me grown
make me groan make me mone? moen? moan? make me sleep
on cardboard make me sleep on concrete make me sleep in the
gutter make me mourn make me suffer make me cry make me
wish I would die make it hurt make it sting make it bend make
it bruise make it bleed make it break jus make it for a purpose
just make it for a purpose my purpose is my story my purpose

is literary take it or leave it take my blankets take my bags my
sleeping bags take my sleep I can always find another an endless
supply of blankets and sleeping bags from donation boxes to the
street from the street to the dumpster and then to the dump a
big dump just filled with everything I lost on the street it's just
stuff you can take nothing with you it is easier for a camel to
threat I mean thread the eye of a needle than be rich and get into
heaven well I am preparing my way for heaven by sleeping on
cardboard and in church basements out of the rain is the church
not for me as much as you few churches let us in on the ground
floor only the basement only the basement won't even let us into
go pee everybody gives us three day old bread and circuses I
remember what you taught me and know thyself and nothing
in excess and panta rhei and everything changes and you can
never be drowned in the same jordan river twice and three day
old bread and no circuses three day old bread and basements and
muffins and everybody wants to call that caring I feel you I feel
you you try you did what you didn't knew how to do but nobody
lets us go pee nobody wants to take that step and let us pee with
dignity and I know how much you care for dignity Father J and
then they get mad you go in the alley well if you don't let us in
do the math at lest at lest? leest? least? leste? there is the eatons
centre bay center and the libary and they have that one out door
one now off pandora its great for those its great for which is
those that pee standing up and there is centennial square and
our place and the clinic too but sometimes theres people you just
dont want to see there for reasons I wont ever tell you but even
then sometimes you just cant get to those places in time but i I
mean I am thankful for the library and the eatons centre bay
center more than bread and muffins but thank-you for the bread
and the muffins that I never took though I knew you gave I know
you meant well with the bread and the muffiins I mean muffins
I know you mean well you mean well you no mean you not mean
you don't do mean and you do mean well for which for reason
for why for why did I come back to you that night of all drizzly
nights because I really was kicked out of the apartment but I was
often kicked out or had nowhere and didn't come back to you you
want to know what my brain is like this is not even it really its
it's own thing in my mind there are no typos and I know how to
spell everything but you want me to say I love you don't you you
want me to say it because I don't say it in life but you need me
to say it you need some one to say it I won't say it I can't say it
not even in my mind it isnt something I can say sincere maybe
one day or two days but not today this is not a snetimental space
and life is a khaos river with neither bed nor banks and you got

breakfast you got the day at the park I gave you that day in the park with your manic magic ginger pixie though she really is a lovely woman if only you'd get to really know her and you are a decent fellow if only she'd get to know you but that's why I gave that gift of a day to you and to her be greatful its more than a lot of people ever get so remember it and the other one I don't remember and i I mean I want you to be brave with her so you can be with her so she can say she loves you and make new sentimental memries to remember if you hafta make up stories make up good ones be spontanious sometimes stop obsessing over evry implication or life passes you by but also I will give you this that you are the best person in my life I will say that if it makes you feel better because you mean well I know you meen well and the cel phone and the Facebook groop and dinner with my friends and all the stuff you think was useless you think was vanity of vanities all in life is vanity well it was that kinda vanity that made me want to come back that night of all the drizzly nights because you did different from when you didn't fight when you just let things happen just let my father take me back but now you fight for me and thats a better story so fight for her take chances for her make a good story for her because life is short and you deserve to live it because you mean well and that means something well and good

Didn't mention the Deacon once, thought James. She was probably just faking about that.

Chapter
38

"Why didn't you tell me if you weren't going to show up?" The Deacon was giving him quite the tongue lashing, even though James had shown up now, three hours before the scheduled service. Ready to celebrate. True to his word.

"You might notice I'm a complete mess."

"I know injuries, James. You could have made it. Now you don't know what to do or when."

"I know how to celebrate a Eucharist."

"Do you know how to do it one armed?"

"I'll figure it out. I have other worries right now in case you hadn't been made aware."

"You're right. I'm sorry." He didn't sound sorry. "I'm just a bit stressed out. I've worked so hard on this. It's my first real introduction to a lot of these people, my first real project as a priest and it could rock. It could help bring a lot of souls back to Christ except that everything's screwing up. Rodger. You. This wedding, which is suddenly my responsibility. We're behind with the leaflets. The band is going to 'wing' a lot of the songs. I had a calling to do this. At least I thought I did."

The Deacon looked, for a moment, to be sincerely filled with a doubt that James did not wish on anyone. A doubt bordering at times on complete existential despair.

"I can do the leaflets."

* * *

James would probably get blamed for turning the *U2charist* into a "disasterpiece" (a term he'd originally composed to describe

Spiderman the Musical). Granted he was partly responsible, but not entirely so.

Before the service even started the Fiancé's band played an obnoxious song. As James was busy being annoyed, one of the servers asked, "Is this song really about God?" It was the exact thing James was thinking. (Nearly. In James' brain "really" was replaced with "even".)

"It's about his mother", said the Rector.

"He wrote a number of songs about her", said the Deacon. "She died when he was in his early teens."

That almost made Bono human. But he didn't have to share his private pain for all the world to see and what's with the sunglasses?

"But what's with the sunglasses?" asked the same server. It was uncanny.

"He has an eye condition", said the Deacon. "He's very sensitive to light."

Luckily the discordance of the music continued to keep James' discontent alive. So too did the accusative eyes as he stepped into the nave during the processional "hymn". The Fiancé might have forgiven James (though obviously not really) but the vast majority of people were still outraged at the (in)actions of a man they briefly saw as a spiritual hero.

Had they come to church just to be judgmental or were they hoping to watch a train wreck? (That sort of behaviour had fuelled the riots.) Or did they actually like this so called music? These so called hymns?

Did they just sing about gyrating hips in a church service?

Then there was that screaming portion where no one could hit the screaming note.

The Fiancé and his rock and roll band were set up in the transept, blasting out the music, attempting to make up for its obnoxiousness with volume. Everyone and their eyes were still judging James, but it was hard not to laugh at them swinging their hips, raising their arms and swaying. Some of them in tears thinking it was beautiful. James concentrated on the pain from his broken elbow and ribs so as not to giggle at his fellow clergy "shaking it up" as they processed up the centre aisle.

Once everything had settled down the Deacon started with a regular, ugly BAS Acclimation and Gloria, then the perfectly adequate Kyrie and Trisagion, the ugly again Collect and Proclamation with the Psalms set to another twangy song. The gospel procession came and went along with *Mysterious Ways* and lyrics that, recontextualized, made God a woman.

Via media! What are you talking about? This is nowhere near *media*. This was *via extrema*.

But it was still a thing indifferent. The Deacon looked so earnest and hopeful. James didn't know if he should laugh or cry.

The Rector's sermon was on the school they would help build. The value of education. How westerners take so much for granted. James found nothing disastrously wrong with it, despite his best efforts.

Then the Nicene Creed. Strange saying "The Father Almighty" when we just called Him "She". But gender is a human construct after all. Not a holy one.

Then came the prayers of the people led by a fourteen-year-old who apparently thought ripped jeans made appropriate church-wear. "Let us pray for the children who will benefit from our humble generosity." Their generosity literally had amplifiers. The (yes, seriously) smoke machine, as if to emphasize this point, released an acrid puff of cloud.

What was that ringing? Had one of these cads left his or her cell phone on? That just tops it. It goes off right in the middle of the prayers of the people no less. James shook his head, simultaneously scanning and judging the room. Where was it coming from?

His own pocket!

Don't do anything. Nobody will know. The ringing finally stopped. Phew.

It was quickly replaced with repeated beeping.

James searched under his robes. Found the phone. He really was about to turn it off, but the missed call and new text were both from

Jo-Marie. No, he couldn't check... He had to check. He looked as apologetically as he could at the Deacon's surprisingly good death stare. "She needs you to take a risk for her. That's how people work." Was it? Didn't sound right, but what did James really know about people anyway?

He turned off his phone as he stood up to invite the congregation to Confession. "'Dear friends in Christ, God is steadfast in love and infinite in mercy. He welcomes sinners and invites them to His table. Let us confess our sins, confident in God's forgiveness...'" Everyone then recited together, "'Most merciful God, we confess that we have sinned against you in thought word and deed. By what we have done. And by what we have left undone. We have not loved you with our whole heart. We have not loved our neighbours as ourselves. We are truly sorry and we humbly repent. Have mercy upon us and forgive us.'" James absolved them all, even though they probably wouldn't have absolved him, given that they were a bunch of jerks.

Now we have confessed our own sins but how can we expect God to forgive us if we cannot forgive our neighbours? So we have the Peace. The reconciliation. Everyone shaking each others' hands. I just get stare downs mostly. The occasional handshake (of James' left hand as his right elbow was broken) but mostly just stare downs. Do you actually think you are ready to receive the sacrament you foolish generation when you cannot even symbolically forgive someone who has never done you any wrong?

But the Rector offered peace, the Deacon offered peace, Melissa offered peace. The Fiancé offered his hand, aggressively shaking James' injured arm, whispering, "Don't worry. You didn't really have a chance."

The Deacon, in his worry and excitement, had forgotten to publish the marriage banns before the service started. The peace, informal in the way they were doing it, seemed to him an appropriate time to make up for this. As people settled back to their respective pews he said, "'I publish the Banns of Marriage between Melissa Jane Wembley and Christopher Philip Knowles. If any of you know cause or just impediment why these two persons should not be joined together in Holy Matrimony, you are to declare it.'"

Every eye and ear in the building turned to James in an instant.

They had spoken ill (and typed ill) of him behind his back. Had condemned him already. He who had worked extra hours. He who had set up Market Place to go along with New-To-You. He who had visited their parents and grandparents when they were too busy to care. He who had given time to their children. Who broke bread with them. Gave them countless Communions. Gave them intellectual yet entertaining sermons. He who had been passed over for promotion after promotion. He who had fought a losing battle for the BCP. He who had (partially) opened his heart to them at Easter. They had condemned him without speaking to him. Without asking his side of the story. He who had stayed loyal to them and to God even though he no longer felt His love. They had condemned him based on rumours and hearsay. So what if he'd written a sonnet? He hadn't sent it. So what if he'd inspired her songs? He hadn't liked them. So what if he'd let her stay the night? So what if he'd let her kiss him good-bye? He had pretty much always done the right thing though it killed him. And yet they condemned him.

And there, among the eyes in the front row, stared Jo-Marie, wearing her Sunday best dress. Had she snuck in during the peace? He knew what her eyes were saying. They could be quite convincing those eyes.

"Yes I love her." James stood up. He looked at Melissa, sitting three rows back. "I declare it before God…" (if He exists) "…and all present, though it may cost me this job to which I have devoted nearly my whole life. Her fiancé doesn't appreciate her. He doesn't appreciate what a wonderful and talented person she is." James looked to Jo-Marie, beaming. "What amazing music she makes. Music that has her share private pain at times like Bono does also. Music that I am honoured to have helped inspire. Music that she should record. I'd love to help her do that or anything she'd ever want to do because I love her. I hope she feels the same for me."

All eyes and ears then turned towards Melissa.

"Could we talk about this privately?" she asked.

"Oh yes", said James. "Of course."

The Fiancé turned to James and smiled. "That was a 'no', in case you didn't understand."

It wasn't necessarily! She just wanted to talk about it privately... Who am I kidding?

Walking back towards his prayer desk the whole humiliating event seemed somehow familiar. Maybe because it was so similar to his very worst nightmares.

Or maybe because it was like that time at church camp.

Chapter
39

How does one maintain dignity after a moment of heartbreaking embarrassment felt in front of hundreds of peers, colleagues, and loved ones?

Continue on as if nothing embarrassing has occurred.

"The Offertory will be *The Sweetest Thing*", said James with authority. "Found on page five of your leaflets." The band looked to the Fiancé who shrugged, then counted them in.

The eyes pitied him now. Well he pitied that their owners couldn't sing in key. Pitied that they had to watch each others' bodies dancing—now less enthusiastically than before the banns (though to an outside observer they probably looked less ridiculous).

James prepared the gifts. It took longer than normal but he had figured out how to manipulate things one armed in the days since he'd been released from hospital. It just looked silly. Washing one hand with the lavabo was awkward. Raising only one arm to the Lord as he said the Eucharistic Prayer made him look like he was about to begin an interpretive dance.

The Communion hymn started with a long organ intro— several misplayed notes and no sense of pacing. Mrs. Mathers was actually quite nice, but her musicality was dismal. James hoped people would talk more about that afterwards than about his minor embarrassment.

* * *

Jo-Marie had disappeared again, but James received a text when he arrived at his office (where he had chosen to disrobe rather than in the vestry): "You'll laugh when you tell this story in ten years."

Then, about three minutes later: "Do you mind if I use this in a story I'm writing?"

A knock on his office door.

"May I come in?" Stop being beautiful! Just stop!

"Of course."

Melissa closed the door behind her. "I really admire what you did."

"Great."

"It was brave. Incredibly brave." Normandy was brave. "I think it shows a lot of growth on your part." Tumours show growth.

"Thank-you."

"Listen, James…" Oy! "…before Chris came back, a part of me was ready to be with you and Jo-Marie. Most of me was. But when I was with him again I remembered why we fell for each other in the first place."

"Why is that, exactly?"

"He really is a wonderful guy, if you actually got to know him. I say the same thing to him about you actually."

"He doesn't appreciate you. He doesn't appreciate your talent." (James, on the other hand, definitely planned to learn to appreciate it.)

"He does. He heard my new demo and was genuinely impressed. He's called in a few favours. We're going to record it properly after the wedding."

"Oh", said James. "But he left you for *Ontario*."

"He's an indecisive person. So am I. It's why I kept switching majors. It's why I could love him then you then him again. I never know what I want."

"Except now."

"You've helped me so much with that. I told Chris if I'm going to be with him, it can't go back to the way it was before. I could have been with a very wonderful man."

"I'm glad I could be of use."

"James…" She looked him in the eye. "The time I spent with you was the happiest of my life. It really was."

Was it?

Really?

"Then why go with him? Are you afraid that I'm packaged with a troubled child? Are you afraid of the responsibility?"

"I'm afraid I'm going to leave. Or I'm going to want to leave and feel trapped and act out and that's just as bad. I know what it's like to live with someone like that. It's no good."

"Then change that."

"I've tried to. My whole life I've tried. I'm too much like my father." The blue eyes struck James with their resoluteness. "Change is my only constant."

Part of James considered it very manipulative of Melissa to paraphrase Heraklitos like she did. Another part of him found it almost touching. A third part of him said, "That almost sounds like Heraklitos."

"Listen, James, I hadn't written songs in years before you came along. But I saw you suffering and I just knew I had to help you through it somehow. You awoke something in me." (She was supposed to have wakened something in him.) "When I had the band before our songs were chicken shit. I was chicken shit. Afraid people would laugh at me like they did at the words on my wall. But, sharing my story with you and Jo-Marie, seeing how much that helped you both, I knew I had a purpose and that it was a good one. You guys gave me so much self-confidence. Not to mention a garden oasis in which to work." (The oasis was struggling again without her.) "You taught me so much about myself and about life." (Melissa was supposed to have taught him so much about himself and about life.) "You're like my muse. It was a blessing to have gotten to know you."

"I'm a person", said James. "I'm not anyone's blessing."

Chapter
40

Joss's Evil Lawyer argued that Jo-Marie's issues with her father stemmed from their car accident. "And it truly was an accident. The other driver didn't even take him to court. Jo-Marie only started blaming my client for this tragedy…" (colloquially, I will give you) "…because her mind has been poisoned by a charismatic preacher…" (I don't have one ounce of charisma, thought James. I make a point of it.) "…so lonely he mistakes his role of godparent as that of an actual parent." The Evil Lawyer used the little outburst at the U2charist as evidence of James' loneliness and recklessness. He argued Jo-Marie's texts and typings were created by James himself to slander his client.

It would be libel, thought James. Not slander. A lawyer should know better.

The not slander, along with Jo-Marie's penchant for running away, did cast doubt on Joss' fitness as a father. For this reason the Judge ordered that she stay in a temporary foster home until the custody trial was resolved and as soon as anyone could find her.

James asked the "Good" Lawyer how he could make up for his outburst. "Maybe do some charity work… oh wait." He laughed. "Write an apology to all parties involved. State that it was a one time thing and that you've learned from it."

James had already done that.

"Can you go back in time and stop yourself?"

"Of course not."

"Then you've officially done all you can do."

He expects payment for this crap?

* * *

James parked his new used car—a 2006 Honda Fit hatchback—at the Jubilee Hospital. He walked up to cardiac care. Nodded a hello at the nurses' station. Entered the room.

"'Peace be to this house…'"

"'…and to all that dwell in it'", said the Old Man from his bed. He smiled.

"Your strength is coming back."

"Thank-you for humouring me, James."

"It was a minor heart attack at best."

"At worst you mean."

James thought for a moment. Shrugged.

"I hope you're not still cross with me."

"Cross with you for what?"

"For not making you rector."

"We can't all be rector."

"You emulate your father. You want to be like him." James nodded. "It's good you do that. He was a good man but, you know James, I knew both your parents very well. I watched you grow up. Do you want to know what I noticed?"

Absolutely not. "Sure."

"You're more like your mother than him. You should accept that about yourself. Nurture that. I think you might find that it's the best part of you."

Now pardon me while I throw up.

No. It was nice to hear.

* * *

"How's our patient?" asked Canon Conroy, taking a sip of oatmeal stout.

"He's looking well", said James. "But he thinks he'll have to retire."

"Welker will become bishop no doubt", said the Venerable McCall. A murmur of displeasure spread through them at the mention of Welker's unholy name.

"I'm sure that's just a rumour", said James.

"He'll reinstate you somewhere", said Canon Conroy. "Maybe with St. Barnabas' or the Cathedral. This will all blow over in time."

James nodded vaguely.

"What is your opinion of gay clergy?" asked Zi-Wei, for no apparent reason.

James smiled. "You always ask that."

"What do you answer always?"

"*Via media*", said the Reverend Doctor Leonard White. Everyone smiled. One day I will visit each of you in hospital. Each of you t...

Each of you *also* shall pass away.

Somewhere. Sometime. But not today.

* * *

"This sure is a long line."

"Go back to Langford if you don't like it."

"In five minutes I'm going to have to", she looked at her watch. "We have to do extra Safer Churches meetings thanks to someone."

"The coconut is fantastic."

"You've mentioned."

"Have I?"

"Once or twice." Ashley smirked at him. "I hear they might reinstate you soon."

"That's just a rumour."

"How do you feel about that rumour?"

"Same as any rumour."

"I thought it calmed you not being a priest."

"The calm passed."

"The crisis is over?"

"No," he said painfully, "I still can't say I have faith."

"I don't *have* faith either James", she smiled. "I don't own it. It's not something I decided to have one day and that was it. Sometimes it's been strong, simple and easy, but sometimes it's not been there at all. Faith is something we strive for, not something we possess."

James let the words slowly sink into his mind before asking, "You just did a sermon on that, didn't you?"

She kissed him on the cheek. "You inspired it." James aimed his death eyes at Ashley as she took her turn to order: a waffle cone of coconut. "It got me thinking, though. Jo-Marie was so sure you'd abandoned her but you never did. She simply didn't understand your reasons. Maybe, just maybe, you don't understand God's."

"'When you see only one set in the sand, it was then that I carried you.' Yes, I've read *Footprints*."

Ashley punched him fraternally, but harder than his still healing body would have liked. She looked at her watch. "I have to get going sweetie but I'll see you in court tomorrow."

"You don't have to come. It's really okay. I'm sure you're very busy with…" James had been working on this form of social interaction: "Thank-you." She squeezed his shoulder as she left.

James purchased two scoops, one of nocciola and one of hazelnut. He was feeling nostalgic.

As he was coming to the door who should walk in but Melissa and the Husband?

"James", said Melissa. "Good to see you."

"Good to see you also. Yeah. Definitely." All eyes were on them now. For a whole month after the embarrassment he'd had to endure the eyes (and a viral YouTube clip and even a small article on page A5 of the newspaper) and now they were back again.

"My nanna thinks she should have chosen you", said the Husband.

"Oh yes? Ha ha."

"She never liked my hair."

"How amusing", said James.

"My album's a hit", said Melissa, "a minor hit."

"A major hit with the geeks", said the Husband proudly.

"I do have lots of geek cred", Melissa smiled.

"She's making more money from it than I ever did." She'd turned pain into compassion into music into success.

"Who cares about that?" asked Melissa. The Husband raised his hand with mock sheepish hilarity. "People love your music", Melissa continued. "People love my music. I got this letter, well Facebook fanpage message, from this little fourteen-year-old boy telling me how my songs are helping him get through his parents' divorce. That's why I do this." Her misery had a fan club.

"That YouTube clip was great publicity", the Husband told James.

"Chris", said Melissa, shaking her head.

"It was. I want him to know there's no hard feelings."

"It's amazing how things work out sometimes", said James. "Like a higher power is shaping our actions, rough hew them as we will." Melissa and the Husband both nodded. "I want to say how happy it makes me... whatever I said before, whatever my past foolishness... I'm happy to have had such a positive effect on both your lives."

"Thank-you, James", said Melissa, squeezing his hand.

"Of course", James said. "All the best."

"You too", said the Husband and Melissa in unison.

James stepped into the sunlight, sucking in the warm fresh air, finally breathing again.

Why had he thought humiliating himself in public would solve his problems? If he hadn't, the case with Jo-Marie likely would have been decided already. Why had he thought he could find happiness by changing a part of himself he did not even consider a vice? He was a private man who did his best to make sensible decisions. There was nothing wrong with that.

When he helped the streetpeople, faced the pawnbroker, faced Joss, faced having a cell phone, he showed courage for the sake of things he believed in. Hitting the Choir Master, speeding in his car, confessing his love in a public setting: mere recklessness. He should have known better. He was a man wasn't he?

It was Jo-Marie's influence. What was wrong with him? Yes she'd known more than her fair share of suffering, and yes she'd been right about the spaghetti lasagna, but these things didn't give her insight regarding adult relationships.

James had a superstitious belief that maybe, just maybe, he was wrong about absolutely everything, while everyone else had a secret knowledge of how to live which had somehow never been revealed to him. He even believed thirteen-year-old girls who had recently spent months homeless knew how to live better than he did. If there was something he needed to change about himself it was that superstition.

A group of joggers passed James as he crossed Fernwood in front of the school. Middle aged, trying to keep in shape. People talk about what a great achievement it is to change and grow but, in actual fact, the opposite is just as true. James looked back to the joggers, now well up the road. It takes effort to hold on to your youth. Effort to hold on to who you are.

Some change was good, to be sure. You should be willing to change if it would truly help. Robert Stanfield had stepped back from the abyss of socialism. But he kept his best ideals. Didn't throw out the blessed baby with the unholy bathwater. It's a hard thing to do. Like trying to grasp a concept with your hands.

(I should write that one down, thought James.)

You can never step in the same river twice. Every moment new waters flowing past you. Every moment it becomes an entirely new entity. But just try to stop that flow. Freeze the river and it's no longer a river. Dam the river…

It becomes a lake.

(Where was his pen? He always kept a pen.)

Why should he have to fight? There was honour in being a pacifist. Why should he have to make a grand romantic gesture? There was honour in stoically doing what is right. If the new generations wanted to live their brave new lives in their brave new worlds, let 'em. But James' way of life was as right as anyone else's.

Better to listen to his own heart. It sought constancy, not change. It sought something eternal. Eternal life through Christ? If it existed at all, it existed in the kingdom to come. In the next world. James wanted something constant in this one. Just one constant thing (other than change) in the here and the now.

What fit that particular bill? Nature was not constant. Culture was not constant. Church was not constant. Liturgy was not constant. Hope was not constant. His faith in God was not constant. Happiness was certainly not constant.

Nor was misery.

As James stepped into his house he saw Jo-Marie mixing a freezie with iced tea crystals.

"I can't believe you still eat that."

"It's better than gelato."

"You're crazy."

"Besides, I thought a good Christian wasn't judgmental."

"I do judge you to be human. That's the diet of an arctic hummingbird." James sat down beside Jo-Marie at the kitchen counter. "They'll eventually find out that you visit here."

"It won't change the verdict." She ate a scoop of the cold sticky mess.

"The judgment. A verdict is when there's a jury."

"Whatever."

"A writer should care about these things."

"Speaking of which, I'm still pissed you submitted my typing as evidence. You weren't even supposed to read it."

"You read my sonnet."

"Well, you should be more mature than me."

"Okay. I won't read your writing without permission again. Or give it to a court of law."

"I hope you told them it was just practice typing." Jo-Marie swallowed another scoop. "I would do much better if it were for real."

* * *

She was reading *Howl*. He was making notes on Plato's *Kratylos*, but not really.

"I'd like you to take me to my father's."

"But he hits you."

She looked at him. He'd read her work. No getting around that. "He won't", she finally said. "Not right before the trial."

"Why would you want to go there?"

"He's had a rough life."

"That doesn't matter."

"It matters. He thinks no one understands what he went through. I understand."

James looked at Jo-Marie with grave compassion. Her face was pinched and defiant. "You don't have to go."

"Just take me, all right?"

* * *

The sharp pains from his neck during shoulder checks and his arm (supposedly coming along nicely) during turns were but a cruel underline that it was all wrong—dropping her off at the lion's den. But what else could he do? Lock her in her room? Then he'd be as bad as the lion.

Jo-Marie said, "You probably feel bad that I don't love you."

"You can't force these things."

"I couldn't write it. It would have been dishonest."

James came to the corner of Shelbourne and Hillside. He slowed down, looked all around. Let the intersection clear completely, and then made a left hand turn without incident.

They continued, wordless, on to Joss' house. James pulled the car over.

"Don't take it personally. Love is just this sentimental thing people think exists. Everybody that gives it wants it back. Even you. You want love back. You need it."

"I'd like it", said James. "It hurts to live without it, but what I feel for you doesn't need anything back. Doesn't expect anything back. A little bit of respect, maybe. To be treated with dignity. Everybody should expect that of everybody. But no, when it comes down to it, I don't even need that."

"Oh", said Jo-Marie, pondering this. "I don't believe you."

James smiled with a heart both broken and warm. "I don't need you to."

Jo-Marie released a rapid burst of laughter, which she quickly stifled. She carefully hugged him good-bye and got out of the car. Before slamming the door way too hard like she always did, she looked back. "He called my cell yesterday. If he wins he'll take me to Llodyminister…"

"Llodyminster, Alberta." James corrected before he could process.

"Saskatchewan", she corrected back. "He's got a job lined up at a refinery there. He wants to make a new beginning." James felt saliva sliding down his esophagus, reacting with stomach acid. "I told him it would never happen. That you and me were gonna win the verdict."

BANG! James was sure the window would shatter one of these times.

As he watched Jo-Marie leaving he thought, I suppose, in my life at least, there has been one constant thing.

He did not feel he was being sentimental.

Chapter
41

James arrived at the courthouse, resolved to feel optimistic.

The trial had started out terrifying enough. His personal life paraded through the court. The Evil Lawyer (a.k.a. "the Lawyer Lawyer") alleged that James was an out of control letch and certainly not fit to raise someone else's child. He brought up the recent events of course and even managed to dredge Suzanne Cumberbatch from the distant past. James had always been the sort to abuse his position of authority. He hadn't changed.

But the Rector stood up for James, saying the latter had gone through proper channels when dealing with Ms. Cumberbatch. He was not a rule breaker by nature. Yes he had to suspend him for the *U2charist* incident, but that was not a reflection of James as a person.

"I know that if I went missing he'd stop sleeping and showering until I was found."

While somewhat hyperbolic, this was essentially true for Jo-Marie and for Ashley and the Old Man. James wasn't positive he'd do it for the Rector.

"He has never lost himself. No matter what happened in his life, he's never stopped being who he is. And while we have had our differences I will say this: it takes incredible bravery to stay who you are when who you are doesn't bring any tangible rewards."

James loved his house, was in sound financial shape and had always enjoyed ministering to the elderly.

"He is one of the bravest people I know."

The Rector smiled at James. James smiled back. What's his agenda? To protect the parish? To get publicity? To impress with his oratory? Or maybe he was sincere. Like Smirky Jack turned out to be at the end of his life: a man can smile and smile and not be a villain. Maybe the Rector actually meant those words. No. It was probably a combination of all of them except that.

Still, James appreciated the flattery.

The Evil Lawyer could find few people to testify against James. Yes his "fans" no longer thought much of him, but there was little they could testify to other than rumour. The Deacon had forgiven James for ruining the U2charist and spoke enthusiastically on his behalf. One of the employees of the gelato place felt he didn't tip enough, but "cheap" was very easily spun into "frugal", which was hardly an argument against him as a guardian.

James put himself in good stead when the sonnet was brought forth as evidence of his immoral sex life.

"I don't have any sort of sex life. The fact that I write acrostic sonnets should be proof enough of that." People had laughed.

He hadn't meant it as a joke.

The Evil Lawyer called the Organ Master (that's wormwood!) to the stand.

"Yes, he attacked me", said the Organ Master.

"So he's violent? An unstable man?"

"If you'd seen him fight you'd know he didn't make a habit of it."

The Organ Master smiled at James when he said it. He'd blindsided the Evil Lawyer. Was he seeking some sort of forgiveness, James wondered. It's not me who has to forgive.

James had been consistently James for thirty-six years. He did not normally get in car accidents (even ones that weren't his fault) and his outburst was completely out of character. It almost seemed endearing to some (Ashley!). The "Good" Lawyer construed it as a release of stress after spending so much time and energy trying to find the child in question. Did this make him human? Absolutely. Unfit to raise Jo-Marie? To the contrary.

Melissa did something that James found very moving. He appreciated her glowing assessment of his parenting skills, but it wasn't that. It was the fact that the Husband volunteered himself to the "Good" Lawyer as a character witness for James. "He did nothing wrong. He simply fell in love with a wonderful woman." Melissa must have used a fair amount of relationship capital to get the Husband to help a man who had tried to steal her away, no matter how beneficial that attempted theft had turned out.

James thought about his time with Melissa. It still hurt him immensely, but he'd not been wrong making an attempt to woo her. He wished he hadn't done it in front of the whole congregation mind you, but the woman had been lovely with Jo-Marie. She helped smooth things over between her and him. He never would have known what clothes to buy, or how to deal with the feminine hygiene situation that, he discovered, she had discussed with Jo-Marie without ever mentioning it to him. (If only Jo-Marie had shown the same discretion he never would have had even to think about it.)

Maybe a higher power was at work. He'd been drawn to Melissa mysteriously. She to him. Was it merely so she could revive her music career? She'd been there the night Jo-Marie came home. Was that merely coincidence? The Lord moves in mysterious ways. Maybe James' attraction to Melissa was a mysterious way.

Or maybe he just had a thing for manic redheads. Maybe he was just projecting the mystery. Either way, he was thankful for her.

The whole Sewing Circle took the stand, including the Old Man, just out of hospital. James had prayed when he'd lost his mom, and then they had appeared in his life. But maybe he was projecting that too.

And maybe he was projecting when he saw his love for Anne as having the grander purpose of bonding him with her daughter.

Jo-Marie, being a minor, did not take the stand, but she did speak to the Judge, saying that she wanted James to be her legal guardian. She recounted all the details from this in the longest text message James had ever received. She'd spoken glowingly of him, occasionally exaggerating how wonderful he was. Her only complaint was that he hadn't taken her in three years ago. James hoped she'd have said the biggest reason she couldn't stay with Joss, but she didn't. She did, however, say he was alcoholic and had a volatile temper and she did confirm the writing James submitted as genuine, though not her best work.

James had high hopes for the judgment. Joss's character did not come off very well. There were many stories, consistent stories, confirming what Jo-Marie had said about his drinking and temper. The "Good" Lawyer told James they had a more than decent shot but, in the end, everything was up to the Judge. It was out of their hands now.

So James did the one thing he could do. He prayed. Prayed that, whatever happened, Jo-Marie would have a stable childhood from now on. That she would know she was loved. That, whatever happened, God must watch over her. She was too good a kid not to be watched over.

James looked up to heaven (purely symbolic) and felt a wave of faith wash over him. Flood around his whole being. He was not certain that it was a faith in God, but he had true faith that things would work out for the best.

His hope again was strong.

And he had never, not for one moment, gone without love.

As the Judge gave the decision, James felt his heart lift up towards the sky.

And it was bold to say,

She is blessed!

She is blessed!

She is blessed!

THE END

Glossary of Classical Words and Phrases

Greek

ἀγάπη (agapē): translated sometimes as "love", sometimes as "charity". Self-giving love. Contrast with *στοργή* (storgē-"love of familiarity"), *φιλία* (philia-"love of friendship/mutual affection"), and *ἔρως* (erōs-"love you might feel in the loins"... C.S. Lewis defines this differently, but he was quite the prude).

δεῖνος (deinos): "Awesome", "awe inspiring". Sometimes translated as "awful", but in the archaic sense (i.e. "full of awe"); or "terrible", but in the same sense as "Oz the Great and Terrible" and not, "That was a terrible putt." It put the "dino" in "dinosaur".

Μέλιττα (Melitta): James himself gives a better explanation than I'd care to repeat.

πάντα χωρεῖ καὶ οὐδὲν μένει (panta khōrei kai ouden menei): Did you read the novel? I have nothing to add. No, wait. I have one thing to add: the related phrase *πάντα 'ρεῖ* (panta rhei) is sometimes used to express this concept. Jo-Marie does so in her writing.

ὕβρις (hubris): James, like so many grade 11 English teachers before him, has defined this as "overweening pride" but I find that slightly misleading. All Greek heroes, tragic and otherwise, have levels of pride that dwarf that of wide receivers, pro-wrestlers and the greatest of rap battlers. Heroes could have as much pride as they liked relative to other mortals but, if this pride led them to believe they were actually on par with the gods, well that's hubris. Put simply: a hero could call himself (or occasionally herself) "godlike",

241

but not "god". Unnecessary example: it would not be hubris for Bellerophon to say, "Look at those people. Do you know why they suck compared to me? They're not on a flying horse, that's why." But if he were then foolishly to conclude, "Let's fly to Olympus so I can hang out with my equals", he would be asking for trouble.

Latin

Carpe diem: If you don't know this phrase I will say that *Dead Poets Society* is a film that exists. I'm not saying it's good, but it does exist.

Quam minimum credula postero: The concluding words of Horace's Ode 1.10. They directly follow "*Carpe diem*" and literally mean "as possible the least trusting in the next", and are a good example of why Latin poetry is rarely given a literal translation.

sola gratia: "by grace alone". One of the five solas that certain protestant churches espouse as the only way into heaven. Other solas: *sola scriptura* ("by Scripture alone"); *sola fide* ("by faith alone"); *solus Christus* ("by Christ alone"); *soli Deo gloria* ("to the glory of God alone"). Yes there are five of them. Yes they all mean "alone". No, I have never accused these particular protestant churches of "mathematical consistency".

via media: Literally, "way middle". (Again, it's not a good idea to translate things literally.)